AND THEN YOU

UNTIL
BOOK 2

BRIAR PRESCOTT

Copyright © 2023 by Briar Prescott

All rights reserved.

No part of this book may be reproduced in any form or by any electronic or mechanical means, including information storage and retrieval systems, without written permission from the author, except for the use of brief quotations in a book review.

This is a work of fiction. Any resemblance to persons, living or dead, or business establishments, events, or locations, is coincidental.

All trademarks are the property of their respective owners.

Cover artist: Cormar Covers

Editing: Heather Caryn

Proofreading: Kate Wood

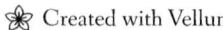 Created with Vellum

ABOUT THIS BOOK

Here's the thing: I am not—I repeat *not*—boyfriend material. I'm a good time for one night, and that's it.

Figures I manage to get myself into a situation where I have to pretend to be in a relationship.

Ah, well. Not much else to do but suck it up and get it over with.

I'm in. I'm out. I'm done.
But then Quinn says he's curious.
He says I'm a liar.
He says he wants to see the real me.
Honestly, I can't run away fast enough after that.
Because he doesn't know.
Doesn't know that I'm a landmine.
That he's trudging so close.
That he's about to step on me.
And then I'll ruin him.

Trigger warning: death of a sibling.

AUGUST 10TH, 2013

GENTLE WIND WHIPS through my hair and droplets shower the arm I'm holding above the water while I lie on my stomach on the deck and stare at the deep blue beneath me. I breathe in until I can't anymore. Fill my lungs with the smell of salt and seaweed. Suck it in until it starts to hurt and only then let it go.

We're leaving tomorrow. September is fast approaching. Mom's leading the troops packing up the house. All our memories and lifetimes of summer are placed into identical cardboard boxes, Mom overseeing the process with the iron fist of an Army general, wielding a Sharpie like a weapon, and slapping labels on boxes.

September is different this time around. We'll be in Washington, D.C. In some fancy-ass private school Dad picked out for us. And it's not that we're afraid we won't fit in or make friends. We will. Mostly, though, we don't care. We don't care about Washington and school and our new life there. We don't care about Dad's amazing new job and ridiculous paychecks and the new house and the promise of a new car the moment we blow out sixteen candles on the cake.

We don't care.

But every person who has the authority to do something about the fact that we don't care doesn't care that we don't care.

Which means this is the last time.

Last time we're running down the trail that leads to the dock.

Last time we're lying on the beach after a day on the sea, watching the stars appear one by one until the whole world is nothing but lights and endlessness.

Last time we're taking the boat out.

Droplets of water fall into the ocean from my fingertips. One after the other. Like a clock counting down the minutes we have left here. *Drip, drip, drip. You're leaving. Drip, drip. Pack your bags. Drip.*

Bare feet pad over the deck.

Cool skin presses against mine.

Sky's temple knocks against mine for a moment before he drapes a hoodie over my back like a blanket. I'm not cold, but Sky and I grew up in a shared world of *we*, and some habits are hard to break. When he's hungry, we're hungry. When I'm tired, we're tired. Tonight, he's cold, so we're cold.

It's hard to want to become an *I* when being a *we* comes so naturally.

Sky and Steph.

Steph and Sky.

Two halves of one whole.

Double trouble. As per Dad.

My two dragonflies. As per Mom.

"Ready to go back and face the music?" I take a glance toward the sky. The dark blue dome stretches toward the edges of the world, pushing the last of the sunlight behind the horizon. "It'll be dark soon."

"A few more minutes," Sky says. He knows I need more time, so he's giving it to me.

"I bet Mom's freaking out," I say after a little while.

"When isn't Mom freaking out?" he says lazily and rolls himself over onto his back.

I copy him until I'm lying right next to him, ocean under and universe above us.

The swaying of the boat feels more natural than the steadiness of dry land ever has. Sky and I grew up surrounded by boats and the sea, wind and waves.

We can fish with a pole or a net, from a pier, the shore, boat, or a kayak. We know how to clean marlin and fillet tuna. We can tie a knot and splice a rope. Row a boat with one oar and navigate by stars.

We recognize the feathers and songs of all sea birds, know which plants are edible, can smell storms, and know every inch of this land and the surrounding waters like the backs of our hands.

The sea is our stomping ground.

Our new house? It's in the middle of the city. 128.8 miles from the ocean.

"*The Potomac River*," Mom said, stubbornly obtuse.

"A river," Sky scoffed like she'd said there was a bathtub in the house.

"Chesapeake Bay," Mom continued, infuriatingly calm and determined to keep that elusive silver lining firmly in our sights. She'd always been a staunch believer in a happy ending. *It will all work out in the end. Always and forever. If you send positive thoughts out, the world will take care of you.*

"It's not the same!" Sky and I snapped in unison.

I can't imagine leaving.

I don't *want* to imagine leaving.

Why would I? This is home. The only one we've ever known.

I turn my head toward Sky and ask the question. The one that brought us here and now. To this pathetic, ultimately pointless rebellion.

"Do you think they're really going to do it?" I swallow through the dryness in my throat. Merely saying the words feels sacrilegious. "Sell. The house. And our boat. Maybe they'll still change their minds?"

Sky's head falls against mine, and he lets out a gloomy sigh, equally as unhappy. Equally as frustrated. Equally as angry. "All the moving boxes are kind of a dead giveaway."

The fight has left us increment by increment over the course of the last twelve hours. Sure, we dramatically ran away from home when Mom and Dad broke the news, but I think we all know we'll go back. What else is there to do?

"We could run away," Sky muses like I've said the last part out loud. We've always been good at that. Hearing each other without having to say a single word. Hearing each other when nobody else does. "Take *Sun of a Beach* on a real adventure." He pats the deck affectionately. His calloused palm strokes the scuffed teak boards like the boat is a beloved pet.

"We'll go to Panama first," I say.

"And then straight across the Pacific." Sky slashes his hand down like he's trying to cut the world open, his head moving against mine, dark brown strands tickling my cheek. "New Zealand. A pitstop in Australia. Wherever the heart takes us."

"We'll travel the world."

"Document our adventures."

"Write a book."

"Make a movie."

"Have fun."

"Fuck school," Sky says, and his vehement tone makes me laugh.

"Fuck Washington," I supply.

"Fuck it."

"Fuck all of it," I agree.

I push myself up and look around. Nothing as far as the eye can see. Sky clasps my extended arm, his long fingers around my wrist and mine around his. I pull him up, and he wraps himself around me. The ever-familiar salt and ocean smell of home fills my nostrils. It'll be gone once we're in Washington. He's going to smell like the city then. Exhaust fumes and concrete. Foreign. Wrong. I push my nose into his neck and inhale. Hold my breath. Trap *ocean* and *home* inside me. Keep it in until my lungs start to protest.

"We could stay the night?" Sky asks hopefully.

"We're already in trouble."

"Serves them right."

But we get the boat ready and ourselves ready, and head back anyway.

The wind's picked up a little. It's nothing to worry about, but we better hurry if we want to get back before Mom alerts the Coast Guard. Dusk has fallen, the day and our rebellion done.

I rub my forearms. I feel weirdly cold, even though it's still warm outside. Sky's holding the wheel, navigating the now-somewhat-choppy waters with calm confidence. We're moving closer to the shore, so every now and then there's a glimpse of other boats on the horizon. The distant rumble of an engine. A lone sail on the skyline. All of us headed back home.

Sky throws me a look. "Go get dressed. And then take over for me for a sec?"

I nod and rub my icy hands together to get the blood moving again before I head below deck.

I throw on warmer clothes and grab Sky's pants.

"Where the fuck is your jacket?" I shout.

"Same place as yours," he yells back.

"Well, it isn't," I mutter and start rummaging around. Not like we packed anything when we stormed out of the house, but this isn't our first impromptu outing, so there are always some supplies and clothes here.

"Steph."

"Still looking!" I yell back distractedly.

"Steph!"

My head snaps up.

My heart jumps into my throat, and terror pounds in my stomach. It twists my gut until I feel sick with it. It comes out of nowhere. Blink of an eye. Sky's voice. Fear so all-encompassing I can't think.

Everything else happens in a second.

One moment I'm tossing our things around, cursing under my breath, the next I'm thrown against the wall, and the floor is suddenly not where it's supposed to be.

Sound is cut off. I can see things flying around, but they don't make any noise when they fall. The only thing I hear is the static in my ears.

The back of my head smacks against the wall. The crack of my skull echoes inside my brain.

The world goes dark.

When I open my eyes, the boat is upright again, and the sound rushes back like a wave crashing over me.

"Sky?"

It's a pathetic squeak. Barely more than a whisper. Inaudible. Useless. I swallow hard and try again.

"Sky?"

My heart pumps in a sickening staccato in my throat. My

fingers brush the skin there, just to make sure everything's still normal. That every part of me is where it's supposed to be.
It's not.
Sky.
I can't seem to breathe properly. A gasp of air, but when I try to breathe in again—nothing. Another gasp. And nothing.
The boat creaks and groans around me, swaying from side to side.
"Sky!"
I fight through the debris. Shaky legs carry me toward the stairs. Shaky fingers grapple for purchase. Shaky heartbeat hammers in my throat.
Up.
Up.
Up.
Stumble on the steps.
Hit my knee.
Through the hatch.
Outside.
Breath still stuck in my throat.
The deck is empty.
I slip and slide and fall and scramble on the soaking wet boards.
"Sky!"
My voice disappears into the wind. The sea silences it, carries it away.
Nothing.
I'm alone.
I try to breathe, but I can't. The air is choking me. Strangling me. Salt and water in my lungs.
I'm drowning.
He's drowning.
We can't breathe!

There's no air.

I can't think.

Somehow, I'm sinking on dry land, heaving in breath after breath, gasping, wheezing, praying for something to stop this. Terror like nothing I've ever felt before washes over me and leaves a metallic taste of blood in my mouth that I can't swallow down any more than I can stop any of this from happening.

I don't want to die.

I don't want to die.

Please, don't let me die!

And then.

Just like that.

It's over.

It only takes one moment for a life to change.

One moment for a we to become an I.

STEPH

PRESENT DAY

IT IS a truth universally acknowledged that I am a bit of a fuckup.

Let's put it this way: if ever you find yourself in need of a boyfriend who'd impress your parents, I am not your guy. I'm more like the dude you bring over to convince them that the ex-boyfriend they despise is actually a pretty decent pick when compared to what else is out there.

Unless, of course, your parents are the kind of people who find lack of ambition endearing and think being in possession of a college degree or having the ability to keep a job are overrated, in which case, look no further, you've found the one.

I'm a charming fuckup, I'll give you that. It always takes people a bit of time to catch on, but once you get a look beneath the surface you can't really fool yourself into thinking there's anything impressive there.

When it comes to me, the word impulsive is thrown around a lot. Spontaneous and free-spirited are also among the more common labels. The nicer ones. Most people tend to go with variations of "a fuckup," "a screwup," "a flaky idiot," "a certifiable disaster." There are more, but I don't think there's much point in listing them all.

To be fair, I'm not working overtime to prove anybody wrong. This moment right here is an excellent example. Because today? Today, I'm bringing my A game.

It's a strange law of nature that when you're late and trying to sneak into a room, every sound is amplified. You push the door open, as slowly and carefully as you possibly can, and it screeches like a banshee—a vocal neon arrow pointing toward you. *Here! Here! This slob didn't arrive on time! Bring out the tar and feathers.*

Your footsteps suddenly make you sound like you're walking with all the grace of an elephant on stilts. Your clothes rustle like you've accidentally dressed yourself in a suit made of parchment paper. Your breathing sounds like an approaching asthma attack.

You'll inevitably get a hankering to sneeze. Or you'll stumble into something. Trip on somebody's feet. The choices are endless, but the result is always the same. Your arrival will be a chaotic experience. Cacophony and chaos rolled into the perfect storm.

It's made all the more terrible when there's a priest staring daggers at you while you're doing your thing, the bride looks like she regrets ever meeting you, and all the people who know you have that resigned expression on their faces that says they weren't really even hoping you *wouldn't* screw up for once.

I don't usually step foot in a church at all because, as I understand it, fugitives aren't generally supposed to show up at the precinct of their own volition.

I made an exception for today.

"Do you?" the priest asks loudly, sounding impatient in a way that seems pretty inappropriate for a priest if you ask me. Then again, what do I know?

AND THEN YOU

All the eyes that weren't on me now are.
I look around. Do I what?
"Pardon?" I ask.

"Do you object to this marriage?" the priest asks, even louder this time, voice echoing between the majestic archways of the church.

Do you... Do you... Do you...
Object to this... Object to this... Object to this...
Marriage... Marriage... Marriage...

The bride is staring daggers at me, and the maid of honor looks like she's trying to decide where to stab me with an ice pick later to make it look like an accident.

"No?" I say slowly and shake my head before I put some conviction in my tone. "No objections. Carry on."

There's some more staring and a few snickers, but eventually, the priest turns his attention back to Casey and David, and I slide to the side, taking up position behind the rows of uncomfortable-looking wooden pews that seem to be a church staple.

I let out a slow, silent breath.

"That was quite an entrance," a low voice says from next to me.

My shoulders slump.

Great.

I glance to my left and up at Quinn Henris. Friend of the groom. The bane of my existence. He's looming over me like one of the horsemen of the apocalypse. Six foot three inches of glaring disapproval in a Tom Ford suit.

When our eyes meet, we both scowl at the same time. The look in his eyes is one part judgment, one part annoyance, and one part exasperation. It's the look that says if he saw me fall off a cliff, he'd turn up the music so my screams wouldn't interrupt his very important mission to be as pompous as humanly possible at all times.

Not to say I'd do anything differently if the roles were reversed, so it would be hypocritical to come back to haunt him for that. Plus, I already spend way too much time in Quinn's presence alive, so I wouldn't want to ruin my afterlife.

"Interesting look for a wedding," he murmurs. "It's rather... sweaty. Is that in this season?"

"You look like a funeral director," I reply cheerfully while I smile and nod at Casey's mother.

A hot funeral director, but a funeral director nevertheless. He's dressed in black, head to toe. Does he look good? I suppose, objectively speaking, one could argue his height, broad shoulders, and wide chest combined with the perfect bone structure, cobalt blue eyes, and black hair is appealing. I just happen to be one of those people who doesn't judge a book by its cover.

The view from my high horse is splendid, if anybody's interested.

Let's make one thing very clear. I do not hate Quinn Henris. No matter what my friends seem to think.

To hate somebody means to have them occupy a large portion of your thoughts and poison your mind with their presence.

I have more enjoyable things to do with my brain.

Generally, I try not to think about him at all.

Not so generally, while I don't hate Quinn, I also don't like him. He's an annoyance. A splinter underneath my nail that refuses to come out. A papercut that doesn't heal. A pebble in my shoe.

He's annoyingly perfect and perfectly annoying. And I'm extremely aware of his judgmental presence next to me.

"Just out of curiosity, do you have a personal vendetta against time? Is that why you refuse to use a watch?" he asks, tone deceptively mild. Like if a tiger stops next to you and bumps his head against you, so you think to yourself, *It's fine.*

See? He just wants you to pet him. Next thing you know there's a tiger sitting on your chest, and you're short an arm.

"Clocks are for people who are so boring they only get asked to go places because they're guaranteed to arrive on time. Filler bodies until the interesting guests arrive. Thank you for your service." I stretch out my neck and peer past him. "No date?" I ask. "You should give Tinder a go." I widen my eyes. "Just think about the possibilities. You could be the first robot that finds love."

"So you keep telling me. Why the persistent interest in my love life?"

"Scientific advancement has always fascinated me." I wave my hand toward him. "You look so lifelike in certain lights that I sometimes forget you're not a real boy. Will you put in a good word for me when the robot overlords take over?"

"You shall be missed," Quinn says.

"It'd sound so much more sincere if you'd wipe that hopeful look off your face."

David's grandmother turns around and gives us both a murderous look.

"Shh!" she hisses.

So I clamp my mouth shut and stare straight ahead for the rest of the ceremony.

IT'S one of those stupid coincidences life sometimes throws at you that Quinn and I are both at this wedding today. It's obviously not enough that I already have to deal with him being a part of my friend group. And, yes, *my* friend group. I got there first, so it's mine.

And, of course, today, I know the bride, and he knows the groom, so here we are.

Casey's my cousin. David is Quinn's college roommate. There are eight billion people in the world, but somehow Casey and David picked each other out of all the potential spouse candidates, dated, and then decided to have one of those weddings where they invite everybody and their mother to witness them entering into holy matrimony. What are the chances, right? I swear, there are days when I'm fully convinced the universe has it out for me and that's why it's trying to force Quinn on me again and again.

As it is, Casey and I aren't that close anymore, but she *is* one of the few people from my extended family who still talks to me, and somehow it felt like I needed to acknowledge that by attending today.

It's yet another bad decision in a row of many—as is customary with me. Approximately one-third of this crowd is related to me in some way or another. I haven't seen most of them in years, so curious glances follow me around, eyes shine with the promise of juicy, juicy gossip, and people in the know compete with each other for who gets to gleefully tell the ones still in the dark all about me.

Did you see him? Shae and Morgan's kid. Such a tragic story. Such a tragic family.

By what feels like the five thousandth time I hear somebody whisper my name and try and sneak a better look at me, I give up the pretense that I can take the scrutiny sober and decide there's not much else to do other than get methodically drunk.

So I do shots, because it seems like the most efficient means to get me where I need to be. I avoid Quinn. I dance with Casey's sorority friends. I avoid Quinn. I give a toast. I avoid Quinn. More shots. More avoiding Quinn.

It's going really well until I stumble into him at the entrance to the tent a few hours later. He's standing there like a security guard, all stiff and imposing. Mildly more tolerable now that I'm not stone cold sober anymore, though, so there's that.

"Having fun?" I ask.

"Of course," he says tonelessly. "Nothing I enjoy more than crowds, drunk people, and the fifth hundredth repetition of 'Dancing Queen.'"

"You know what they say. If you can't beat 'em, join 'em." I shove my champagne in front of his face. "Want one?"

He sends the glass a horrified look. "You just drank out of it."

I shrug. "So? It's not like I spat in it."

"Backwash," he says shortly.

"Eh, what's a little saliva between two"—I try to think of a good word to describe us and eventually settle on—"acquaintances."

Yeah. That'll do.

"I'd rather we both kept our saliva to ourselves," he says primly and adjusts his cufflinks.

"You're losing out on a lot of fun with that philosophy," I say and finish off the champagne.

"I'll also lose out on things like bacterial meningitis."

"Because that's running rampant in these parts? Where's your sense of adventure?"

"I imagine in the same place where you put your sense of self-preservation."

"The what?" I blink innocently.

He stares back. An unmovable, unshakable object. Pristine and emotionless like a statue.

I could leave.

Of course, I don't.

He's too perfect. Always has been. Never steps a foot out of line. Never makes waves. We're three hours into the reception. Everybody's starting to look at least a little rumpled. Jackets are off. Ties are loose. Heels have been abandoned in favor of bare feet. Quinn looks like he's heading to a job interview. He has an untouchable air about him. Royalty among commoners. A step above everybody else.

The DJ puts on another ABBA song. Quinn sighs.

"Lighten up," I say. "It's a party. You're supposed to enjoy it."

"Thank you for explaining the rules."

I tilt my head to the side. "What's with the face?"

"I'm not sure I understand what you mean," he says.

"You've got very judgmental eyebrows. What is it this time? Are we having fun wrong?"

He opens his mouth, but then, instead of saying whatever it is he was going to say, he shakes his head and says, "You're drunk."

"Not yet, but give me another twenty minutes."

He sighs and looks like he's about to traverse the perilous grounds of existential crisis.

"Stay here," he finally says. "I'm going to get you some water." The prospect of doing something nice for me clearly hurts.

I know receiving help from him hurts for sure, so I suppose I can relate.

"Sparkling," I tell him.

He raises his brows.

I widen my eyes innocently. "Still water bores me."

He sighs like the weight of the world is on his shoulders. "Of course it does."

By the looks of it, he counts to at least a hundred in his head before he starts moving. The moment he disappears inside the tent, I walk out of there and grab another glass of champagne while I'm at it. I stroll into the backyard where fairy lights have been strung between the trees, flowerbeds are filled to the brim with roses, and the grass looks like somebody's trimmed each blade with the help of a ruler and a pair of nail clippers. It all looks just a little too perfect. I half expect the roses to be made of plastic. They're that flawless.

I assume there are unspoken rules in place about how you're not supposed to walk on the grass, but I ignore those and make my way to the weeping willow standing majestically in the corner of the garden. Once there, I take a seat and press my back against the rough bark of the tree, hidden from sight by the low-hanging branches.

I pluck a few blades of grass and tear them into small pieces before I let them rain down on the ground.

I will take this to my grave, but I used to be a tiny bit obsessed with Quinn back when I was fourteen and he was the twenty-three-year-old swimming prodigy. It was the year of the London Summer Olympics, and he was about as famous as an athlete can get. Everywhere you looked that year it was all *the meteoric rise of Quinn Henris* this and *the fiercely private national treasure Quinn Henris* that.

The Henrises are one of those high-profile families. Quinn's mother is an actress. A sort of living legend. Everybody knows her, even if she's been gone from the spotlight for years now. Quinn's father's a former vice president of the United States. There is also a sister and two brothers, all younger than Quinn. Most of them make occasional appearances and have their pictures taken at charity events or premieres or tennis matches.

I had a somewhat serious case of hero worship, which Sky found excessively amusing. Amusing enough to buy me an issue of *Sports Illustrated* with Quinn on the cover. He tossed it at me when he got home from the store and snickered, and I pretended to be annoyed and dropped the magazine under my bed, where I dug it out later that night when Sky was already asleep. I flipped through the pages, a flashlight between my teeth while I was searching.

And there he was. Page five. An article and a spread of photos. One of them a bit bigger than the others. Quinn midway out of a pool, water cascading down his impressive abs, cobalt blue eyes smoldering with intensity, a lock of hair plastered to his forehead, muscles flexing. Something hot and weird and *unknown* settled in the bottom of my belly. Heart skipped a beat and then did a few extra ones in quick succession to catch up.

That summer, I watched the Olympics like it was my job and I had a performance evaluation approaching.

Over the next year, I'd secretly buy more magazines and scour the internet for more articles. I devoured everything I could find about him. I took note of things he said, watched videos of his training sessions, and joined the swim team. I tried to emulate him when I was in the water. I wasn't good enough to go anywhere with swimming, but I was decent enough to be a medium-sized fish in a small pond.

He was the only secret I ever kept from Sky.

And then August 2013 happened, and Sky and I became just I, and I spent the next year in a thick fog. And the year after that in that same thick fog while pretending I was not as lost as I really was.

I moved to my grandmother's house in Maine. Started tenth grade all over again because I had failed every single one of my classes the previous two years. Met Blair and then Jude. And they didn't know the Steph from before. They didn't know I used to be a *we*. I fixed a smile on my face. Created a new Steph. Pulled him on like a costume over that hollow shell of an I and kept going.

Nobody suspects a smile. It's the most useful lesson I've ever learned.

And then I met him in real life. The great Quinn Henris. I hadn't thought about him in a long time. The magazines and my collection of articles hadn't made it with me to Maine. Nothing of my previous life had. My fascination with Quinn had died along with my old life.

But meet him I did, by some shitty twist of fate on a sunny June morning in Central Park. Blair and I had taken a road trip to New York to drop her off, because we were done with high school and she was moving to the city, ready to conquer the world of ballet.

Quinn was sitting on a park bench, all alone, like I'd somehow conjured him out of thin air during one of my early morning runs. And for the first time in years, I felt the old Steph stir somewhere inside me. For the first time in years, I felt actual, startled, tentative excitement. A tiny spark that was so faint I didn't even dare hope it'd turn into a flame. But it was there.

Go, a tiny, amused voice whispered inside my head. *Go and tell him you two should become buddies.*

Shut up, Sky!

You know you want to...

I went.

Not because I actually thought we'd hit it off and it'd be the start of an epic friendship. Not because I wanted anything from him at all.

I suppose what I was after was a reminder. A reminder that maybe, just maybe, I could reclaim some of that person I used to be. Some tiny spark of hope that even people who've been lost at sea for years can maybe one day find their way back home.

All I managed to get out was an, "Excuse me. Are you—"

He looked at me then. Cold blue eyes in an impossibly handsome face filled with nothing but disdain.

"Fuck off," he spat out, got up, and stormed away.

And that last little remnant of the old Steph died.

They say never meet your heroes. I guess there's a reason.

And then, because life wasn't done with me yet, a few years later Blair met Nora. And with Nora, the elusive Quinn Henris found his way back into my life for the third time. And in the end, he's proven to be everything that I now expected from him. Cold. Stuck-up. Unpleasant. The kind of person who looks down on others and doesn't bother to be subtle about it either.

A pebble in my shoe.

A papercut that refuses to heal.

Dislike is a snowball. It starts with a flake. At first, you can ignore it. But little, inane things build up over time until all the small things you can usually look past start to irritate the living shit out of you. And that fuck off he handed to me all those years ago was a shovelful of flakes in the face at once, so I had a good head start in the dislike department.

I stare into the darkness with an unseeing gaze and hate him just a little bit for the moment. Hate him for everything he unknowingly destroyed that morning way back when.

He didn't even recognize me when Nora introduced the two of us once she and Blair were getting serious. Not that I expected him to. We exchanged small talk and each went our own way, but when you share friends you're forced to interact from time to time, even if you happen to live clear across the country.

I visited.

The snowball kept growing.

I shake my head and wince. I'm clearly at that unfortunate point of being drunk where I turn toward self-pity, and nobody needs that. Time for a refill.

I start to get up.

"...Shae and Morgan, yes."

I sink back down like a stone when I hear my parents' names.

"What are those two up to now?" one of the voices asks.

"Still begging for money, I imagine," a woman's voice says. I know that voice. Nice going, Aunt Kathy. "You know how it is with them. God, it's just getting embarrassing at this point, isn't it? Listen, I know it's tragic what happened, but they're milking the hell out of it, aren't they?"

"Did you get their email?" a man asks.

"We *all* got the email, Justin," the first woman says.

I close my eyes and swallow down the bile that gathers in the back of my throat.

"The whole family needs therapy," Aunt Kathy concludes.

"Here, here," Justin says. "I'd consider donating for that, to be honest. Not this... whatever this mess is. I can't support that in good conscience. The kid's dead. Time to stop exploiting it."

They keep talking. My ears are buzzing so hard I can't really register what else they're saying as they move away, voices dying down.

Once it's silent again, I push myself to my feet again, teeth gritted so hard I think I might be doing permanent damage to my molars, and storm inside. I grab a bottle of vodka from the bar and head back outside.

Fuck them.

Fuck them all.

STEPH

AS FAR AS being unimpressive goes, I'm pulling out all the stops this morning. My face is smothered in a pillow, dried drool glues my cheek to the soft cotton of the pillowcase, and even lying completely still, my head hurts like a bitch. My mouth is so dry swallowing hurts. Even goddamn blinking is painful.

Here's a fun fact: I have no idea where I am.

Which is to be expected. That should, ideally, ring some alarm bells. Nudge my self-preservation gene into action.

I wait for a moment. Will something to happen. Heart palpitations. Tightness in my chest. The smothering claws of fear around my throat.

Come on, Steph. Feel something.

But no. No dice.

Oh well. I gave it a try.

Thing is, I don't really care what happens to me.

Haven't for years now.

It is what it is.

I do my best to only move my eyeballs while I check out the room. The little I see of it. As far as surroundings go, I could've picked a worse place to crash. It's all very stylish with its sand-

AND THEN YOU

colored, exposed brick wall with a large window in it, and the contrasting deep green wall behind the headboard. And the bed itself smells like a summer's day, so I stuff my face into the pillow and inhale until my lungs feel like they're about to burst, pushing the reality out of my mind for a moment longer.

All in all, I've woken up in worse places.

Eventually, I get out of bed and take my first proper look around the room. Seriously, whoever decorated this place, nice job. It's all calming earth tones and subtle details that give the place character.

I assume I slept with whoever lives here, seeing that I'm naked. I can't see my clothes anywhere, but on the dresser, I find a pair of dark green sweats, and a plain white T-shirt with the Columbia University logo on it, so I'm just going to freely assume I can borrow those. The other option is to do my walk of shame nude, and I'm not that keen on being arrested. Nora will murder me if she has to bail me out again, and my head hurts enough that I'd rather forgo the lecture that'd surely follow the murder.

I tuck the clothes underneath my arm and head to the en suite bathroom, where I gulp down a gallon of water and then take a shower because I feel like I'm sweating excess alcohol at this point, and I'd like to get it off me.

Once done, I get dressed and find a staircase.

Somebody's definitely speaking somewhere. Muffled voices and an occasional bout of laughter carry up the stairs and give me a moment's pause. But it's not like I have many options about what to do here.

I might as well make it interesting for myself. Let's play a round of Who Did Steph Sleep With?

Man? Woman? Threesome? A wedding guest? Some random person? A familiar face? Somebody I don't know?

This might take a while. And I'm too hungover to get really

invested in the game, so I'm gonna say it was a man because of the clothes I just borrowed. Or stole. We'll see how this plays out. I'm also going to say it was a wedding guest because I don't remember actually leaving the wedding. Not that it means much. It wouldn't be the first time I ended up somewhere without the ability to retrace my steps.

Time to see if I was right. Drumroll, please. How exciting.

At the top of the black metal staircase, I take a look around. Below me is a spacious living area, and from the direction of the muffled voices and an occasional clatter of dishes, I'm guessing there's a kitchen somewhere below and out of sight. The front door might as well have a halo around it and an angel choir singing next to it by how it's calling out to me. I could just sneak down, slip out, and call it good, but in addition to my clothes, I've also somehow misplaced my shoes, phone, keys, and wallet, and looking for them would probably create enough noise to draw attention to my great escape.

Suppose I'll just go and face the music.

I pad downstairs as quietly as I can, but seeing that I'm also looking around and taking this place in, I misjudge how many steps there are left and come down hard on my right foot. I land on it all wrong, and a bolt of fire shoots through my ankle.

"Ow! Shit! Fuck!" I let out a few more curses while I hop around on one foot, trying to shake the pain off.

"Stephen?"

I whip myself around at Quinn's voice.

And stare.

What in the—

Here I am. Painfully hungover. Dressed in somebody else's clothes. My ankle on fire. Staring at a bunch of people.

There's Quinn. Because of course there's Quinn. I simply cannot catch a break when it comes to him.

There's a young woman, probably somewhere in her midtwenties.

There's a very familiar-looking woman.

And an equally familiar-looking man.

Not familiar as in I've met them before. Familiar as in I've seen their faces on TV, on my laptop screen, newspapers, and magazines countless times over the years.

"Mom. Dad," Quinn says in an extremely measured tone. "This is Stephen." There's a beat of silence before he turns toward me. "Stephen, these are my mother and father, Caroline and Philip. And my little sister, Rubi."

The silence that follows is the most painful thing I've ever experienced in my life. It goes on. And on. And on. Before some tiny part of my brain realizes that the ball is in my court. That I should probably say something.

"Hi?" I'm pretty sure I look as horrified as I sound.

I had sex with your son.

I hope to God they're not mind readers. And have terrible deduction skills.

"Hi," I repeat when nobody says anything. "I was just..."

I draw a complete blank. What do I say? I was just stopping by to borrow a cup of sugar? Thankfully, Quinn's mom shows me some mercy and takes over. She squeezes her husband's arm. Raises her brows at him. Smiles. At him. And then at me. Not the stiff, strained smile I usually see on her son's face. An actual, friendly smile.

"Stephen," she says as if testing my name. "How nice to meet you. And I do apologize for all of this. We were in the neighborhood and decided to drop by on a whim. I realize now we should've called."

"Pssh!" Yes, that's the actual, goddamn sound I make. "No. What? No. It's..." I swallow through the tightness of my throat and try to find the right words. "I mean, it's family, right?"

Somehow my total inability to find even a smidge of dignity in this situation seems to endear me to her because her smile widens. "It's an absolute pleasure to finally meet you."

"Likewise?" Aside from the fact that everything I say sounds like a question, I could do worse. I could've trekked downstairs in my birthday suit, so, you know, silver linings. I wave my hand in the air like I'm conducting a symphony. "This is... great," I say. "I've... heard a lot of great things, so it's... great meeting you. Just... great."

I'm sure I could stuff the word 'great' in there a few more times if I really tried.

"Great, indeed," Quinn's sister says and rests her chin in her palm, eyes moving over me like I'm some interesting discovery. "On the other hand, Quinn here has been extremely tight-lipped about *you*."

"Rubi," Quinn says. There's a clear warning in his voice that Rubi ignores.

"What? It's not like you've exactly been a well of information."

"Rubs, leave your brother alone," Philip says.

"Yeah, like you two aren't dying to—"

That's when the doorbell rings. Yes! Divine intervention.

"I'll get it!" I say so loudly they all jerk their heads toward me. I send them a tight smile, elbow Quinn out of my way, and hurry toward the front door. With any luck I can slide past whoever's out there and escape.

I pull the door open.

And come face-to-face with Nora. Seriously, universe? What's with the sabotage?

She frowns and hikes Hazel higher on her hip. "Steph? What are you doing here?"

"Dying," I whisper. "Save me!"

"From?" she asks. Hazel starts wiggling, and she pushes her into my arms. "Here you go, Uncle Steph."

"No, I'm supposed to—" I start to say, but she's already heading inside.

I look down at Hazel. "You want to run away with me?"

She pulls the fist she's been chewing on like her life depends on it out of her mouth and pats it against my cheek before she turns her head toward the voices coming from inside the apartment and starts cooing and waving her chubby arms.

"Thought so," I mutter before I kiss the top of her head, let out a deep breath, turn around, and make my way back into the kitchen.

Nora's busy kissing everyone on the cheek and saying hi, so I quietly stand to the side and hope to God nobody notices me anymore.

Hazel sells me out immediately when she starts to babble. All eyes back on me.

"What are you feeding that sweet angel?" Caroline asks and comes and stands next to me, smoothly taking Hazel off my hands. "She just keeps growing!" She starts talking to Hazel, bouncing and tickling her, and she lets out a happy little gurgle.

"Like a weed," Nora agrees and drops the huge bag of baby supplies in the corner. "I'd be careful with your dress. She's teething, so there's drool everywhere."

"What's a little drool?" Caroline says happily and starts giving Hazel small kisses on her cheeks.

I take a step back. I think I can sneak out of here now that Hazel's taken one for the team and is distracting everybody. Who needs keys and wallets and phones anyway? I can bribe Blair to come and get them for me later and just camp on Jude and Blake's couch until she gets around to it.

Perfect plan. In theory. I take another step back and slam straight into Quinn. He lets out a soft, "Oof," and puts his hands on my hips to steady me. Or possibly he was aiming for the neck and missed.

And everybody's eyes are on me again. I just can't catch a break today, can I?

"How was the wedding?" Nora asks and helps herself to a handful of grapes and sends me a toothy grin. "Did you two have fun?"

"It was nice," Quinn says, and I nod my agreement distractedly while I try to maneuver myself past him as inconspicuously as I can. Does he have to be so fucking wide? It's like trying to get past a boulder.

"Any highlights? Anybody drop the cake?" Nora asks.

"Is that something that happens often?" Philip asks with a chuckle.

"I've seen it," Nora says.

"I've been to a wedding where the best man danced into a champagne tower," Rubi says thoughtfully. "The floor was so sticky for the rest of the night that it was like walking on Scotch Tape."

"Well, this was just your regular wedding," Quinn says. "Speeches. Dancing." He makes a deliberate pause and says, "Drunk people."

I narrow my eyes at the side of his face. *Asshole.*

I force out a short laugh.

"You don't have to undersell it. It was a really beautiful wedding," I say before I turn toward his family. "Quinn got so emotional. When Casey and David were doing their first dance, he leaned toward me and said, 'I can't wait until it's my turn.'"

Rubi blinks and starts to laugh. "Quinn said that? Our Quinn?"

"Aww," Caroline says. "Sometimes you just need to find the right person, Rubs."

"All you need is love," I say with a nod, turn my gaze back to

Quinn, and widen my eyes. "Hey! Isn't that also the song you said you'd like to use for the first dance? Or was it 'Can You Feel the Love Tonight?'"

"I have a different tune in mind right now," Quinn says through clenched teeth.

I pat him on the chest. "You don't have to be embarrassed. That dream wedding you told me all about last night sounds wonderful. And it's sweet you have a binder with all the details planned out. And those inspiration photos you showed me where you've cut off the model's head and photoshopped your own there instead just really showcased your vision. It's nice that you care so deeply about it."

Quinn looks like he's about to murder me. My job here is done. Fuck you with your 'drunk people' comments and judgment.

"Can I have a word?" he asks with all the pleasantness of an alligator about to attack.

"Probably best to save that for later," I say and swipe my eyes over the people in the kitchen. "We've got company."

I say company, but I mean witnesses, which means I'm going to stay close to them. And Quinn says I lack self-preservation. Shows what he knows.

Philip gets up from his seat and drains his coffee cup. "Don't mind us. We have to get going anyway. We have a meeting in an hour."

Caroline glances at her watch. "My God. Is that the time already?"

She hands Hazel back to Nora and gathers her things.

"I'm so sorry we have to run like this. And we didn't even get to properly meet you, Stephen. Terrible timing on our part, really. We'll need to remedy that as soon as possible."

She stops in front of Quinn and gives him a hug. "I will call you later, son of mine."

Quinn nods and kisses her cheek. It's unexpectedly sweet. Or just normal. I don't know what I thought was going to happen, but mainly I'm just used to him being stiff and cold, so it seems weird when he shows human emotions.

He also hugs his dad and then Rubi. She murmurs something in his ear, and he rolls his eyes and says, "That's disturbing, Rubs. Thank you for that."

"I'm just saying," Rubi says and waggles her brows. "Upgrade."

And then Quinn's mother is in front of me, and I find myself engulfed in a hug too, and... I don't know what to do. I just stand there, frozen like a statue. She's still holding on to my forearms when she takes a step back, sends me a warm smile, and says, "I hope you'll consider coming with Quinn when he comes to the camp. We'd all love it if you would."

I don't know what to say. Other than 'why the hell would you want that?' But it doesn't seem like the politest of things to say, so in the end, I simply nod and say, "Sure."

Maybe it's some famous-people thing where they invite random people over to their house to stay? I have no clue.

"Oh, wonderful. Everybody else will be there, too. They can't wait to meet you."

The who? Everybody else?

But she's already halfway out the door with the rest of her family behind her and in another fifteen seconds, the front door falls shut behind them.

I turn back toward the kitchen. Nora's stuffing grapes into her mouth like she's trying to stock up for winter, eyes roaming between me and Quinn. Quinn still looks like he's one step away from becoming the main character in a true crime podcast.

"So," Nora says and moves her forefinger back and forth between me and Quinn. "This is an interesting development. How long have you two lovebirds been together, then?"

I stare at her. "You know, you should really be a better role model for your kid and lay off the drugs," I say.

"Hey, you were the one who practically told your boyfriend's parents he was planning to propose." She tosses another grape in her mouth. "I'm glad somebody's enjoying herself."

"No, I didn't." I wave my hand toward Quinn. "I was giving him shit."

"By insinuating you two are in a relationship and getting super serious," she says and nods. "Well, you showed him."

"I wasn't insinuating anything. Come on. Who in their right mind would think he and I are together?"

"I bet you five billion dollars Caroline and Philip think that," Nora says.

I turn toward Quinn. Usually I wouldn't, but desperate times. "Can you talk some sense into your friend? Your parents do *not* think that you and I are together."

Quinn drags his hand through his hair and lets out a mirthless laugh. "Oh, I can guarantee you my parents definitely think we're together."

"See?" I tell Nora before what Quinn said fully registers. Once it does, I whirl back toward him. "Wait. No, that's not what I said." I take a deep, calming breath and scowl at him. "You are exceptionally irritating today. Good job. Can we stop this nonsense now?"

"Believe me, if I could, I would," Quinn says.

"Honey. Sweetie. Darling. You're dressed in Quinn's clothes and based on the hair and the bed face, you clearly slept *and* showered here. And then you stand there, all pressed up against him and start talking about love and proposals and dream weddings. What did you think was going to happen?" Nora asks.

First things first, I take a huge step away from Quinn. It's not my fault I was trying to escape, and he was in my way.

"I'm not—" I look down at that damn Columbia University T-shirt. "This could be my shirt," I say while I try and fix my hair as subtly as possible. "I could be the neighbor."

"You came downstairs from my bedroom," Quinn says.

"Or was it the guest room?" I say pointedly.

"I don't have a guest room."

"You were on the Columbia University swim team?" Nora asks in the meantime and blinks innocently. "Tell me more."

"Why are you even here?" I ask her.

"Your boyfriend's supposed to babysit," she says. "But that was before I found out about the love affair of the century. If you two are overcome by your feelings and can't resist the urge to elope, feel free to say so. I think Blake was free, too."

I shove my hand in the pocket of my sweats, then pull it out, holding my middle finger up toward her.

Nora's smile is downright evil now. "I'm going to enjoy this relationship."

"There is no relationship," I grit through my teeth.

"There kind of *is* a relationship," Nora says. She plucks another grape and tosses it into her mouth. She chews it slowly, eyes on me the whole time, before she says, "And you've just cast yourself as the boyfriend."

I cross my arms over my chest and glare at her. "No. Absolutely not. Nuh-uh. Sorry. Not doing that."

"Yeah, that's not necessary," Quinn agrees. "I'll figure something out." He sends me a quick side glance. *Something that doesn't involve him.*

"Consequences of actions," Nora says firmly. "*You*"—she points to Quinn—"shouldn't have lied. And *you*"—her finger is now aimed in my face as she purses her lips—"well, your involvement is sort of accidental this time, true, but you owe me about a thousand favors, so I'm cashing them in right now."

I stare back at her.

She quirks her brow, daring me to argue, and... Well, I can't really, can I?

I look away.

Straight at Quinn.

Shit.

STEPH

IT'S safe to say I have a bit of experience with comeuppance.
I've been arrested.
I've been stranded.
I've woken up in unmentionable places and next to unmentionable people.
I have multiple scars on different parts of my body that would probably tell a story if I could remember fuck all about how I got them.
I bet my photo is up on at least some bedroom walls with darts conveniently placed close by.
I'm pretty sure I'm banned from Arkansas altogether, but that's neither here nor there.
It's life. Play stupid games, win stupid prizes. Stupid does the heavy lifting when it comes to me. It's not to say I've enjoyed any of those stupid prizes. All I'm saying is I've got a lot of experience with the consequences of my actions. Mostly unpleasant ones. And I'm not exaggerating when I say I'd take any of those other consequences instead of this—this cruel and unusual punishment.
The worst part about this mess? I volunteered.

Sort of.

I cross my arms over my chest and tuck my hands underneath my armpits. Quirk my brow the tiniest increment. The air that was already cool is now downright icy.

Hazel doesn't seem to notice, happily dozing in Quinn's arms like a tiny sloth. Nora took off a few minutes ago, and ever since the door fell shut behind her, Quinn and I have been engaged in silent warfare where the loser is the person who either looks away first or speaks first.

Childish? Yes.

Am I going to be the bigger person, break the angry eye contact, and discuss this problem we now have? No.

Hazel giggles in her sleep, and my eyes snap down to her.

God damnit!

When I look up again, he doesn't gloat. That's beneath Quinn. He's too perfect for that.

"If you agree to do this," he says in a low voice, eyes on Hazel. "If we're going to pretend... We have to do it properly. I know everything's all fun and games to you, but..."

He doesn't finish the sentence, and instead chooses to let me fill in the gaps.

It's all fun and games to you because you're an irresponsible fuckup, but it's important to me because I'm awesome and great and will not tolerate anything other than perfection.

Or something in that ballpark.

"It has to be convincing, is what I mean," he continues. "We have to get our stories straight."

"Our stories?"

"Facts," he reiterates. "How we met. How long we've been together. We have to be able to leave the impression we know each other. At least a little bit. Basic likes. Dislikes. Habits. Allergies. Et cetera."

I stare at him. "Are you expecting your family to conduct a green card marriage interview?"

His jaw twitches. "We have to be convincing. There's no point in doing this if I have to later explain to my family that I was lying and have been lying about having a... a..."—he seems to be lost for words for a moment—"a love life for the past year," he finally concludes.

"Yeah... What's the deal with that? Why did you say it in the first place? Why make up a boyfriend? If you wanted one, you could probably find somebody. I mean, to the average viewer I guess you're not totally off-putting, so it doesn't sound like it'd be impossible to find at least some takers."

"Thank you," he says dryly.

I just shrug. We both know where we stand with each other, so I don't think either of us needs to sugarcoat our opinions.

His gaze stays on Hazel, and he's silent for the longest time before he says, "It was just easier that way."

"*Was* being the operative word," I mutter.

"Yes, well, I didn't really plan on you," he says.

He looks up then. Eyes meet mine. Searching for something. I don't know what, and even if I did, I doubt I could give it to him. But for once, he regards me with something other than cold distance in his gaze. For once, the door is open. *Come. Come inside. Sit down. Let me see you.*

My heart speeds up, apprehension worming its way through my insides.

No, thank you.

"Not many people do. I don't know why," I say flippantly. "I'm a really good time."

The door slams shut.

"Lack of preparedness tends to be the one contributing factor that always makes natural disasters worse when they occur, doesn't it?" he says.

"A natural disaster," I muse. "I'm flattered."

"It wasn't a compliment."

His eyes are still on me. There are these moments with Quinn sometimes when it feels like he's curious. Like he's trying to find something when he looks at me. Not the uncomplicated, pretty facade, but the truth beneath the surface.

It's yet another one of those things I thoroughly dislike about him.

No one's allowed to see me.

Which is why it's not a good idea to increase the time I spend in Quinn's presence.

"You sure you want to do this?" I ask.

He quirks his brow in question.

"Introduce me to your family," I clarify.

"Changing your mind already?" he asks tonelessly, like this is exactly what he's been expecting from me. To abandon ship once I've run it onto a reef.

"I'm giving *you* a chance to change your mind. Look, we both know I'm not exactly boyfriend material, right? Please, please, please tell me this is one of those rare moments when we're on the same page."

"You can relax. I'm not vying for your hand in marriage here." He gives me an assessing look. "Blair says you participated in a ton of school plays when you were in high school."

"Yeah. So?"

"So I assume there's a reason you did. Which means you can act like you are boyfriend material for a few days," he says, like it's that simple.

"You do realize you also have to act like you can stand me?" I point out.

"I'll do my best," he says with a tight smile.

I suppose 'do my best' is the best we can hope for here.

"We're also going to have to act like a couple," I continue

listing all the flaws in that plan. "We have to... do stuff." Already this relationship is making me revert back into an awkward teenager.

"Do stuff?" Quinn repeats. "You really have a way with words."

I give him the stink eye.

He quirks his brow. "Do you think my family expects us to jump each other in front of them to prove our commitment? Because I assure you, they don't. Yes, there has to be at least some physical contact between the two of us to make the relationship seem believable, but I promise you, nobody expects us to engage in excessive amounts of PDA in front of everybody. In fact, I strongly suggest we avoid anything that resembles PDA."

Well, I suppose that sounds reasonable. Maybe even doable.

"You don't think it'll be extremely awkward?" I ask. "Considering..." My voice drops off, and I execute some sort of hand motion that is so nonsensical even I'm having trouble figuring out what it's supposed to mean.

"Considering?" Quinn prompts.

"The thing," I say. Because I'm a fifth grader now.

"Uh..." he says slowly. "What the hell are you talking about?"

"You know. The sleeping together thing. That happened. Between us," I say.

It's almost comical how his face transforms from confused to straight-up horrified. "You think we had sex?"

I blink and stare. "We... didn't?"

"You think we slept together?" he asks, still with the thoroughly scandalized look. He seems to be having a bit of trouble finding his words before he sputters, "Wha—Why—?" He starts shaking his head. "No! No. No, no, no. No." More head shaking to the chorus of more noes follow. "No, no. No. No—"

"Do you have a word count you have to fill?" I interrupt.

He clamps his mouth shut, and we stare at each other for a second.

"Why would you even think I would ever do something li—" Quinn starts.

"Oh, I don't know. Might be because I was naked in your bed."

"Yes, believe me, the striptease last night was entirely unwelcome. Maybe next time we could avoid that. Also—"

"I get the picture!" I snap.

Look, yeah, I'm a disaster, but I'm a disaster with feelings. And when somebody is so intensely horrified about the prospect of seeing me naked those feelings get hurt.

We both fall silent. It's uncomfortable as hell and is starting to make me all fidgety.

"Now what?" I finally ask.

"Pray?" he suggests dryly.

Yup. Sounds about right.

STEPH

MY SHIT-TASTIC DAY only gets worse when I unlock my front door and immediately stumble on a bag and only manage to avoid faceplanting on the floor by landing ungracefully on my arm.

"Shit! Ow! Shit!" I snap and glare at the offending piece of black luggage by my feet.

Jude's voice carries into the hallway. "Steph?"

"The one and only," I mutter.

Jude's head appears in the doorway, and he frowns when he sees me on the floor. "Why are you crawling around the hallway?"

"I don't know about you, but I happen to like being on all fours," I say.

He laughs, comes over, and pulls me to my feet.

"Thanks," I say and wipe my palms over my ass. "Why are you putting up booby traps all over the place? Oh! Did Blake hack the wrong people, and now we're all running from the law, trying to prove our innocence? I'll get my stuff!"

He smiles and raps his knuckles against the top of my head. "What a fascinating acid trip this place must be."

"Really makes you wonder how I ever get anything done." Jude laughs and nudges the suitcase against the wall.

"What brings you to my humble abode?" I ask.

Next to Blair, Jude's my other best friend, and we're technically roommates. The kind of roommates where I live in the apartment we rent together, and he lives a few blocks away with his boyfriend.

I'm only about twenty-five percent bitter Blake stole him from me. Maybe thirty. It's not jealousy. Or at least not the traditional kind of jealousy. It's just that when your best friend falls in love, you drop in the rankings of the most important people in his life, and sometimes one likes to be a selfish dumbass and feel left out.

Not that I'd ever say any of it out loud. Jude deserves to be with somebody who makes him come alive. That person is Blake. The less enjoyable part is that now that they're really serious, I need to get my shit together, because as long as I don't have alternative living arrangements figured out, Jude will officially stay in this apartment out of some misguided sense of loyalty.

"Blake needed some sort of wire," Jude says. "Apparently the five thousand ones we have at home just won't cut it. Go figure." He goes to Blake, who's sitting in the middle of the living room, sorting through something that looks like a hundred wires were turned into a ball of yarn and then a cat went to town on it.

"I need the one that can perform keystroke injection attacks," Blake says distractedly. "I swear, I have it somewhere."

"What does it look like? Maybe I've seen it," I offer.

"It's white and has a doodad on one end and a doohickey on the other," Jude says.

"Ah. I've only seen the ones with either two doodads or two doohickeys. Sorry."

"Maybe it's in one of the boxes I put in the closet in the bedroom." Blake looks around and scratches the back of his head.

"When did you have time to put crap in the closet?" Jude asks with a genuinely perplexed expression.

"I ran out of room at home," Blake says and gets up. "And since you don't own anything, it seemed like a waste to leave all that closet space empty."

Jude crosses his arms over his chest. "What do you mean I don't own anything?"

"I mean you... don't own anything," Blake says. "You're like an extreme minimalist. I keep expecting Netflix to stop by and ask to do a reality show about you. You don't even have a laptop." He makes it sound like Jude's trying to exist without air.

Jude sends him a dubious look. "Why would I buy a laptop when you have three?"

"Kitchen supplies?"

"You know I don't cook if I can help it, so why would I voluntarily buy kitchen shit?" Jude asks.

"And you're wearing my clothes," Blake adds.

"Well, if I can't even wear your clothes, what's the point of being in this relationship at all?" Jude raises his brow. "You know, some people find frugality hot."

Blake glances at me. "I trapped him with my sweats collection."

I make a face. "Thanks for the warning. I'll be sure to throw out every pair I own lest somebody get ideas."

"Yeah, no," Jude says. "You probably don't need to trap anybody now that you're all in love and shit." He sends me a sly smirk, just shy of wiggling his eyebrows.

"Damn Nora and her big mouth," I mutter.

"Technically, it was Blair's big mouth." He thinks about it for a second. "Well, she tried to break the news, but she was laughing so hard I couldn't understand a word, so Nora had to translate."

"With great reluctance, I imagine, since we all value privacy and discretion so much, right?" I say.

"Oh, yeah." Jude snorts. "We're all about tact and not sticking our noses into anybody else's business in these parts. You've got that spot on."

I sigh and shake my head. "We could be," I say hopefully. "Picture this: a new group dynamic. One where we all respect each other's boundaries and won't talk about each other behind the other's back. Huh? Wouldn't it be nice?"

Jude looks at Blake with a frown for a second and then they both start to laugh out loud.

"Sounds boring," Jude concludes once he's calmed down.

I can't say I'm loving this new, in-touch-with-his-emotions Jude. I miss the days when we could both peacefully ignore our issues and just be screwed up together. Now it's just me left in that corner.

"Seriously, though," Jude says. "Why did you agree to this? You hate Quinn."

I lift up my index finger. "I do *not* hate Quinn. I don't hate anybody." Neither Blake nor Jude says anything. They both just send me identical skeptical looks until I start to fidget.

"I don't hate him," I repeat. "I'm ambivalent." They're still staring. "It's mutual," I say defensively. "Some people just don't click. He finds me difficult to tolerate. And I find him more palatable in moderation," I add, even though it's starting to feel a bit like the lady doth protest too much. "Like wasabi."

"You hate wasabi," Jude points out.

"No. I'm fine with wasabi as long as it's not anywhere near me."

"Case in point."

I shrug and drag my fingers through my hair. "Yeah, well, I

can kind of admit that the whole thing is partially my fault. Mainly his, but I did have a hand in leaving the impression that we might be... seeing. Each other."

"You might want to practice saying that out loud a few times," Blake suggests. "The gagging doesn't exactly scream eternal love."

"Aww. Never given a proper blowjob?" I ask.

Blake just laughs. He's the kind of person who is almost impossible to piss off. I'm one of the few who've managed. By accident, mind you. How was I supposed to know I shouldn't mention I've slept with Jude to Blake? Yeah. It took some time for Blake to get over that one.

"We'll go visit his family for a few days and then we'll go our separate ways," I say. "He'll tell them we broke up after a little while, and we can put it all behind us."

"A week," Jude corrects.

"Otherwise known as a few days," I say. "Can you work with me here?"

"Sure. My bad. All the seven few days."

I flip him off. "Anyway, there'll be a bunch of people there, so it's not like we have to be attached at the hip."

"Absolutely," Jude says and nods seriously. "Couples in love are known for staying far away from each other."

I look at Blake. "Can you tell your boyfriend not to be such a buzzkill."

"I would, but he's making some valid points."

I roll my eyes. "You're already dating him. You don't have to keep sucking up."

"Don't listen to him," Jude tells Blake. "Suck up all you want. I love hearing that I'm the bestest." He glances toward me. "I'd take notes about the proper boyfriend etiquette if I were you. Learn from the best."

Blake grins at him and heads to the bedroom to search for his wire, and Jude sobers.

"You sure this is a good idea?" he asks.

It's my turn to laugh. "No. But when has that ever stopped me?"

"True. But still. You don't actually have to if you don't want to."

I wave him off. "I'll be fine. I can act like I like him for a few days. How hard can it be?"

"No offense, but I don't think you're *that* good of an actor."

I flip him off again.

I am *that* good of an actor. My whole life is an act.

And I can do this.

Piece of cake.

STEPH

I'VE ALWAYS LIKED the beginning of *Love Actually*. The very first few scenes where Hugh Grant's voice talks about the arrival gate at Heathrow Airport and how there's love everywhere.

And secretly, deep down inside, I've always wanted somebody to greet me like the people in that movie do. With tight hugs that squeeze the breath right out of your lungs, and wide smiles that let you know you're the one they've been waiting for.

Instead, I get Quinn, and I get a scowl that says he has a bunch of other destinations in mind for me. Gates of hell. The edge of an active volcano. Locked in an arena with a pack of polar bears.

For a moment, I entertain the idea of hugging him. Just as an experiment. I'd like to see what he'd do. Burst into flames and turn into ash most likely, which, I'm not going to lie, isn't a terrible prospect.

"You're late," is his joyful greeting. I couldn't get off work, so Quinn arrived two days before me.

"Yeah, my bad," I say and drop my suitcase in front of my feet and slam my hands on my hips. "See, the moment we took off from JFK, I realized we weren't going to make it on time, so naturally I went to the cockpit and told the pilots I'd take over. I really think you would've been impressed with me. I was just oozing authority and can-do attitude. So much so that everybody was cool with me flying the plane because things like that happen all the time on commercial flights, and whenever the flight is delayed, they actually expect the passengers to come in and save the day. Anyway, I did my best, but there's only so fast I can make a plane go, and now here we are. Late. I take full responsibility. *Mea culpa.*"

"You could have texted," he says after a moment.

"I could've," I agree. "Everybody knows that once you board the plane, the cell reception is going to be excellent. Did you know they give you extra bars the moment you get your ass in that seat?"

"What a fun story," Quinn says without a trace of emotion.

I look toward the ceiling and count to ten. Is it too late to get back on the plane, hide in the bathroom, and pretend I never arrived in Portland? It's the perfect plan. Save for the fact it requires time travel.

"Let's get going," Quinn says. "We'll have about three hours of driving ahead of us before we get to the camp. I figured it was enough time to get our stories and facts straight."

I stretch my lips into a smile. "Can't wait."

"Clearly. Once we arrive, could you try and sound less like you're headed to get a lobotomy?" he suggests.

I stretch my neck and look around excitedly. "Are they offering those here? 'Cause I'll take two."

It might just be my imagination, but his lips twitch a tiniest bit. Of course, it might just be that the idea of torture makes him happy.

"WHY ARE YOU TAKING I-95?" I ask when Quinn takes a left.

"It's faster."

I let out my most derisive snort. "Where? In your head?"

"On the map."

"Be serious. You know it's not. I-295 is shorter."

"I didn't say shorter, did I? I said faster," he says.

"It's not. Are you really going to argue with somebody who used to live here?" I ask.

"My family's had a camp here since I was born," he counters. "I take this road every few months. I *just* took this road five hours ago to come and pick you up."

"You take the wrong interstate every few months?" I ask. "I wouldn't brag about it so loudly, but I guess it's admirable you own your mistakes."

His fingers grip the steering wheel, and he draws in a long, slow breath.

"We'll have to merge onto I-95 midway through anyway, so what's the difference?"

"Your way is longer," I say.

"Well, I'm driving, so tough."

"Tolls," I point out.

"Who the fuck cares?" he grouses.

The next few miles go by in silence as Quinn navigates us out of Portland. Calmly and competently. It would be a turn-on, honestly, but it's Quinn, so adhering to my I'm-opposed-to-everything-Quinn-does principle, I now like wimpy drivers. Are you insecure behind the wheel? A real danger to all the other travelers? Mmm, yeah, baby. Do me.

I pair my phone with the car and put on some music. Miraculously, he doesn't have anything to say about my choice of songs.

"We should probably figure out what we're going to tell people about us," Quinn eventually says.

"What have you told them so far?" I ask.

"Almost nothing," he says. "Seeing that I made you up."

"Yeah, that's what I'm worried about. I'm pretty sure your imagination doesn't do me justice." There's also the fact that the few of Quinn's dates I've seen over the years have been pretty much the polar opposite of me. They've all been interchangeable blond, polo-shirt-wearing, khakis-loving, golf-playing, investment banker types. Whenever I can't sleep, I just have to remember any of the mind-numbingly boring conversations I've had with some of those dudes, and it works better than any sleeping pill. "What exactly is your family expecting?"

Quinn throws me a questioning look. "What do you mean?"

"I mean, whatever you told them, I have to *be* that person. So help me out here, would you? Unless you want me to improvise. Actually, can I improvise? Let's see. Who do I want to be?" I narrow my eyes for a moment before I flick my fingers. "Got it. Simon Merryweather. Royal Navy assassin."

He sighs. "A, they already know your name. B, I'm pretty sure assassins don't introduce themselves as assassins. It defeats the purpose. C, the Royal Navy is the United Kingdom's naval force."

"Stephen Hartley. Astronaut."

"Do you know anything about space?"

"That shiny, round object you see in the sky at night is called the moon. Fun fact, the name moon comes from the Greek word moo. The sound cows make. Because the moon is made of cheese, and you can't have cheese without cows."

"Well, you obviously have extensive knowledge. We'll let NASA know about you."

"Stephen Hartley. Forensic scientist."

"Again, do you know anything about forensic science?"

"I can definitely almost certainly tell a dead body from a live one. The trick is to see if they're moving or not."

"We'll get you a badge first thing tomorrow morning."

I wave him off. "I'll make something up as I go."

"That's what I'm afraid of." He sighs and stares ahead for so long I'm starting to think he's spaced out on me. "They don't expect you to be anything," he finally says. "You should just be you."

I blink, completely stumped for a moment. The person who actively dislikes me tells me to be myself. It feels like a trap.

"Besides," he continues. "I don't think you'll be very convincing as somebody else."

"You underestimate me. I'm a chameleon."

He glances toward me and then back to the road. "You know, not everything I say is meant to be taken as an attack on your person."

"At this point, it's just an automatic reaction."

He lets out a grim laugh. "This is going to be a disaster."

"You're a pessimist," I say. "Aww. See? We're already learning things about each other."

"A realist," he corrects.

"Otherwise known as a pessimist. I heard you loud and clear the first time."

"It'll be a miracle if we don't kill each other by the end of this," he says. "How's that for optimism?"

"Yeah," I say before I gasp. "Oh, fuck! I'm agreeing with you on something. Didn't the Mayans say it was one of the signs of the end of our civilization?"

"Yes, Stephen. You're such a force of nature, the Mayans predicted you four thousand years ago. Can we just try and stick to the topic for once?" Quinn asks with an exasperated huff. "Just tell me something useful. Some relevant facts about yourself, so it'll look like I know you at least a little bit. Anything."

It takes a long-ass time to find something I think I'm okay with him knowing. "My middle name is Christopher."

He mulls over it for a second. "Stephen Christopher Hartley."

"What's yours?" I ask.

"Benedict."

"Quinn Benedict Henris," I say, mimicking his tone.

"Alexander," he says.

I send him a confused look. "Your name is Quinn Benedict Alexander? Since when?"

"Quinn Benedict Alexander Henris," he says.

I snort. "Somebody's overcompensating."

He sends me a withering look.

I aim a toothy grin his way. "It suits you perfectly."

"What else do I need to know?" he asks. "Favorite food? How do you take your coffee? Allergies? Job? Education?"

"You're really stuck on those allergies. I'm beginning to think that if I tell you, you'll use that knowledge to 'accidentally' kill me." I add the finger quotes. "Oh, oops. How could I possibly forget Steph was deathly allergic to penicillin? Oh well. What's done is done. Let's bury the body in the backyard and move on."

"Why would I do the dirty work myself? I'll just hire one of those Royal Navy assassins," he says dryly.

"You probably have to, seeing that I have no deadly allergies. Sorry."

"Packing all those bees and nuts in my suitcase was a waste of time, then."

Ladies and gentlemen, let this day be marked in the history books as the day Quinn Henris made a joke. I'm too shocked by this turn of events to laugh.

"A complete waste," I agree. "Also, still a college dropout and still working in a bar. You're still coaching, I assume?"

"Teaching swimming," he says.

I wave him off. "Same thing."

"Not really."

I sigh and try to remember the rest of the questionnaire. "I don't like coffee, and my favorite food is potatoes."

"Potatoes," he repeats.

"The Gaffer's delight, and rare good ballast for an empty belly," I say.

He's staring again.

"What?" I ask in an exasperated voice.

He turns his gaze away. "Just didn't expect you to start quoting *The Two Towers*."

"Because you didn't think I could read?"

He sighs and shakes his head. "Yes, Stephen. You caught me. I absolutely figured you were illiterate. To say I'm shocked you're not is an understatement."

"It's why we've been happily shacked up for so long. I keep you on your toes. All new surprises every day. Are we living together, by the way? I feel like I should know that."

"No, we don't live together," he says. Another mile passes in silence before he says, "It's my sister's favorite book series. *The Lord of the Rings*. She's dyslexic, so at first, I used to read it to her. A lot. I think I can still quote half the book by heart."

As always, it stumps me when he shows his human side.

"Rubi?" I ask.

He nods. "I'm the oldest. Then it's Rubi, Axel, and Reid's the baby of the family."

I knew that already. From all my stalking days.

"When Rubi was thirteen, I told her Tolkien was having a book signing in our local bookstore," Quinn says. "She stood in the corner for three hours with her stack of books until one of the assistants asked her if she was lost."

My mouth falls open as I stare at Quinn's profile and the

slight tilt in the corner of his lips. I'm not shocked about the prank. But I'm definitely shocked about how fond he sounds when he talks about his family.

"That's both incredibly evil and incredibly funny," I finally say once I've regained my ability to speak.

"She got her revenge." He sends me an amused look. "No siblings?"

Such an ordinary question asked in such a casual way.

Not even a question, really.

A comment.

Almost careless in its delivery.

It shouldn't feel like this. The lightheaded feeling of drowning shouldn't be there if a question is so simple.

I should laugh it off, but I can't.

What do you say? How do you answer if he *was* but no longer *is*? If you *had* but no longer *have*? How do you explain a void so endless it sometimes feels like your whole existence is made up of an absence.

And why does it even matter? To Quinn. I don't care about Quinn.

So I simply shake my head.

No, no siblings. No nobody.

"What's that like?" he asks, the slight tilt of humor in the corner of his mouth is still there. "Being an only child."

I stare at him. Is it stab the scars day or something?

"What the fuck does it matter?" I snap, even though I try to keep my voice level. Try and fail.

He sends me a strange look. "Call it curiosity."

It's already too late when I realize that wasn't so much a question but maybe something like an olive branch. An offer to both take a tentative step toward no man's land. Maybe meet in the middle and make this weekend a bit less painful.

An olive branch that says, *hey, this is a harmless, pointless question you can turn into small talk. Take it. Maybe we can make this easier for the both of us.*

And even while realizing all of that, the words I need to say just aren't there.

Because I don't know what it's like to be an only child. I only know what it's like to be a lonely adult.

Instead of explaining any of that, I force out a strained laugh.

"I don't think your family will ask you how I feel about being an only child," I say. "So that's irrelevant."

He's quiet for a long time then. "Right," he finally says, voice tight. He straightens his shoulders and stretches his neck, and then he's all business again. He packs away the memories of siblings and funny stories. And good for him. It's better if he keeps them for somebody... somebody better.

"It's probably easier if we stick as close to the truth as possible, so we'll say Nora introduced us, which is true," he says. "And we've been seeing each other for about nine months now, which is about the time you've been in New York, so it checks out."

I nod and slouch lower in the seat and try and get my head back straight. I'm feeling slightly more off-balance than I'd necessarily like.

Any other day, I'd shrug it off. Tuck those feelings away. Out of sight, out of mind. I'm good at that part.

Right now, I'm tired and apprehensive about what's to come, so it's hard to dismiss the feeling that I've somehow disappointed Quinn.

And I shouldn't care. But I do. Creating disappointment seems to be my lot in life.

"Sounds good," I say belatedly.

And then we go back to silence.

QUINN

PEOPLE AREN'T REALLY SUPPOSED to lie. It's something we're taught early on. Books. Kids' shows. Movies. People lie, and they get into trouble until both you and the main character of whatever form of entertainment you're currently consuming learn a valuable lesson. Do. Not. Lie.

Clearly that lesson didn't stick in my case, and that one little white lie I've been spinning for quite some time now has come back to bite me in the ass at the most inopportune moment and in the most inconvenient way.

It's my own fault. Not because I lied in the first place. It's my own fault because I brought the consequences on myself by being too responsible. I should've just let Stephen take care of Stephen when I found him holding a private party with a bottle of vodka. Instead, I dragged him home and put him to bed from some misguided sense of loyalty to Nora and Blair.

Things really got out of hand, and now I'm on my way to the camp, getting ready to spend time with my family, with a pretend boyfriend in tow.

All my fault, of course. Nobody forced me to tell my family I was dating somebody. Nobody forced me to keep the lie going just because it stopped Rubi and Axel from trying to fix me up with people like they were afraid being single was punishable by death. Just because it stopped my parents from sending me worried looks about my apparent loneliness.

I had one glass of champagne too many and told them all I was seeing somebody sometime during my parents' anniversary party, right after Rubi tried to set me up with the bartender.

I figured I'd come clean, but then something great happened —they stopped meddling. And I kept lying.

And now here we are. As if the pretend boyfriend part isn't bad enough, I've somehow ended up with Stephen filling that role.

Stephen, who's currently sitting cross-legged in the passenger seat, humming along to the music, tapping the rhythm on his thighs. Long fingers on dark blue denim. Messy hair and the beginnings of a five o'clock shadow. A sharp edge of his collarbone and lips so full they almost look swollen. Green eyes and a distant look he gets in them when he thinks no one's watching.

He's pulled off the hoodie he was wearing earlier and is now sitting there in a white T-shirt. And when he absently scratches his shoulder, he exposes the edge of a tattoo. Transparent wings of some sort.

I mercilessly stomp down the need to ask what it is. Stomp down the strange spark of curiosity I sometimes feel around Stephen. My gaze darts away.

Kill it with fire. This mess is the last thing you need.

My hands grip the steering wheel, and I glare at the road.

It's the flippant attitude, I think. Or maybe the carefree approach to absolutely everything. Or the exceedingly happy-go-lucky nature. Or the fact that nothing about him seems sincere. It's difficult to pinpoint the thing that annoys me most about Stephen. His whole cheerful, never-take-anything-seriously outlook on life grates on me. It's the polar opposite of everything I am.

Stephen is the poster boy of having it easy. He's undisputedly a mess, but there are never any consequences. He keeps fucking up, and people keep bailing him out, handing him chance after chance without a second thought.

And I know my own personal shit is not a good reason to dislike somebody, but here's the interesting part: for all his apparent optimism and cheerfulness? Stephen has absolutely despised me from the moment Nora introduced the two of us.

Yes, he made a valiant effort to hide it at first. He was painfully polite, but it was also obvious that he tried to avoid me as much as he could. Whenever I walked into the room, his whole body stiffened, and the brilliant smile he had for everybody else morphed into a tight-lipped grin when he aimed it in my direction. The forced pleasantness didn't last too long, and over the years silent contempt has grown into snide remarks, stabs disguised as neutral statements, and by now, we've graduated into a full-on war of words.

In its own way, the relationship I have with Stephen is the most honest one I've ever had.

No pretenses.

No hidden agenda.

Just pure mutual dislike.

STEPH

I STARE at the behemoth of a house in front of me before I turn toward Quinn. "Well, this is ridiculous."

Quinn closes the trunk and frowns. "What is ridiculous?"

"*This*," I say and gesture toward the... Log Mansion? Wood Palace? Castle of Spruce? The Great Pine Hall?

He rolls his eyes. "It's just a camp."

"It has towers!"

"Also known as chimneys."

"And this thing's all windows," I continue. "And there are a bunch of little houses. This is no camp. This is a damn compound."

"Okay," he says and rolls his eyes.

"Camps are small," I say.

"I don't think that's a requirement."

"Let's see, shall we?" I pull out my phone. "Ha! Camp. A *simple* cabin, often overlooking a body of water."

"The bay is right back there." He drops my bag on the ground next to him and takes in the house in front of us. "My parents spend their summers here. Family and friends visit. They need room for all the people who stop by."

He starts to move, but I grab his arm and pull him back.

"Exactly how many people will be here?"

"Technically just family, but you never know who decides to invite a friend or two at the last moment."

"Are you—"

I don't get to finish that sentence because the front door is pulled open, and Quinn's mom walks out, cutting through the tension that's growing inside me at the thought of including more people in this sham of a relationship.

"There you two are," she says. "I was beginning to think you got lost on the way here."

She widens her arms even before she reaches us, and once she's in front of me, I'm engulfed in a hug like I'm the long-lost son, instead of somebody she's only met once, briefly.

"The plane was delayed," I say quickly because I wouldn't put it past Quinn to throw me under the bus here.

And she's *still* hugging me.

"Oh, I hate it when that happens," she says brightly and finally lets go. "But you're here now. Let's get you inside, and we'll get you settled."

The camp might not really be a camp, but it's undeniably a gorgeous house. Situated a thirty-minute drive from Bar Harbor, it's nestled among trees so naturally you'd think it wasn't built by humans and one day just grew out of the ground.

"This is a lovely house," I say as she leads me through the front door and into a foyer.

She throws a smile over her shoulder. "Thank you. This land's been in Philip's family for ages. We're actually standing right where the old camp used to be. Of course, it was only one room and a dirt floor back when he first brought me to visit. We've always loved it here, though, so when Phil's brother said he was thinking about selling the place, we couldn't let it go and bought it for ourselves. It's home. Filled to the brim with memories and stories." She points to the fireplace in the large, open plan living room. "Quinn ran into the corner of this thing when he was ten and lost all his front teeth."

I glance toward Quinn and raise my brows. "Those aren't your real teeth?"

"They are," he says shortly like childhood injuries are something to be ashamed of.

"He lost the baby teeth," Caroline explains.

A slow grin tilts the corners of my lips up. "You still had your front baby teeth when you were ten?"

"Yes," he says tonelessly. My God, he's really not selling this relationship at all.

Hell, one of us should, at least, so I sidle closer to him, slide my palm over his chest and smile at him. "Luck of the draw, then, huh?"

He's so stiff I could probably pick him up by his feet and use him as a battering ram.

"Quinn was a late bloomer," Caroline supplies and points out a photo on the wall. "That's him when he was eleven."

I'm not too proud to take the chance to escape Quinn's side. There's a skinny, tiny boy in the photo, all knees and elbows and wide eyes. He looks about seven, at the most. I turn my head toward Quinn and then back to the photo. No way.

"That's you?" I ask.

"Thank you, Mother," Quinn says.

"Oh, hush. You were cute." Caroline pats him on the cheek.

"Very cute," I say, lift my phone, and take a photo. "What?" I ask innocently when Quinn glares at me. "You've never showed me your childhood photos. Are there more? Maybe photo albums? I'd love to see photo albums."

"Yes, we have tons of photos," Caroline says happily.

"And we're moving on," Quinn interrupts and plants his palm on my shoulder and pushes me forward.

"Hey! I wasn't done looking." I crane my neck, trying to get one last look. "Is that you dressed as a banana?"

"Up the stairs you go," Quinn says loudly.

"Quinn will show you his room," Caroline calls after me. "Drop off your things and come outside to the back when you're settled in. Dinner's in an hour."

"Sure," I call from the second floor while Quinn is marching me down the long hallway, a step shy of manhandling me like a damn prison guard. We turn a corner, and he pushes open a door and then pushes me in.

"Holy shit," I say once I get a moment to look around.

The bag drops on the floor, and I walk straight to the window. It's blue. Everything is blue. The sky. The sea. It stretches out in front of me, dotted with little islets and fluffy white clouds that look like cotton candy. This is a photo from a vacation brochure. It can't be real.

I stand, and I stare, unable to move or look away.

It takes effort to tear my gaze away.

"That's quite a view," I say.

The ever-present frown on Quinn's face is tucked away for a change, replaced with an unreadable expression. An improvement, as far as I'm concerned.

"Yes," he says once he catches himself showing something other than disdain. "It's nice. Are you ready to go downstairs now? We better get this dinner over with."

Back to reality.

"Sure, sweet pea. Lead the way," I say.

"Do not call me sweet pea."

"Pumpkin?" I offer.

"How about we skip nicknames altogether," he says in a voice that makes it very clear this isn't a suggestion. "And how about we try and take this seriously, for fuck's sake!"

"Oh, I'm sorry. I forgot that as your boyfriend I'm supposed to look miserable. But don't worry. I'll bring the despair, and it'll be one hundred percent authentic."

He looks like he wants to say something else, but then he turns on his heel and stalks out of the room.

"Coming, honey," I mutter under my breath and follow him.

IT'S MAYHEM OUTSIDE. There's a large deck at the back of the house where everybody has gathered, and when Quinn and I step outside, all heads turn toward us.

The middle of the deck is taken up by a long table and people are milling back and forth to the kitchen, bringing out food, standing around by the grill, laying out plates and utensils.

"Everybody, this is Stephen," Quinn says loudly. "The boyfriend," he adds in a tone people usually reserve for saying things like 'drug mule' or 'cult leader.'

"Hi," I say. Silence. And staring. I'm not sure why. I'm hardly the first person Quinn's dated. Granted, they're all usually the same boring, stock-shares-make-for-riveting-conversation types, so it might be his family's under the impression he's been dating the same man the whole time.

"I usually go by Steph," I say.

And the volume comes back on.

The childhood Quinn obsession pays off at least a little bit because it makes it somewhat easier to remember everybody when Quinn points out all the people milling around.

Rubi greets me with a hug and a kiss on the cheek. Considering how contained Quinn always is, it's a jarring contrast that his whole family is so tactile.

On the opposite side of the table from Rubi is Axel, the two of them in the middle of a card game. Another round of hugs follows when Quinn introduces us.

"You're hot," Rubi tells me before she turns to look at Quinn. "Good choice."

Quinn groans. "Can you stop calling my boyfriend hot? It's fucking weird."

"Why? Are you afraid he doesn't know and will dump you once he finds out?" Axel asks.

"You have nothing to worry about." I slide my arm around Quinn's waist. "I still like you even though I'm hot."

Rubi and Axel grin. Quinn gives another pained smile. He's either a terrible liar or my proximity is physically painful.

Rounding up the Henris clan is the youngest brother, Reid, who smiles and nods at me without saying a word and escapes back to the kitchen shortly after Quinn introduces us.

There's also Rubi's boyfriend, Nick, and Axel's wife, Ivy.

Quinn seems to be having trouble figuring out what to do with his arm. In the end, he drapes it around my shoulders in the most unnatural way possible, so we end up standing side by side stiffly, in the way I imagine people do when it's an arranged marriage, and you only meet your groom five minutes before you're supposed to say I do.

"Can I help?" I ask desperately the next time Quinn's mom appears in the doorway. *Just give me a job. Anything that gets me far away from your son will do.*

"Of course. Grab whatever Reid has set on the counter and bring it outside," she says.

I sprint away from the deck like my heels are on fire.

All too soon, the table has been set and we're all sitting down for dinner. I take the empty chair between Rubi and Quinn, and then everybody starts a coordinated dance of passing around trays and bowls until all the plates are piled high with food.

Rubi taps her fork against the wineglass and calls out, "Speech. Speech."

Phil gets up, lifts his own wineglass, clears his throat, and everybody falls silent.

"Welcome, sons. Welcome, daughters. Welcome, significant others," he says before he looks at his wife and raises his brows.

"And now dig in," Caroline continues.

"Dad always gives the best speeches," Rubi tells me.

"And what makes them the best is the fact that they're so short," Axel adds.

"I don't always give short speeches," Philip argues. "It's just a matter of knowing your audience, and this particular audience does not appreciate my more thoughtful offerings. I'd be casting pearls before swine."

Shouts of protest ring out all around the table, but they're interspersed with laughter. Teasing remarks fly back and forth, and it's all so goddamn wholesome and nice, and ooh, boy, I do *not* belong at this table. I have never felt quite this out of place in my life.

And it only gets worse because I'm suddenly acutely aware that I'm lying to all these people. Pretending to be Quinn's boyfriend for a few days didn't seem like that big of a problem when I was far away in New York and hadn't properly met Quinn's family yet. Now I'm seriously questioning whether it was actually a good idea to go along with this.

All my greatest failures have started with the best of intentions. And now it's too late to do anything other than see it through. Story of my life.

"Steph?"

I snap my eyes up at the sound of my name and blink, focusing back on the present.

"You okay?" Quinn asks.

I nod quickly. "Yes. Sorry. I spaced out for a moment."

Caroline smiles at me. "Quinn was telling us Nora introduced the two of you. How do you know Nora?"

"Oh! She's married to one of my best friends. Blair and I met in high school, so we've known each other forever already."

"Which means you two have also known each other for a while, then?" Rubi asks and motions her fork between me and Quinn.

I glance toward my... boyfriend. "Oh, well, yeah. We've run into each other on occasion. Here and there. Sometimes."

"We've spent time together when we were both in town," Quinn interjects smoothly. "But we only started seeing each other when Stephen moved to New York last year."

"Are you from New York?" Philip asks.

"No," I say. "No. I'm..." There's no real reason to tell them the truth, but I'm already lying so much that I just can't find it in me to add more to the tally. And that's how I find myself saying, "I'm originally from North Carolina, but I moved to Maine when I started high school. And after that I just sort of hopped from place to place for a while."

They all smile at me like I'm the most fascinating thing to ever happen to any of them. These are people desperate to like me.

"Where in North Carolina?" Caroline asks.

My palms are getting sweaty, and I fumble with my wineglass. "The Outer Banks region."

"It's lovely there," she says and presses her palm to her heart.

I nod. "Oh, yeah. It's great. Really... nice."

I don't know why I sound so stiff. I'm usually good at this kind of thing. Small talk. Making people like me. Of course, I usually don't talk about myself and just ask about the other person. It works out perfectly every time. People love talking about themselves.

I take a deep breath and force myself to speak because they're all still looking at me expectantly. "We—I had a real beach bum childhood. I don't think I was properly dry until I moved away."

"Oh! Do you swim?" Caroline again.

"Sure. I'm more of a... boat person, though." Am. Was. What's the difference, right?

Caroline perks up even more. "You like to sail?"

"Love it." Love. Used to love. What's the damn difference, right?

"Where did you live before New York?" Nick asks in between bites.

"LA," I say.

"Oh my God, why would you ever move?" Rubi asks with a laugh. "I'd give anything to be warm once winter hits."

I shrug. "I missed the seasons, I guess." And then, because I'm a good fake boyfriend, I place my palm on top of Quinn's hand and squeeze. "And New York has its perks."

So many happy smiles.

"What were you doing in LA?" Ivy asks.

"School," I say.

Oh, for fuck's sake, Steph! How hard is it just to lie?

This is like a very kind interrogation. I get it. They want to get to know me. But the urge to escape is getting almost impossible to ignore.

Ivy's smile widens. "I'm doing my master's in psychometrics right now. What are you studying?"

I force a smile on my face and some desperately needed carelessness in my tone. "Marine biology," I say. "I flunked out, though. Turns out academics really isn't for me. Not much fun in it, is there? And you have to read a whole bunch."

Quinn draws in a long, slow breath, and his fingers tighten around the stem of his wineglass. So much for me being me. I bet he's regretting that he didn't let me be an astronaut now.

Ivy just laughs. "I've had a few of those moments too, where I'm ready to throw in the towel."

"You shouldn't," Quinn snaps and sends me a glare like he's afraid I'm going to start singing "Another Brick in the Wall" and the awesome musical number will prompt Ivy to rethink all her plans.

There's a beat of awkward silence that follows Quinn's outburst.

"What, exactly, is psychometrics?" I ask, trying my best to cut through the tension. "I don't think I've ever heard of it."

"The science of psychological assessment," Ivy says. "Basically how to properly measure certain psychological concepts like cognition, and knowledge, and personality."

She launches into an explanation and after that the conversation turns to everybody else's college days, and then to work, and the conversations multiply as all the siblings catch up. My shoulders start to relax slowly the longer the spotlight is off me.

When I glance toward Quinn, he looks like a statue. No relaxing for him. No, sir.

This damn week can't end fast enough.

"WHICH SIDE DO YOU PREFER?" Quinn's standing beside the bed like one of the King's Guards—perfect posture, no smile.

It's not like it's the first time I'm sharing a bed with somebody, but usually the person in the bed wants me there, and Quinn would clearly prefer to sleep next to a porcupine instead of me.

"Whichever," I say. "I don't care about sides."

He takes the right.

I take the left.
He turns off the lights.
I close my eyes.
One day down. Six more to go.

STEPH

MOSTLY, I don't give a shit. Bad decisions? I'll make them. Stupid stunts? Direct them to me. Mistakes? What's one more.

Mostly, I'm the fun one. The first to jump. The first to say yes to anything. The first to agree to everything.

But then there are those moments. Late at night. When the world around me is so quiet there's nothing that'd hide my thoughts from me. It's my hour of the wolf. When regrets tumble on top of me until I'm buried six feet under. When every 'what if' laughs in my face until it starts to feel like I'm going insane.

It's a process.

One I've gone through countless times.

I wake up. Middle of the night. No reason at all, but my eyes fly open, my palms are clammy, and my breath is stuck in my throat. Maybe I was dreaming, but if I was, I never remember. Just deal with the aftermath.

It takes a moment to realize I'm not drowning.

Right on schedule, it's time for flashbacks, and then I *am* drowning. Again. And again. And again.

And then it's game time.

What if you could make a deal with the devil, Steph? What if you could get the other half of you back? What if you could trade? All the people you now have in your life. All the people you now love. Jude. Blair. Nora. Hazel. What if they disappeared out of your life for good? But you got Sky back. Would you make the trade?

That's the part where I usually throw the covers off and get out of bed.

Because I know the answer.

And I'm not sure I like the person who chooses the way I would.

I creep toward my duffel and silently open it, careful not to make a sound. Careful not to wake Quinn. Grab the pair of shorts and a T-shirt. I pull the shirt I slept in over my head and drop it on the floor. Lose the pants next. Then get dressed in my running gear. Take my shoes in my hand and tiptoe out of the room and then out of the house.

It's that hour before dawn when the world is still teetering between awake and asleep. The sky is dark blue, but there's a hint of light on the horizon. A few brighter stars are still visible, but all the other ones have packed it in for the night. The air is cool, just shy of cold. Enough to make goosebumps appear on my forearms.

Out back, I sit down on the edge of the deck and put on my running shoes. Lace them up and look around. There's no clear path to follow, but fuck it. I'll just go straight until I can't anymore and then come back.

I hate running. With a vengeance. But that hate has come in handy a lot over the years because at some point, inevitably, when my legs are starting to give out underneath me, the thoughts about how much I fucking loathe running will drown out everything else going on in my head. It's the only reason I put myself through the torture multiple times a week. If my brain stopped waking me up every few nights, I wouldn't have to do this shit.

I get up just as the door slides open.

When I turn around, I find Quinn scowling at me, eyes like storm clouds in the low light of predawn.

"The fuck are you doing?" he asks.

I can handle Quinn any other time of the day. Not now, though. Not when I'm already feeling like somebody's peeled my skin off, exposing every nerve ending.

I draw in a slow breath. "What does it look like I'm doing?"

"Being a pain in the ass," he says.

"I'm more of a thorn in the side type of person, seeing that I always treat asses very nicely." I pause thoughtfully. "Of course, some people are into that whole pain thing, but I've never been much of a fan."

"You don't know the surrounding area. Please tell me you're not going for a run while it isn't even light outside yet." He crosses his arms over his chest, the furrow between his brows as deep as a crater in Mars.

"Okay. I won't tell you I'm going for a run while it isn't even light outside yet. Happy?"

He sends me an unimpressed look before he closes his eyes and sighs. "Give me two fucking minutes. I'll go and get dressed."

"Take all the time you need."

The moment the door slides shut behind him, I turn around and take off running. I make my way down to the beach. There's a narrow strip of sand, but most of the shoreline is rocky. Not ideal ground for running, but I'll make do. Whatever I told Quinn, I don't fancy getting lost, so I'll stay out of the forest for now.

Whatever running as a form of exercise lacks, it only gets worse when you try and run on a rocky beach. It fucking sucks. I usually prefer to go hard and fast from the start to exhaust myself as quickly as I can, but it's impossible here, unless I plan to twist my ankle or fall against a rock and give myself a concussion. A slow jog it is. Running turns ten times more boring, and it didn't have much excitement to offer in the first place.

I'm barely half a mile away from the house when I hear footsteps behind me.

Be a hot, horny fisherman. Be a hot, horny fisherman.

"I fucking told you to wait," Quinn snaps.

I turn around and jog backward. "And I didn't. You really don't know how to take a hint, do you? Why are you following me?"

"Clearly I hate myself." He grabs onto my arm and pulls me to a stop. "And you're an idiot. Stop running. You'll break a leg."

"I'll take my chances."

"Based on how things go for you usually, you'll also break an arm and your head in the process. Just follow me. There's a trail in the woods."

Annoyance rushes to the surface and while I can hide it any other time, I can't right now. "Okay. Point it out to me, then, and go away."

"I'm already out and dressed. I might as well keep an eye on you. It'd be a pity to waste search and rescue's time when you get lost."

"*If* I get lost," I say like that distinction somehow makes all the difference.

Quinn lets out a mirthless laugh. "I know you, Stephen. It's a when, not an if."

"In that case, I hereby grant you permission not to inform the authorities and leave me to deal with the fallout myself."

He scoffs. "You never deal with the fallout yourself. Why should this time be any different?"

"Oh, fuck off, you goddamn condescending prick!" I snap.

As much as Quinn and I verbally spar with each other, it's never come down to straight-up insults before.

Come on. Say something. Tell me what you really think of me.

He doesn't. Of course he doesn't.

Instead, he just crosses his arms over his chest and sends me a level look.

"It's the trail with me, or you get your stubborn, irresponsible ass back inside the house. What'll it be?"

I squint and concentrate like my life depends on it, but wishing he'd get a torturously itchy rash just doesn't work.

"The trail," I grit through my teeth. I doubt it's the last early morning run I'm going to have to endure in this place, so it'd be better to know where the trail is for next time.

He sends me a suspicious look like he's expecting me to take off again once he turns his back, so I suppose I'm now forced to follow him to prove him wrong.

Turns out there really is a trail behind the first rows of trees. It's barely wide enough for a single person, let alone two, and since Quinn is already in front of me, he takes the lead.

"Mind the roots," he says.

"Mind your own fucking roots," I grumble under my breath.

Whether he hears me or not is anybody's guess because he just starts to run, so I follow him.

He heads down the trail with the steady, confident gait of a person who's familiar and comfortable in his surroundings. He's probably taken this trail hundreds of times over the years, so he knows every one of those roots he warned me about.

The good news is that soon enough I'm fully occupied by not tripping on the uneven ground. The bad news is that it doesn't take me long to realize running alongside a motherfucking Olympic Champion a bazillion times over might not have been my brightest idea. I usually limit myself to a few miles of this torture. Provided I go hard and fast, it does the trick.

Surprise, surprise, Quinn's one of those people who does this shit for fun. About a mile in, when the trail goes in two different directions, he glances over his shoulder.

"Just tell me if it gets too much," he says, and I immediately bristle. Of course he thinks he can run faster and farther.

"Wait, this isn't a warm-up?" I ask and squint at him. "You mean you run this slowly on purpose?"

Never mind that I'm pretty sure I'm going to die.

"All the way around the lake, then," he says with a smirk like he doesn't believe I can run around his stupid lake.

So I elbow myself past him and pick up speed, knowing full well this is a terrible idea, and that I have to run farther and faster than I've run in years.

Then again, I'm pretty sure my hatred will fuel me at least a good few more miles.

QUINN

I'VE NEVER ACTUALLY FIGURED people could kill themselves with stubbornness. Surely, at some point self-preservation and common sense must kick in.

Then again, it's Stephen we're talking about.

There is about zero chance he planned to run fifteen miles this morning. Or ever. Neither did I, for that matter, but Stephen looks like he's a step away from collapsing when we finally stop in front of the back deck. The sun's already up, and my parents are sitting on the wicker chairs, cups of coffee in front of them on the round wicker table.

"Good morning," Mom says and raises her brows at me. "You two are up early."

"My positive influence," Stephen says. I think. His words are a bit difficult to understand due to the loud wheezing. "Not much of a runner, this one."

"Yes," I say dryly. "I'm generally against exercise as we all know."

Mom and Dad laugh. Stephen looks like he wants to throw something at me.

"Did you take the trail to the bay?" Mom asks.

"No. We went around the lake," I say.

They both gape at me.

"How long have you been up?" Dad asks.

Stephen mutters something inaudible. It looks like the smile he forces onto his face hurts. "A while."

"I admire the dedication," Mom says and lifts her coffee cup. "But I choose this."

Stephen plops down on the edge of the deck, elbows on his knees, head down, as he tries to get his breathing back under control.

"Rubi was talking about going for a hike later, but it seems you two have already gotten all the exercising you can take."

"I'd love to go," I say. "But Stephen's probably tired."

Stephen lifts his head and glares at me. "A hike sounds great."

"They're going in the evening," Mom says and turns to Stephen again. "Oh, and before I forget, how do you feel about lobster? We were thinking of having it for dinner."

For some reason, Stephen looks startled. Like the question doesn't make sense. Like nobody has ever cared enough to do something nice for him.

"I like lobster," he eventually says.

"Corn on the cob?" Mom continues.

Stephen nods. "Sounds great."

"Coleslaw?"

He smiles. "I think everybody likes that. I'm honestly not that picky about food."

"Okay, but is there anything you don't like?" she asks.

"Can't think of anything."

"Veggie fries?"

"Sure," Stephen says.

"Any preferences with salad?" Mom continues.

This could take a while. Mom opens her mouth again.

"He doesn't like bell peppers," I say. "So anything without those."

Stephen's eyes snap to me.

I roll my eyes. "You keep picking them off whenever there's some on pizza."

He just keeps staring at me like I'm an alien life-form until he finally catches himself and clears his throat. "Yeah, okay. I guess I'm not the biggest fan of bell peppers."

"He does like potatoes," I continue. "And he likes cheesecake."

Another startled look from Stephen.

"Nora's thirtieth birthday party two years ago?" I prompt. "You kept going on and on about how you were going to kidnap the pastry chef?"

Stephen straightens himself and pushes his hair back.

"It's cheese and cake. What's not to like?" He smiles then. A ray of sunlight falls over the right side of his face, and he suddenly looks impossibly fresh-faced and soft, all his sharp edges tucked away somewhere. More genuine than I've ever seen him before. Somehow more real. And all the more dangerous for it. I've never seen somebody switch between personas as quickly and often as Stephen does. It's almost as if he has a selection of faces always at hand, and he dons the one he deems necessary at any given moment.

"Baked potatoes, in that case," Mom says.

And there. With a snap of fingers, the softness is gone, replaced by the usual effervescent smile.

"Can't wait," Stephen says. "Well, I better go take a shower."

"Breakfast is served in the fridge," Mom says. "You two just grab whatever you feel like eating."

"Copy that," Stephen says, gets up, and saunters into the house.

My eyes get stuck on his ass before the reasonable part of my brain catches up and makes me tear my gaze away. When I look up, I find two sets of eyes on me.

"He's interesting," Dad says. "And locked up like a vault."

"More like reserved." Mom takes another sip of her coffee. "I imagine it's stressful meeting your boyfriend's family for the first time."

Dad hums noncommittedly. I can see gears turning in his head. His uncanny ability to read people has always been his strong suit, so it's not exactly common for him to fail at doing that.

Mom frowns. "Do you think he feels welcome here? Should we do something to make him more comfortable?"

I hate myself. I hate that I'm putting them in this situation. I hate that I lied. I hate that I'm not a better son.

"You don't have to do anything," I say.

Mom quirks her brow. "Excuse me, but I'd prefer that your boyfriend liked us."

"He does," I assure her. "You don't have to worry about that."

"I absolutely do have to worry about that," she argues. "You haven't had a serious relationship since—" She catches herself and sort of waves her palm in the air for a little bit. "Which means Stephen's important to you," she continues. "Which, in turn, means we need to make a good impression."

This is a fucking mess, and it's all on me.

"You could never make a bad impression, Mom," I say, and lean down to kiss her on the temple.

She smiles and squishes my cheek between her forefinger and thumb. "You're sweet. Full of crap. But sweet."

"Is that any way to talk to your firstborn?"

"Yes. Now go take a shower, and then you have my blessing to wake up all those lazy people upstairs I call my children."

That draws the first genuine smile out of me in what feels like days. "Consider it done."

RUBI SENDS me a glare as she plops down at the table with a huge yawn. "China had something good going on with that one-child policy."

"I hate to break it to you, Rubs, but I'm the oldest, so that means I'd be the chosen one." I tear off a piece of bread and stuff it into my mouth.

"I prefer to think Mom and Dad would've gone with me if they knew they only had one shot at a decent child."

"What are you guys talking about?" Axel asks.

"Who's the favorite child," Rubi says and closes her eyes.

Axel tilts his head to the side. "Just in general or in a *Sophie's Choice* type of situation?"

"Does it matter? A favorite is a favorite," Rubi says.

"Absolutely, embarrassingly wrong." Axel points his fork at Rubi. "If it's just in your general, everyday setting, you can go with your gut feeling. If there are stakes, you have to make your choice based on a wholly different set of criteria. Like, you have to pick the *actual* best one. If I had to choose just one of you to spare, I'd like to make an informed decision and base it on things like intelligence, physical shape, talents, personality, and so on."

Rubi and I glance at each other.

"Okay, well, we know Axel's out of the running since he's clearly a psycho," Rubi says. "That has to be at least a hundred minus points."

I lift two fingers in the air and nod. "Automatic elimination."

"You're not the parents," Axel scoffs. "You don't get a vote."

"I don't see why not," Ivy pipes up. "Let's say you're all trapped in a cave. There's only food for one person. You're all civilized people, so you decide to vote on who gets to live to tell the tale. And, hon? In the span of a minute, you got two people voting against you. Think about what you'll accomplish in a few days in a cave? They'll off you before you can nominate yourself as the survivor of the month."

"We'll sacrifice him for good luck," Reid says in that toneless, deadpan way my little brother has about him. "Or for food. I'd eat human meat if it was a desperate situation."

Ivy points at him. "See?"

Axel gasps and slaps a palm on his chest. "You're supposed to be on my side. And I'm sorry, but right now it kind of feels like you two are going to start swapping recipes."

"A goulash," Reid says. "Or something spicy to mask the taste."

"Oh, so we wouldn't have food, but we'd have spices in the cave?" Rubi asks.

"We're not savages," Reid says.

"Aww, babe. Stop looking so glum. I'd plead your case. I would. But I'm not there, so..." Ivy smiles at Axel sweetly, and he just shakes his head, struggling to keep the indignant look in place.

"You could be. We could be one of those romantic 'you jump, I jump' couples."

"We all know how that played out in the end. If you say you want to explore a dangerous cave, you have my blessing, but I'm not coming with you."

"I'm learning so much about my marriage today," Axel says.

Stephen, who's been listening to the conversation silently while loading his plate with absolutely every variety of carb available in the kitchen takes a seat on my right and digs into his breakfast.

"What about you, Steph?" Rubi asks. "Any brothers or sisters to sacrifice in a cave?"

He takes a long time with his answer, just like the time I asked the same question, and then, too, he doesn't really say anything. Just shakes his head.

"An only child's automatic favorite status," Axel says. "See, that's clever. You get all the food. Nobody will kill you."

Everybody's eyes move to Stephen again. He's smiling, but it's not his usual smile. Not the blindingly bright, happy one he usually wears. There's something unsure and insecure in this smile. Something almost fragile. Like it's glued together from the pieces of something honest. A pale shadow of the real thing.

"That's me," he eventually says. He straightens himself and grins. "The brains of the operation."

There's another one of those personality switches happening right in front of my very eyes.

"Did you two actually run around the lake this morning or was Mom lying?" Rubi raises her brows at us, changing the topic.

"Not lying," I say. "Want to come with the next time?"

"If you ever see me wake up before seven voluntarily it's because I've been possessed." She moves her forefinger between me and Stephen. "But it's nice to know you two are equally insane. I'd like to extend a humble thank you from all of us, Steph, for taking him and his incessant begging to go running or swimming off our hands."

"Me asking if you want to come with me is incessant begging?" I ask.

"I was being nice. You guilt people into coming with you." Rubi turns toward Stephen. "Is that how he got to you?"

"It's how I got to him," he says.

"Oh, good. There's two of you," Rubi says, and Stephen laughs.

"Not really. I fucking loathe running," he says. A glob of chocolate falls on his plate from his donut. He swipes over it with his finger and my eyes get stuck on the way he licks the finger clean.

"You must really like Quinn, then," Rubi says. "Ivy, would you run fifteen miles for Axel?"

Ivy purses her lips and squints her eyes at her husband. "Run? No. I'd drive, though."

"And I get it," Axel says. "Who the fuck runs when we have all those different types of wheels?"

"Oh, yeah," Reid says. "There's this famous song about it. I would scooter five hundred miles, and I would scooter five hundred more."

"You know what? We should rent electric scooters and take a ride around town," Axel says.

"I can already see us rolling down the street. Like a motorcycle gang but a million times more pathetic," Rubi says. "Let's order jackets."

Axel flips her off.

All my siblings start shouting and yelling over each other. Teasing remarks and insults fly around the table.

I lean back and just listen to the bickering. Feels like home.

When I look toward Stephen, he's smiling. One of his rare, real smiles.

Fragile again, though.

And filled with something that looks suspiciously like longing.

STEPH

I STARE at the rocky path in front of me. The snort that escapes is downright hysterical at this point. Uphill. Of course. Goddamnit, I'm gonna die today.

Caroline and Philip dropped us off at the beginning of the trail on their way to town for their date night. Reid, Axel, and Ivy bowed out of the hike to go catch a movie, but since Quinn smugly suggested I should take it easy after this morning, me and my water bottle were the first in the car.

"There's a bus that goes to town every fifty minutes. The stop is about a mile that way," Quinn says from next to me and points to the road on my left.

"You're going back already?" I ask. "I guess we'll... Well, not me personally, but some people will surely miss you."

Rubi stops next to us, bouncing on her heels as she adjusts the straps of her backpack.

"Three-mile loop or the six-mile one?"

Quinn quirks his brow at me.

"Stephen would probably prefer the three-mile one," he says, and ruffles my hair like I'm a fucking labradoodle. "He's a bit winded after this morning."

"Who, me? No," I scoff. "Thanks for worrying, love bug, but I'm great. Six miles sounds good. Unless it's too much for you?" I smack him on the ass, and he jumps and glares at me.

Rubi glances at her smart watch. "If we hurry, we should make it to the lookout point in time to see the sunset."

"Great," I say. The hysterics from the earlier snort have now traveled to my tone. "We should definitely hurry, then."

It's Quinn's hand that lands on my ass this time.

"Brisk pace, pumpkin," he says.

I swallow down the dejected sigh and the plethora of swear words on the tip of my tongue and start walking. The first fifteen minutes, I'm fueled by pure contempt.

The next fifteen go by with me daydreaming about throwing myself off the first cliff I find.

I don't get a chance to start looking for a place to jump because this is where I get a moment of reprieve when there's a sound of retching from behind me. I turn around, hope singing in my heart. Who would've guessed my most fervent dream was to find Quinn puking into the bushes?

Instead, it's Rubi.

"What's happening?" Quinn asks and rushes back down the trail to where Rubi and Nick are standing.

Rubi waves her hand weakly and gags some more. Nick is sliding his palm up and down her back, holding out a bottle of water.

"Are you okay?" I ask pointlessly, because clearly she's not, but I don't do well with feeling useless.

"She's fine," Nick says. "It's nothing. Don't worry about it."

"Dude, she's vomiting," I say because I'm all about useless remarks today.

Rubi lets out a deep breath and pushes herself upright. "I'm fine. I think I'm done for now." She takes the bottle of water

Nick hands her, sips and spits the water out before taking a drink. Nick hands her a few tissues, and she wipes her mouth.

"You okay?" Nick asks.

Rubi nods.

"What the hell is going on?" Quinn snaps.

"Calm down," Rubi says and rolls her eyes. "It's just some run-of-the-mill morning sickness."

Quinn stares at her. "What? Morning? It's eight-thirty in the evening."

"Yes, well, this baby thinks it's the proper time to make me puke my guts out."

Quinn keeps staring at her.

"You're pregnant?" he says.

"Surprise," Rubi's voice is dry as a desert. "We were planning on telling everybody this weekend, but I guess you two now have early access to the news."

For a moment, Quinn is completely still, but then he's in front of Rubi, wrapping her in a tight hug.

"Seriously?" he asks. "You're pregnant?"

"Either that or it's the world's longest hangover."

Quinn laughs. "That's... Congrats, you two! This is great news." And now he's hugging Nick, and Rubi is laughing.

"Congratulations," I echo Quinn. This is very much a family moment, and I'm the intruder.

"Yeah," Rubi says. "This baby better be really cute, though, to make up for the vomiting. I don't think I'm making it to the lookout point today."

"Why are we out here when you're—" Quinn starts to say, but Nick waves both his hands wildly behind Rubi's back and then starts slashing his hand in front of his throat.

"Walking is great exercise," Nick says pointedly.

"Fresh air usually helps," Rubi grumbles and makes a face.

"Something smells really disgusting here, though. Can we move, please?"

"It's really a shame we're going to have to cut the hike short," I say and try to look regretful. Two seconds is all I can manage. "Ah well. Shall we?"

I'm going to buy this baby a pony as a thank you for saving my life.

"Hell no," Rubi says. "I'm not gonna ruin your evening. You go ahead and finish the hike. I'll stop by every bush to puke anyway, so we should make it down around the same time."

Sorry, baby. No pony for you. Blame your mother.

"You might need help," Quinn argues.

"With vomiting? I've been practicing for two months. Believe me, I'm an expert. Just go."

"But—"

"I have Nick. Go," she says and points to the trail. "Shoo."

"I'm not a horse," Quinn grumbles.

"Definitely more of a mule," Rubi says and points toward the trail. "Get going."

Quinn rolls his eyes and turns around.

"I guess we'll be going, then," he tells me.

For a moment, I consider puking too. It seems to get people out of this torture. Too bad I haven't learned to vomit on command.

I'm not sure if it's me or if the trail has actually gotten more difficult, but it seems impossible to keep up with Quinn once we start moving again. Moving is putting it lightly. We're practically running. Again.

Sweat is running down my back, and the bottoms of my feet are on fire as I drag myself toward the end of the trail, one step at a time.

I give up somewhere between the fourth and fifth mile.

Fuck it. I'm done. I'll just die here and have Quinn figure out what to do with my body as my last act of petty revenge.

I plop down on the ground and stare at the slivers of darkening sky visible between branches and leaves.

It's quite nice, actually.

Until Quinn's face appears in front of me and ruins the view.

"Are you taking a nap?" he demands incredulously.

I lift both my middle fingers up and then lower my arms over my eyes, still holding my middle fingers up. There's some shuffling, and then a thump as Quinn sits down next to me.

We're both silent for the longest time before he asks, "How are your feet?"

"No idea. Can't feel them," I mutter.

"Yeah," he says and drags his hand through his hair. "This was not a smart idea."

I snort. "I rarely have those, so that's nothing new. Must be a novel experience for you, though."

"You think I've never done anything stupid before?" he asks.

"Oh, please, *please* tell me about that one time you jaywalked. I bet that's weighing heavily on your conscience."

He lets out a short laugh. "You're so unbelievably self-absorbed sometimes."

"Go fuck yourself," I say without much heat.

We fall silent again.

"So you're going to be an uncle," I eventually say and lift my arm to glance at him.

He nods. "Seems so."

"Happy?"

"Is there a person who wouldn't be?"

"Yeah, hi. Me." I shrug. "Kids scare the crap out of me."

His eyes stay on the side of my face. "You seem to handle Hazel well enough."

I ignore that comment. "Who in their right mind would ever want to have kids? To be responsible for keeping another person... alive. Who the hell wants that?"

He looks into the distance, eyes unfocused. "I might."

"Of course you do. Have fun in your house in the suburbs with your white picket fence and your golden retriever puppy."

Sour grapes is what they call it, I think.

Instead of replying, he gets up. "We should probably get going."

So I push myself up and follow him. My feet might never work the same again, but we make it to the lookout point.

Quinn stops abruptly once we emerge from the trees, and I step past him, only to still, too.

"Well," I say. "I'm almost tempted to say this makes the torture worth it."

The sky seems to be on fire. Bright yellows blend into orange and then subtly morph into purple and dark blue hues.

"Almost," Quinn says softly.

So we stand there, shoulder to shoulder, and watch the sun sink behind the horizon, and all things considered, the urge to shove him off the platform is marginally less intrusive than it usually is.

STEPH

YOU'D THINK after yesterday I'd sleep in, but that's not how I operate. Instead, the cold gray light of early morning finds me lacing up my sneakers once again.

And once again, the door behind me slides open.

"If you think about it, it's really nothing short of a miracle nobody's hired a hitman to take you out yet," Quinn says conversationally as he sits down next to me to lace his own running shoes.

"I think it comes down to cost," I say and yawn. "Assassins are pricey. I did some research when Nora first introduced us."

It's a cooler morning than yesterday, and I take the lead when we start to run. I'll be damned if I let him drag me around that fucking lake again. I also keep the pace slower than he did. It's the morning of miracles because he says nothing, just silently follows me.

At the crossroads, I take the second trail—the one that leads far away from the lake—and hope for the best.

In another few miles, the trail suddenly just ends. It's there and then it's just gone. I stop and blink for a second, trying to figure out if excessive running has made me blind.

"It's not a loop. We have to turn back," Quinn says from behind me.

Which I do. Only I don't account for the fact that he's standing right behind me, and because I'm an economical person, I start to move forward as soon as I've turned around, so I end up bumping straight into him. Chest against chest, toes against toes.

He doesn't move away. Just stands there, plastered against me. And I'm suddenly hit with the realization of just how very tall he is.

Tall and wide-shouldered and steady. Two feet firmly on the ground. Knows where he's supposed to be and what he's supposed to do.

I'm not like that. I flail and stumble and smack my way through life, bruises and cuts all over me, hopelessly lacking that kind of quiet confidence where somebody just *knows* what the right answer is.

If I have two options laid out in front of me, I pick both or neither because the chances to choose wrong go down significantly that way. But Quinn? Quinn would know, wouldn't he? He'd *know*. And he'd calmly point out the right choice and go on with his day.

I don't know what I'm doing.

Never have.

I'm adrift and aimless and without purpose, and I really don't appreciate the fact that right here and now, he makes me feel... safe. Like being lost is okay. A temporary situation. Because he knows how to find me.

"You're in my way." My voice comes out all wrong. Brittle and tense.

He doesn't move. Instead, he sends me a contemplative look.

"Want to see something?" he asks.

I'd say no, but that'd mean running again, so I nod.

He stays still for another moment before he starts to push past me, which only ends up rubbing his chest against mine.

I fix my eyes on the bush on my left and stare at it like my life depends on it until he's past me.

He goes off the trail, makes his way past a few shrubs, and I follow him.

He takes me to a tree. Even though tree seems like an understatement. It's a huge oak, so wide you'd probably need ten people to make a circle around it. Low branches spread out like the tree is trying to occupy as much space as it possibly can. It somehow seems out of place here, between the rocks and pitiful excuses for pine trees, but at the same time exactly where it's supposed to be.

I glance toward Quinn. He's frowning again.

"Ever climbed this thing?" I ask him.

He stares at the tree for way too long.

"Yes," he finally says.

"So it's not some super protected, special, national park tree. Good to know." I go to the tree.

"What are you doing?"

I grab one of the lower branches and hoist myself up. "You said it's okay to climb it."

"You need to get your hearing checked. I said I *have* climbed it."

"And I took it as permission." I grab the next branch.

"You really shouldn't have."

A few seconds pass in silence while I climb.

"You're going to bash your head in when you fall," he calls after a moment.

"My God! Can you lighten up at least a little bit? Smell the fucking roses for once."

"Some of us grew out of our ten-year-old selves," he says.

"And there's your first mistake." I look down and quirk my brow. "What's the matter? Scared?"

"Of a tree?" he asks.

I look up thoughtfully. "I guess I can see it. All these scary, scary leaves..."

He glares at me. I can practically hear his thoughts. *I will not be provoked. I will not be provoked.* He's no better than I am in that regard, though, so in the end, he lets out a loud curse and grabs one of the branches. He scales the tree with annoying agility, passing me with ease on his way up.

Once I catch up to him, he's already settled in on a large branch, back pressed against the trunk, one leg bent at the knee, the other dangling in the air, eyes taking in his surroundings.

"Look who finally made it," he says smugly.

I find my own spot and sit down. "Spoiler alert, you'll be slower too, once you evolve further away from a monkey."

His lips twitch. If he's not careful, I'm going to start thinking he finds me funny.

We both fall silent for a little while, but it's lacking the usual tension of our silences.

"I used to love coming here when I was younger," Quinn says out of the blue and then looks down.

"This is your secret spot?" I ask.

He laughs. "I guess you could say that."

Well, that's nice. There's a glaring issue, though.

"Why are you showing this to me then?"

He's silent for a long time before he shrugs one shoulder. "You know how sometimes one person can completely ruin something for you?"

I blink at him. "Is that a hint?"

"What? No." He rolls his eyes. "I meant this place doesn't exactly hold a lot of great memories anymore, so unless you plan to push me off this branch, you can't really make it worse." He pauses. "You seemed to like the lookout point. And the view from my room. I just figured you'd appreciate this, too."

This is weird. Being civil to him. Having him be civil and do something nice for me.

"Thank you," I say. Gratitude has never felt quite so awkward. I hesitate, but curiosity gets the better of me. "So what happened?"

He's silent for so long I'm beginning to think he's not going to answer.

"I was young and stupid and trusted the wrong person. As one does."

Since I usually communicate through thinly veiled insults when it comes to Quinn, I now have no idea what to say to that.

"It was a long time ago," he says, as if sensing my discomfort with finding the appropriate response.

"Things from a long time ago can still hurt. There's no time limit to these things."

He sends me a funny look. Surprise, surprise. Seems I got it wrong again. But then he looks away from me and frowns, but it doesn't look like a bad frown. More like a thoughtful one.

"Is this personal experience speaking?" he asks.

My automatic reaction is to make a joke. But... he brought me here. Because he thought I'd like it. I don't know what to make of it, but it doesn't inspire me to lie, at least.

"Yes," I say.

He stares straight ahead. Tilts his head to the side for a moment. Looks straight at me.

"Tell me something real," he says.

This time there's no subtle olive branch. Just a straight-out demand.

"Uh... mosquitoes are the world's deadliest creatures? The sun is a star? You'll have to be more specific."

He rolls his eyes. "About you."

I fiddle with the bark of the tree. "What do you want to know?"

He shrugs. "Anything." He turns his head, eyes wandering up and down me, taking me in, before he leans forward and presses the tip of his finger against the narrow scar that bisects my left eyebrow. "Where'd you get that?"

Straight for the jugular.

And the not-lying-because-of-gratitude plan goes straight out the window.

I stretch my lips into a grin. "Excellent question. And an excellent story. I was on a bus on my way to work when suddenly a cop jumped on board and said there was a bomb. And we had to keep the bus going over fifty miles per hour or the bomb would explode. Anyway, like with the plane earlier, I took over. I'm an awesome person like that. Really dependable in a time of crisis—"

"That's the plot of *Speed*," he says, an unimpressed look on his face.

"It's based on my life. I'm very famous."

He sighs and pulls his fingers away, and for a delirious second, I want to tell him to put his hand back. To touch me again.

He turns his gaze away.

I swallow down the next unhinged wish—for him to keep looking at me.

Instead, I clear my throat and gesture around. "This is great, by the way. I mean, if you don't want to keep it as your secret spot, I can totally ruin it some more and take it off your hands."

He sends me another thoughtful look. "I'll let you know."

I nod.

He nods.

And then we just sit.

And it's not totally unpleasant.

QUINN

I DON'T TRUST my dick.

Unlike my brain, my dick's remarkably shallow. It simply reacts, disregarding all common sense and logic, and it doesn't really have any standards other than physical appeal. Basic biology is a bit pathetic that way.

Be that as it may, yes, I can admit my dick appreciates Stephen Hartley. Has ever since the first time I met him.

There's something about him that on the most basic physical level just affects me in a way very few people ever have.

And yes, the first time I saw him standing next to Blair, I did a double take. I saw him, and I *wanted*. An undeniable moment of insanity, complete with flashes of soft lips, fingertips digging into skin, harsh exhales, and green eyes filled with the same want that had burned through me moments earlier.

Insanity and stupidity.

Lust is not something to trust. It doesn't care about common sense and logic. It just is.

And then it isn't.

And you're done.

Give it enough time, and lust will pass.

Lust *has* passed.

But then I'm sitting on the edge of my parents' deck, elbows on knees, sun on my face, when Stephen saunters out of the house. He walks past me. Board shorts, T-shirt, bare feet. The toenails of his right foot have been painted light purple. Not on his left foot, though. Like he forgot about it halfway through. There's a smudge of green on his calf. A stray blade of grass plays peekaboo in his hair that's still wet from the shower he took after this morning's run.

We ended up going to the oak tree for the second morning in a row. I don't know why. But we climbed that damn tree again and sat for a while.

I asked him where he went to school in LA, and he told me all about his time at UC Sunnydale. Where he killed vampires.

He almost fell out of the goddamn tree while climbing down.

He's hopelessly messy and impractical, and I have no idea how anybody's supposed to handle him if they actually have him for real.

"Incoming!" Axel yells and sends a basketball Stephen's way.

He catches it with ease and moves toward Axel, bouncing the ball, laughter and taunts following in his wake. He makes the shot and the ball whooshes through the net.

"Oh, I see how it is." Axel laughs.

For a while, the gentle rustle of the leaves and the distant noise of waves lapping at the shore is accompanied by the muted thud of feet on the ground, and the bouncing of the basketball.

There's no proper court here. Just a hoop rigged up on an old, out-of-use utility pole. The hoop is crooked and the dirt underneath it is hard as concrete from years of feet trampling on it.

Somewhere in the middle of friendly insults and laughter, Stephen pulls off his shirt, and my gaze gets stuck on the sun-kissed skin of his back and the flight of dragonflies on his shoulder blade. Nine altogether.

He's still laughing when he glances over his shoulder and catches me watching. He holds my gaze when he very deliberately walks to where he dropped his shirt earlier and pulls it over his head again. That metaphorical door is slammed shut so hard I can practically feel the impact reverberate through me.

What's worse than lust?

Curiosity.

I DEBATE NOT FOLLOWING when my bedroom door closes behind Stephen with a quiet snick.

He's seen the trail by now.

I won't put it past him to get lost. I won't put it past him to fall off a cliff. But he's a grown man. He can handle himself.

And it'd do me some good to put some distance between us. To not entertain the curiosity.

I stare at the whitewashed wooden ceiling and count the thick beams that hold the roof above my head.

I take my phone and scroll through my messages.

I list all the ways sleeping alone is superior to sharing a bed with somebody.

Then I curse and get out of bed.

I expect I'll need to go faster than usual to catch up to him, but when I push the door open, I find him fiddling with the laces of his sneakers. A pair of battered old things that no sane person would run in, which is to say they're completely in character for Stephen.

He's taking his sweet-ass time to tie those laces, too. In

another thirty seconds, I'm starting to think I should ask him if he needs help.

As if on cue, he glances toward where I'm standing and nearly lands on his ass with the way he jumps.

"Shit! Sneak up on people like a serial killer, why don't you?" He scowls. Crosses his arms over his chest. Taps his foot on the ground. "I see you insist on tagging along again. Quite stalkerish, if you ask me, but I suppose you have to practice if that's your only move."

Fucking curiosity again.

He waves his hand in front of my face. "Hello? Anybody in there? Are you coming or not?"

He takes the shorter route and doesn't stop when we get to the end. Instead, he pushes forward until we're at the oak again. He doesn't look at me. He doesn't say a word. Just grabs onto the branch and starts climbing.

I follow. Again.

I take my spot, and he takes his.

Everything is quiet.

Stephen's gaze rakes over the landscape in front of us. The shore in the distance. The pines. The rocks.

"It's weird this tree is here, right?" he eventually says. "Doesn't really seem to belong."

I frown and look around, too. I've been here so many times over the years, but I've never much contemplated the oak's right to grow here. It just is. Always has been.

Lukas and I used to come here a lot. I figured this place was ruined for good, but somehow when I look around, I don't think about Lukas anymore. There's too much Stephen everywhere, and he's pushing all the ghosts to the periphery.

"Or maybe not weird," Stephen muses. "Just unlikely. Like it's claimed this corner for itself here. And maybe it wasn't easy, and it had to push and shove and kick and scream to carve out a place for itself in the world, but it managed. Thrived, even."

Leave it to Stephen to turn a tree sentient.

"I'd pick this place, too," he continues with a nod.

"For?" I ask.

"Living. If I were a tree. This is where I'd grow."

"You'd never be a tree, though," I say.

He glances toward me then. "Why? Not dignified and stately enough?"

"I can't imagine you standing still in one spot for hundreds of years. You're too alive."

He frowns at me, but this might be one of the few times he hasn't taken insult in what I've said.

"Okay then. If I can't be a tree, what would I be?"

I'm not quite sure how, but somehow he's dragged me into this game of his where I'm now seriously contemplating his question.

"A bird," I eventually say. "A seagull."

He starts to laugh. "Fitting. You know, nobody seems to like seagulls, but they're actually extraordinary. Remarkably intelligent. Adaptable. Tough. Superb swimmers. Street smart. Tenacious. It's really a great compliment to be compared to a seagull."

The last statement is delivered with defiance.

"Wasn't meant as an insult," I say. Like always.

"I'd like to be a bird," Stephen muses.

"Why?" I ask.

I don't really expect a real answer, but then his gaze goes distant, and he says, "They seem so... free." His eyes move over me. Up and down. Calculating. Assessing. "You'd make for a good tree, though."

"Would I?"

He nods.

"Sturdy. Dependable. Steady. Roots deep in the ground. You're kind of like this oak if you think about it. No wonder this here is your spot."

"Something to consider if it turns out reincarnation is a thing," I say.

"I'll land on you if I come back as a seagull."

"So you can take a dump on me?" I ask.

"Depends whether you're still annoying when you die," he says. "Guess we'll see."

I laugh and shake my head.

"Seagulls aren't really that known for their love for trees," he says after a little bit.

"So no change there, then," I say.

"No. Even as a tree and a bird, we'll still be the same. Never the twain shall meet."

Somehow, it doesn't sound quite as appealing as I would've figured it would.

STEPH

WE USED to go on family vacations. Sky, me, Mom, Dad. A cross-country road trip to Colorado in a rented RV. Camping and fishing all over North Carolina. Bike rides on every island of the Outer Banks. Hiking. Sailing. A vacation was a vacation only when it was filled to the brim with every available activity.

Quinn's family does things a little differently. They just hang out. There's a lot of reading involved. Lounging on deck chairs. Food and cooking. Board games and talking.

"It's the only time of the year we get to just be and do nothing," Caroline says when I tell her this. "But believe me, just say the word and Quinn will come and bike, run, sail, and hike anywhere you want. I don't really know where we went wrong with him, to be honest. God knows I'm not that athletic, and Phil is much more comfortable in his study than outside of it."

I grin at her, and she smiles back.

I like her. I like all of Quinn's family. I like that they like each other. Most people don't seem to realize that it's possible to love somebody and not like them. I know better. My own parents, for example. They love me. I know they do. But I don't think they like me very much. Not anymore. Not after everything.

Faint echoes of voices carry in through the open window of the kitchen from outside where Quinn and his siblings are in the middle of a heated poker match.

"You must think we're a bunch of slackers around here," Caroline says with a laugh.

"No. It's just different. But it's nice." I pause. "I don't think I've actually said it yet. Thank you for having me here."

Caroline passes me on her way to the fridge and squeezes my shoulder. "We're happy to have you. To tell you the truth, we were all getting a bit worried about Quinn. After all that mess with Lukas, he just became almost like a different person. So cautious. So reluctant to let anybody in. But when he's around you, he's got a spark in him again."

That spark she's talking about is most likely pure, undiluted dislike.

Also, pro tip for anybody who's considering playing somebody's boyfriend in the future: make sure their family is terrible. Unless you want to be a shitty human being, of course. Because if you do, lying to a bunch of thoroughly nice, caring people is a surefire way to accomplish that.

This is uncomfortable. "I'm sure he's dated other people who've been, you know, good for him," I say.

"I wouldn't know. You're the first person he's introduced to us since," Caroline throws over her shoulder distractedly while she's digging around in the fridge. Then she stops. "Since Lukas."

Oh, yay. Awesome.

And who the fuck is this Lukas?

AND THEN YOU

"WHO THE FUCK IS LUKAS?" I ask Quinn.

He snaps his whole body toward me in surprise and almost loses his balance. I have to grab his arm so he doesn't fall out of the tree.

He composes himself pretty quickly, though.

"Who?" he asks, which is just pathetic.

"Your mom mentioned him. So who is he?"

He's silent for a little while before he says, "We moved to Southern California, and there was this group who studied karate at the Cobra Kai dojo—"

"This is just embarrassing lack of originality. So exactly what I've come to expect from you. But find your own deflection strategies," I say. "Who's Lukas?"

"A guy," he says.

"An ex?" I prompt.

He narrows his eyes. "What's it to you?"

I widen my eyes innocently. "As your boyfriend, we should cover those parts. It's essential boyfriend knowledge."

"Right," he says dryly. "Okay, lay it on me, then. List your exes."

"Don't have any."

He rolls his eyes. "You and your commitment-phobic ways."

"It's a choice, not a phobia," I scoff and widen my arms. "Look at me. It'd be a shame to limit all of this to just one person."

"The world truly would be a sadder place if you didn't fuck around. Literally and figuratively."

"Exactly. See? That's good deflection. And it almost worked. It's always a good idea to either talk about fucking or me fucking. Distracts me like this." I snap my fingers. "Now, who's Lukas?"

He sighs. "An ex."

"I've known you for years. I've never seen you with a

Lukas," I say. What a dumb name. Lukas. Sounds like a fancy horse.

"It was before we met."

"And you're still carrying a torch for him?" I refuse to address the annoyance that gathers inside me at the thought of Quinn being into some dude named Lukas. "What happened? Did he break your heart? Ruin you for all other men?"

"Well, aren't we chatty today," he says.

"Not like you're making an effort to provide me with riveting conversation here."

"Tell you what. Tit for tat. Tell me how you got the scar," he says.

"I was working as a bicycle courier and had an accident, so I was in a coma, and when I awoke it turned out a deadly outbreak had occurred, resulting in societal collapse—"

"*28 Days Later*," Quinn says in a bored voice. "Do better."

"I was banking on you never seeing that movie. Too scary for you."

"Yes. I'm sure if I hadn't seen it, the phrase 'societal collapse' wouldn't have told me that you were full of shit."

"Who's Lukas?" I repeat stubbornly. I'm not curious. It's just the only interesting thing about Quinn I've ever heard, so I'm willing to give him a chance to talk about it.

He quirks his brow at me. "Lukas is a cunning thief and criminal. We met when he held Nakatomi Plaza hostage."

"You're creating a lot of mystery around what's most likely a regular story of some dude who dumped you."

"Tell me about the scar and find out," he says.

I clamp my mouth shut for a moment before I shrug. "Fine. I don't really care anyway."

I start to climb down.

"Sure you don't," he says smugly, and I can feel his gaze on me all the way down.

STEPH

"ONE MORE?" Axel asks with a yawn and blinks toward the white sheet he and Nick rigged up against the back wall of the garage earlier. We're all sitting in front of it in lawn chairs, snuggled up in blankets, snacks all around us.

We're two movies in, and it's getting late. Caroline and Philip left after the first movie. Reid called it quits halfway through the second one.

"I'm out," Nick says. Rubi opted out of the whole movie night because of her evening morning sickness.

"Babe?" Axel quirks his brow toward Ivy.

"Depends," Ivy says. "Is it Quinn's turn to pick?"

"It's Reid's," Axel says.

"Reid's not here. So that means Quinn's next in line, right?" Ivy asks.

"Yes," Quinn says.

"Bed it is." Ivy claps once and gets up.

I raise my brows at Quinn while Ivy and Axel pack up for the night. "What's wrong with your picks?"

"They're not in the spirit of movie night," Axel says. "You

want to give your brain a rest and watch people blow up shit. Not learn things. Run while you still can."

"I think I'll stay," I say.

He presses his palm to his chest. "Ah. Young love. The way you still try to impress the other by pretending to be interested in all the boring crap the other person likes."

"Axel told my dad he was into cars," Ivy says. "That was a long, embarrassing afternoon."

"It wasn't that bad. I was being clever and took frequent bathroom breaks to secretly research stuff," Axel says.

"And I told all my siblings it was because Axel had diarrhea," Ivy says.

Axel's mouth drops open. "What? Wait a minute. Is that why they still make the jokes about stocking up on toilet paper every time we visit?"

"It might have something to do with it," Ivy says.

Axel groans and closes his eyes. "Oh shit! That explains... everything. Every weird comment. Every question about my fiber intake. You need to text them and tell them you were lying!"

Ivy quirks her brow. "Don't you think it'll be a bit late four years later?"

"No," Axel scoffs indignantly. "Justice must prevail. Must! Where would we be if the truth about Watergate hadn't come out? Or... the Chernobyl disaster? Bernie Madoff?"

"Totally the same thing as your bathroom adventures," Quinn says.

"You need to fix this," Axel says.

"Fine, fine." Ivy sighs and pulls out her phone. After a second of typing, she waves her phone in front of his face. "See? Done."

"'Axel didn't have diarrhea,'" he reads.

The phone dings. "Cole says congrats," Ivy says while

scrolling through the messages. "And Mom asks if you started taking the fiber supplements she sent you."

"You have to specify when. Right now it reads like you're telling them I didn't have it today!" Axel says. They both start walking toward the house, bickering about the text.

I'm still smiling when I turn my eyes away from them and find Quinn looking at me.

"You have a really nice family," I say.

It takes a little while for him to reply. "Yeah. They're great."

He's frowning at me now, and I roll my eyes. "You can stop glowering. I'm not going to tell them the truth about us."

"I didn't think you would. And I don't glower."

I snort out a laugh. "Please. You always have this broody, unimpressed look that pretty much screams, 'I don't know who you are, and I don't know what you did, but rest assured, I'm disappointed in you.'" His glower deepens, and I snap my fingers. "That's the exact face I was talking about." And then I start to laugh. "And now you look unimpressed with me."

"You seem very in tune with my facial expressions."

"Five years of research. Think of this as me presenting my findings."

"That's some measly research if all you've got to show for it is that I've got a resting disappointed face."

"Not my fault you're so closed off. Come on. Give me something to work with. Tell me your deepest, darkest secrets."

His eyes lock on mine. That terrifying intensity in them makes me feel like he can see right through me, past me, into me.

"I'll tell you mine if you tell me yours."

I open my mouth as if I've been possessed before I catch myself. I lean my head back and wiggle a bit to make myself more comfortable.

"What are we watching, then?" I ask.

"Whatever you want."

"Oh, I wouldn't make that promise. I might get ideas," I say.

"Just pick something," he says. Him and his resting disappointed face. Only not really. Sure, the eyebrows are still slightly drawn, and his mouth is set in a straight line, but there's a spark of something in his eyes as he hands me the laptop.

I scroll through the choices for a bit before I connect the laptop to the projector again and sit down.

"Hand me the chips," I say.

Quinn doesn't react. Just stares at the screen and the opening credits. He only snaps out of it when I wave my hand in front of his face.

"Chips?" I prompt.

His frown deepens, and his eyes stay on the side of my face until I finally ask, "What? You know, if you don't like this, you only have yourself to blame. You told me to pick something."

He's still frowning. "Guess I just didn't expect you to pick this," he finally says.

"Well, if you don't like it, you're free to go to bed. Don't let me keep you up."

"Is that massive defensive streak difficult to lug around everywhere you go?" he asks.

"Not difficult, no. As long as you have a solid grip, you'll barely notice it."

"Clearly," he says, and steals the chips back.

I WAKE up to the sound of birds chirping through the open window. It's light outside. I slept through the night. Just like that. No clammy palms. No regrets wreaking havoc in my mind. No hour of the wolf.

It's so goddamn unusual that it takes me a moment to realize there's something else out of the ordinary going on.

A warm body against my back. An erection worthy of a statue in its honor digging into my ass. An arm around my waist keeping me firmly in place. A palm pressed flat against my stomach.

My own morning wood is trying to poke a hole through my boxer briefs, clearly interested in this new development.

Quinn's breathing remains slow and steady. It whispers through my hair, his nose buried in the back of my head.

My heart picks up speed. My toes curl in the warm sheets. A shiver of excitement rushes through my insides.

Get a grip, Steph!

Figures he'd suddenly get a hankering to spoon when we're so close to the finish line.

Do not think about finishing anything!

I'm stiff as a plank by now, not sure how to proceed. Can I slither out of his grasp somehow? Probably not. I'm not exactly known for my gracefulness at the best of times.

Then what?

Elbow him in the gut and roll away before he's awake enough to realize what's going on?

Only, I'd still have to get out of bed, then, with my cock saluting everything like an especially eager cadet.

"You know, with how stiff you are, I'm starting to think rigor mortis has kicked in," Quinn mumbles into my hair.

I squeeze my eyes shut for a moment.

"Wishful thinking?" I ask, and thankfully I sound relatively normal.

"Is that what people usually do around you? Wish for your death?" he asks and rolls away with a yawn.

"It's probable. Most of them don't get as excited about a dead body as you do, though."

He snorts and throws his arm over his eyes. "It's morning wood. I wouldn't read too much into it if I were you."

"And here I thought we'd finally discovered something interesting about you."

He lowers one arm and peers at me through his narrowed left eye. "Gets turned on by dead bodies is interesting in your book? Not veering toward concerning?"

"Those two things aren't mutually exclusive."

He starts to laugh then, his whole body shaking with it. "It's impossible to predict what comes out of your mouth," he says. "I'm starting my day discussing necrophilia. How did we get here?"

"You started poking me in the ass with your weapon while discussing my death, so that's all on you, buddy."

"Yeah, well, my weapon's now effectively unloaded. I don't think I've ever been this soft in my entire life."

I press my palm to my heart and sigh. "You sure know how to make a boy swoon."

He rolls himself out of the bed. Bare chest. Pillow crease on his cheek. Messy hair.

I push myself up on my elbows as I watch him move around the room.

My throat feels a bit too dry.

My toes curl again.

He looks out the window and absently scratches his chest. Another yawn.

I throw the covers off and sprint into the bathroom without a word while he's still distracted. An ice-cold shower later, I feel marginally more clearheaded.

While Quinn goes to take a shower, I make my way downstairs to the kitchen, where I find Rubi at the counter, drinking something green and unappetizing.

"There's more in the blender," she says when she catches me eyeing her drink.

"You know, I *would*," I say, "but I don't want you to run out."

"Relax. This thing is mostly banana. The grass taste is very mild."

"I'll take your word for it," I say, and go in search of carbs.

"How was the movie night?" Rubi asks after I've parked myself next to her with a plate of donuts.

"Quinn and I stayed up past everybody else, so I think technically we won?" I say.

"He probably made everybody watch one of his nature documentaries. That clears out the room real fast," Rubi says with a laugh.

I stare at her, the donut dangling between my fingers while I digest this new piece of information.

"It was about sea otters," I say after a bit.

"The one where they're not cute, but sick, depraved jerks?" she asks.

"I take it you've seen it."

"Unfortunately." She pretends to shudder.

"It's an interesting movie," I say.

"Not you too. It ruins otters with the truth. They're not cuddly, cute, hand-holding sweeties, but murderous monsters."

"You're viewing it all wrong," I say through a mouthful of donut.

She quirks her brow at me. "Am I?"

"Well, yeah. You're missing the key point. Otters aren't humans. You can't judge them by the same criteria you do humans. And you shouldn't really anthropomorphize animals anyway. It'll just end in disappointment. The way animals behave is normal for them. It doesn't have to be normal for you."

She rolls her eyes. "I swear I had this exact conversation with Quinn not too long ago."

I stuff another bite of donut in my mouth because I have no clue what to say to that. Or how to feel about it. Any of it.

Turns out Quinn and I have something in common after all.

It's not a lot.

And it's not anything substantial.

But at the same time, it's more than the nothing I've always thought we had.

STEPH

"I'M GOING to miss this tree." I pat the rough bark of the oak once and take a look around. The sun is slowly sinking lower. A lone bird is singing somewhere. The air is muggy and warm in a way that lets you know summer is finally in full swing. It's our last day in Maine, and I'm saying goodbye to the oak. No, I'm not insane. Just weirdly sentimental all of a sudden. Quinn just shook his head when I told him where I was going and followed me without comment as I trudged through the woods.

Our flight leaves tomorrow, right before noon, and then it's back to New York and back to the regularly scheduled programming where Quinn and I don't have to hide the fact that we barely tolerate each other.

I should be relieved.

I *am* relieved.

This week has been confusing and awkward and somewhat eye opening. It all just calls for self-analysis, and I am not somebody who enjoys something like that.

If I were, I'd have to consider the problem I seem to have with lying right now, specifically the fact that I suddenly seem to have developed some sort of rudimentary moral compass, even though I've never expressed any interest in having one.

I'd have to try and decipher the cryptic looks Quinn's been aiming my way these last few days. Not exactly infatuated boyfriend material. But not exactly the usual a-wooden-stake-through-the-heart-shouldn't-be-a-treatment-exclusively-reserved-for-vampires look either.

I'd have to admit my need to tackle him to the ground and strangle him has decreased by about ten percent. He's still annoying a lot of the time. But sometimes he's also not totally annoying.

I'd have to face the fact that I've repeatedly come *this* close to spilling the beans to Quinn about what a royal mess I really am. And in the interests of being honest, I couldn't exactly blame sitting in the tree for those bouts of honesty.

All in all, it sure is lucky I'm not into introspection.

"So," I say and glance toward Quinn. "Now that we're a step closer to breaking up, how do you think it'll happen?"

He turns his head toward me and pushes a strand of hair off his forehead. "What do you mean?"

"I mean, what are you gonna tell your family? Why did we break up? Who dumped who? What was the last straw that killed our love?"

"Who dumped *whom*," he says.

"Never mind," I say. "You just answered the why."

He tilts his head to the side and studies me silently. It's been happening lately. For some reason. I'm not sure what he's trying to find, but he sure does seem intent on looking for it. Dignity? Respectable behavior? Good manners? Hah! Good luck to him.

"So how does it all go down?" I add. "'Cause you know I won't go quietly."

"Is that so?" he asks.

"Oh, absolutely. I'll be vindictive. I'll smash your headlights in with a baseball bat. I'll scream your name in front of your building for weeks on end until your neighbors vote to get you evicted. I'll get you fired. I'll crash your future dates. I'll write a song about how you have a small dick."

"I'm starting to think everybody who's ever wanted to be in a relationship with you dodged a bullet."

"You shouldn't have cheated on me," I say with a shrug.

"I don't think—"

"And with our pool boy!" I wail. "All those mornings when I woke up at four a.m. to prepare a homemade lunch for you and feed our twelve cats while juggling three jobs to keep a roof over our head, and the whole time you were boinking Chad behind my back!"

"We really don't know how to budget if you were working three jobs and we still kept a pool boy."

"That's what our financial adviser said! But then we had to fire him because you were doing the devil's tango with him too."

"Wow. I get around."

"My momma warned me you were a lothario, but I thought I could fix you with my love. Now, I forgave the financial adviser thing because you said we couldn't afford to pay him and that you had to make a deal with him, but I draw the line at the pizza boy. I have some dignity left."

"I thought it was a pool boy," he says.

"Excuse me? What was that? You had a threesome with the pool boy *and* the pizza boy? Because you got stuck in the dryer, and they had to bang you free? Talk about a two-man job." I draw in a big breath and shake my head. "Why? Why couldn't you just keep your tiny penis in your pants?"

"That was definitely a story," he finally says. And then he starts to laugh. And once he stops, he looks at me and smiles. It's so simple. And so real. And maybe this whole trip is a lie and coming here at all was a terrible idea, but right here? Right now?

I can't really find it in me to regret it either. Just because of that one smile.

"You've got your thinking face on," Quinn says.

"I would never. Thinking causes wrinkles. It's why I avoid it at all costs."

He shakes his head and looks away. "You're hands down the strangest liar I've ever met."

I raise my brows at him. "I resent that. I'm absolutely upfront that what you see is what you get."

"Another lie," he says calmly like he knows everything, when in reality he knows nothing. The fact that he—accurately—branded me a liar was a lucky guess.

He turns his body toward me and leans his back against the trunk. His eyes bore into me and flay me open with precise cuts. Measured. Calm. Determined.

"Most people lie to make themselves look better. For some reason *you've* decided to go in the exact opposite direction." He pauses, eyes moving up and down me almost lazily. "Can't really figure out why, though. Who would voluntarily present themselves as shallow, self-absorbed, and thoughtless?"

His words slowly scrape the smile off my face. Not because I'm offended.

Because he's stripping me naked, but not in an enjoyable way.

I should laugh it off. Say something shallow and self-absorbed and thoughtless. Banish the curiosity. Cement the narrative.

Instead, I opt for being stupid.

"What makes you think I'm not?"

"I don't think people who are actually shallow and thoughtless hide themselves as thoroughly as you do."

"I don't hide," I say.

"But you do," he says. "Expertly and in plain sight, but you're definitely hiding."

He's very calm, aiming every word perfectly so that it hits at just the right angle. Picking away at my defenses. An archaeologist searching for buried truths.

"It's funny," he says. "I never realized how little I know about you. How little anybody seems to know about you. 'Steph likes to party and have a good time. Oh, that Steph. He sure seems to get into trouble a lot.' That's the main thing anybody ever says about you, even your closest friends. And I'm starting to think it's not true."

My fingertips dig into the branch. It takes almost insurmountable effort to keep my voice level.

"You know what I think you're doing?" I ask.

"Enlighten me."

"I think you want to fuck me," I say. And I don't think he does, to be honest. I'm one hundred percent not his type. But I need him to stop talking. I need to shock him into silence. Distract him. Get him off my case. Above all else, I need him to shut the fuck up.

"And you're trying to make me a bit more palatable for yourself. Can't really figure out why, though," I say, mockingly parroting his earlier statement. "You *can* not like somebody and still fuck them, you know that right? Don't worry, nobody will think less of you just because you find me hot. Lots of people do."

My words don't have the desired effect. Instead of denial, I get another thoughtful glance aimed my way.

"You are attractive," he acknowledges with the same ease one would say that the sky is blue and water is wet.

That is not what I expected to come out of his mouth.

"I'm... attractive?" I repeat slowly.

"You just said you were," he says with obvious exasperation.

"And I find it very difficult to believe you don't know it, what with how often you wax poetic about your looks."

"Permission to rephrase, your honor," I say. "*You* think I'm attractive?"

"I have eyes, don't I?" he replies dryly.

"Two, the last time I checked."

"Well, those eyes also have perfect twenty-twenty vision, and a working connection to the brain."

"You know, it never stops being weird when you agree with me on something," I say.

He just smiles at that. Like the *Mona Lisa*. The smile is there, but what the hell he's smiling about is a mystery to me.

We sit in the tree for a little while longer before we climb back down. I give the tree one more pat and turn around.

Instead of going back the way we came, Quinn starts going down to the water's edge in the distance. I follow him, carefully making my way across the rocky shoreline and once there, we start our trek toward the house in silence. When we reach the small sliver of sand that makes up the beach part of Quinn's family's camp on the beach, he stops, eyes moving to the wooden dock.

"Feel like going for a swim?" he asks.

It's not that I'm afraid of water. It's not that I haven't been swimming since that day.

But nowadays, when I look at the endless expanse of water in front of me, I don't feel at home anymore. There's just fear and tension. Instead of freedom, the only thing that I now seem to associate with the sea is unsuccessful attempts to survive. And the ocean always wins.

"Stephen?"

I snap my eyes to Quinn and force myself to swallow through the dryness in my throat.

"Are you insane? Do you know how long it takes to get my hair to look like this in the morning? I can't make it wet."

I sound relatively normal. Then again, I've had a lot of practice.

"Suit yourself," Quinn says. And pulls his shirt over his head. His pants are next to go, and then he's walking toward the wooden dock, clad only in a pair of skintight black boxer briefs. They leave nothing to the imagination. He's pure muscle everywhere. Long limbs, an ass that looks like it's carved out of marble, and wide shoulders that taper into a narrow waist.

It'd be nice if I could just appreciate the view. It'd be nice if I were normal and could tell him that I find the thought of the ocean a bit terrifying now, and him jumping into the water makes me anxious, and that anxiety grows with every step he takes on that dock.

"The man's an Olympic swimmer," I whisper under my breath. "Stop being an idiot."

Quinn reaches the end of the dock. He glances over his shoulder. He has a cocky grin on his face before he turns back around and dives in.

I see it all in slow motion.

I walk to the end of the dock in the same slow motion.

With every step, my heartbeat grows louder.

I don't see him anywhere.

Something swirls inside me. Uncomfortable and stupid.

"Don't be an idiot," I repeat. "He's fine."

But he's still nowhere to be seen. It's just me and the dock and the sea and he's still not up, even though people need air to survive.

How long has it been?

I have no idea. It could've been a minute from when he went under, but it could be more.

By now, my heart is hammering in my throat.

I don't know what to do.

"Quinn?" I call out.

My feet are stuck on the dock. I start counting in my head. Get to thirty. And I can't anymore.

I pull off my shirt and toe off my sneakers. The left one gets stuck on my foot, and I give a shake, so it flies off and lands in the water.

I dive in. A second later, I crash to the surface and look around frantically. There's still no sign of Quinn. Just water everywhere as far as the eye can see. Impossible to comb through on my own.

I'm alone.

I can feel panic setting in. Moving through me. Cutting off air. Paralyzing my thoughts.

Don't, I plead with myself. *You can't do this here.*

I gasp. Instead of air, I pull in a mouthful of water. I cough and splutter as my throat tightens.

Instead of looking for Quinn, I'm now gasping for breath, fighting off the feeling of drowning.

I don't know how it happens, but suddenly, there are arms around my waist, and Quinn is dragging me toward the shore.

I stumble out of the water and land on the sand, desperate to get some air into my lungs.

It's not working.

Quinn is in front of me then, his big palms on my cheeks as he holds my head still, eyes boring into mine.

"You're okay," he says, infinitely calm and sure and safe. His voice is a low, steady rumble in my ears.

"You're okay," he repeats. "Look at me. I'm going to count to five, and you're going to breathe in."

I manage a single nod.

"One, two..." His voice is a low, steady rumble in my ears. I draw in a shallow breath, force it into my lungs.

"Now out," he says firmly, and starts counting again.

And again.

And again.

The water starts to recede until I can breathe again.

He stops counting once I squeeze my eyes shut. My hands are shaking as I drag them through my hair, sand falling from my palms and clinging to the wet skin.

"Okay?" Quinn asks.

I give a shaky nod.

My mouth tastes all salty, and I fight the urge to gag.

"I'm fine," I croak.

He pauses for a moment before he drops down next to me, plastering himself against my side, and lets out a deep breath.

He doesn't say anything for a little while, and slowly, I get my breathing back under control.

"What happened?" he asks after a little bit.

I stare at the sea. I wonder if my sneaker is still out there. Just bobbing on the waves. Maybe it's on its way to Canada by now. I close my eyes, fighting the hysterical snort of laughter that threatens to escape.

"I panicked," I say quietly. "You didn't come up for air, and I panicked."

He stills next to me. His next words are filled to the brim with confusion.

"Do you know how to swim?" he asks.

"It's been a while," I say. It's as honest as I can force myself to get.

He's silent again. "Maybe," he says in a slow, measured voice. "Maybe next time it'd be a better idea to call for help?"

The snort does escape this time.

"Maybe," I agree.

"I can hold my breath for close to five minutes," he adds after a moment. "For future reference."

I squeeze my eyes shut and take another slow breath. "Show-off," I say.

"If you can insult me, you must be feeling better," he says.

"I'd insult you on my deathbed." The words are normal. The toneless delivery is not.

He laughs and shakes his head. "Of course you would. Guess I'm lucky you didn't just let me drown."

My whole body locks up tight.

Quinn sends me a curious look and opens his mouth to say something.

I scramble to my feet and fight off the lightheaded feeling that accompanies my every move right now.

"I should go inside," I say. "I'm freezing my ass off."

"Yeah, okay," he says, and gets up too. "A shower. And then we'll talk."

We start to trudge toward the house.

"Can we... Can you not mention this to anybody?" I say once we're at the door. I grit my teeth for a second. "Please."

"Sure," he says. "Don't worry about it."

I sneak inside and past the living room where most of Quinn's family seems to have gathered.

I hear Quinn say, "We went for a swim," before I run up the stairs and lock myself in the bathroom.

Once there, I sit down on the lid of the toilet and scrub my palms over my face.

Well.

Fucked up again.

YOU'D THINK it'd be pretty damn impossible to find a ride while you're in the middle of nowhere when it's fuck-knows-o'clock at night.

Lucky for me, I lack some key aspects that are generally considered a necessity for being a good person. Morals, pride, and a sense of decency being the top ones. It really comes in handy when you find yourself in the midst of a middle-of-the-night freak out.

I place the Post-it on Quinn's bedside table as quietly as I can to not wake him. Family emergency. Yada, yada, yada. Didn't want to wake you or make any trouble. Yada, yada, yada.

I take one more look at him. He's thrown his arm over the side of the bed where I was lying a few minutes ago, his breathing deep and even.

Coward, a voice whispers in my head.

Yeah. Tell me something new.

I throw my backpack over my shoulder and sneak down the stairs. Open the front door as quietly as I can. Once outside, I head down the road that leads away from the house. I don't look back. Just keep going.

There's a car idling at the end of the road. I don't recognize it. It's some fancy new model of Lexus that looks like it's just rolled out of the dealership.

I open the trunk and throw my bag in and once that's done, I go and open the passenger door and get inside.

I lean back against the seat and turn my head to the side.

"Hey, Evelyn."

She flicks me on the nose with her long, manicured fingers, and it stings like a motherfucker.

"Ow!" I yelp and rub at the hurt spot.

"You're in my neck of the woods, and I'm only finding out now?" she asks. "With a middle-of-the-night phone call?"

She's not really angry with me. It's a strange relationship we have. She's never been the sentimental kind. I'd go so far as to say she abhors anything that resembles feelings of any kind. We can go weeks without speaking to each other or sending out any signs of life. But she's always there when I call.

"Sorry," I say.

My grandmother sends me a measured look. "You in trouble?"

I rub my palm over my face. "Not any more than usual."

"Good. I'm not dressed for a car chase. Have you eaten?"

"No," I say. There's no point in adding that I'm not hungry. Evelyn loves to feed people. Not in the sense that she likes to cook for them. She prefers footing the bill in a fancy restaurant. I doubt any of those are open at this hour, but if anybody can conjure up good food at this time of night, it's Evelyn Hartley.

"I know a place," she says.

QUINN

THE FAMILY EMERGENCY lie is laughably flimsy. I turn the Post-it around between my fingers, almost expecting something like "Gotcha!" written on the other side. There isn't.

I contemplate the note some more. Pointlessly.

After a minute, I grab my phone and do something I've avoided for years. I type "Stephen Hartley" into the search engine.

I have a few issues surrounding privacy. Namely that I love mine and feel rather strongly about keeping it. Which means I also avoid digging into other people's private affairs on principle. Unless they want to tell me things themselves, I'll stick to my own business.

Until Stephen.

Not that going against my own principles does me any good. There are thousands of results because it turns out Stephen Hartley is a pretty common name, and since there's an actor and a college professor, both with the same name, the results are useless. Stephen Christopher Hartley narrows it down a bit, but the most prominent Stephen Christopher Hartley seems to be a local politician in Idaho.

Eventually, after narrowing and finetuning my search a bit further, I hit the jackpot. All the results are from Stephen's high school years. Nothing before. Nothing after. It's as if Stephen only existed for three years.

Mostly, his name features in honor roll. Year after year. A few hits about scholarships he's earned, all seemingly for exemplary academic success. And awards. For everything. Sport. Science. Music. Is it even humanly possible for one person to manage all this? To have time for all of this?

I sit back and frown.

So why, exactly, does a person, who by all accounts seems to be extremely talented and smart, let the whole world think he's a shallow idiot?

STEPH

I LIE low in Maine for a few days and let Evelyn volunteer me as a stagehand for her community theater project. As with everything else Evelyn does, it's highly experimental, which is another word for god-awful, but keeping busy does keep my mind off Quinn. Almost. Sometimes.

It's not a foolproof method, but it works better than obsessing over the fact that now Quinn really has seen me at my worst.

After four days, though, I have to either get back to New York, or fuck off to parts unknown. And for God knows what reason, I choose New York.

Evelyn drops me off at the airport and waves at me from the car. She's not much for sentimentality, my grandmother, and I'm grateful for that.

Once I get back home, the apartment is empty, as it usually is, but for once, I'm absolutely fine with it.

I'm really not in the mood to talk about Maine.

Probably ever.

WHEN YOUR PAST comes back to haunt you, I expect it'd have the decency to be a mistake from a long time ago. A minimum of two years. A *bare* minimum.

Then again, I've never been one for traditions, so of course it makes sense the past that comes to haunt *me* is barely a week old.

I jog up the stairs to Blair and Nora's apartment for family dinner. It's a thing Blair kicked into gear after her and Nora's daughter, Hazel, was born. Something about reassuring Jude and me we're still an important part of Blair's life, even if she now has a family of her own. I don't quite get the logic behind it, but Blair's been very insistent about the whole thing. The dinner takes place every week on Friday. Attendance compulsory. Only excuse to miss it is being on one's deathbed. Or visiting one's fake boyfriend's family. That also seems to be a viable excuse as experience dictates.

Nora lets me in and takes the six-pack I brought with me with a dubious expression.

"Is this the wine you were supposed to bring?" she asks, holding the beer at arm's length from herself like I've presented her with an animal carcass.

"Close enough," I say with a shrug.

"Yes. I'm sure grapes were involved in making… this."

"Don't be a snob. I shelled out fifteen bucks for this baby. It's a 2022 Great Lake Dortmunder Gold Lager. It's a great vintage."

"Oh my God," Nora mutters, turns around, and walks away from me.

"You'll thank me once you've had a glass of that baby," I call after her.

She turns around in the doorway and sends me a scathing look. "I'm sure it'll go great with the duck we're having."

"That's the spirit."

I'd laugh, but I'm not masochistic enough to want to find out what she'd do to me.

Instead, I sit down on the bench by the door. I put the wine bottle I hid in my jacket on the floor and bend down to unlace my shoes when there's another knock on the door.

"Can you get it?" Blair shouts from somewhere inside the apartment.

"On it," I holler back.

I push my shoes out of the way and open the door. The smile melts off my face the moment I see who it is. I was expecting Jude and Blake. Instead, I get Quinn.

"Oh," I say like an idiot.

Ah, yes. Quinn. Remember me? The idiot who almost drowned himself while having a panic attack? It's not at all devastating to see you again.

He quirks his brow at me when I've spent a sufficient amount of time staring at him.

"Are you going to let me in or...?"

"What are you doing here?" I blurt. Not the politest of questions, I admit, but I did a little covert spying via Nora before I came here, and she told me Quinn was busy. It's the only reason I didn't fake my own death!

"It's always a pleasure, Stephen," Quinn says. Pleasantly.

"Uh-huh," I mutter under my breath. Not so pleasantly. "So nice."

Karma must've finally caught up to me. To be fair, she took her sweet time, and I had a good run. Even so, fuck!

Quinn tilts his head to the side. "What was that?"

"It's nice to see you too," I say a bit louder than distinctly necessary, enunciating every word very clearly.

And there's that lip twitch. That irritating, knowing lip twitch.

"I'm so glad you made time in your busy schedule to be here," I say.

He tilts his head to the side. "Are you?"

I'd answer, but while I was busy being passive aggressive, steps echoed in the hallway, and Jude and Blake clear the stairs and stop behind Quinn.

Jude glances at Blake. "They've hired a bouncer. This place is getting fancy."

Blake's lips twitch. "Let's hope they don't have standards."

Jude looks his boyfriend up and down. "Why? You look very nice, so I think we can fool them."

Blake flicks a look toward Jude. "Your jeans have a rip just below your ass."

Jude glances behind him. "That's for your benefit."

"And your T-shirt says Men Suck."

"So? We do!" Jude says.

Blake grins before he tears his attention away from Jude with some obvious difficulty.

He raises his brow at me. "Do we make the cut? Or do you need to see some ID?"

I quickly take a step to the side. "Sorry. I was just... warming the threshold for you."

Jude sends me a funny look. "Did you hit your head coming out of the shower this morning or something?"

"Let's just go inside," I say.

Jude and Blake stroll into the living room. Quinn stays behind.

"How's the family emergency?" he asks, and his tone makes it very clear what he thinks of my emergency storyline.

"Solved," I reply and stare back with my most impassive gaze.

"And you?" he says. "How are you?"

I narrow my eyes at him and cross my arms over my chest. "What are you doing?"

"Asking about you?" he says.

I scowl at him. "Why? Are you on your deathbed? Stop being nice to me. You're freaking me out. We don't do that."

He leans his shoulder against the wall and watches me calmly. "Why is that?"

I stare at him in complete confusion. "What?"

"Why aren't we nice to each other?"

I open and close my mouth for a few seconds because the words don't seem to want to come out.

"Because we don't like each other," I finally say.

Quinn tilts his head to the side, the picture of polite curiosity, and hums thoughtfully. "We could try."

My stomach feels disgustingly hollow as it dawns on me what he's doing.

"I don't need you to pity me!" I growl. "Fuck's sake, just stop being weird."

This is the part where he snaps at me and order is restored.

Only he doesn't.

Just sends me a mercurial smile and walks away from me, so I'm left standing in the hallway, frowning, and not sure what I should do now. Have dinner, I guess. I sigh and go to the living room. The moment I step foot in the door, Blair aims a shit-eating grin my way.

"Well, well, well. If it isn't the happy couple."

I return the smile and lift up my middle finger.

"I call best man," Jude says.

"What? No!" Blair protests. "That's not how it works. You can't just call best man."

Jude shrugs. "Just did."

Blair crosses her arms over her chest and glares at Jude.

"Don't you think the groom has the right to choose his best man?"

"How is he supposed to choose between you and me? At least I care enough to call dibs and make it easier on him. I care," he repeats. And he's looking at me again. "I'm just that kind of person."

"You choose the person who'll do a better job. And, like, I don't want to brag, but only one of us is married here and knows the process in and out." She looks at me. "It's a complicated affair. You don't want an amateur at your side for this."

"Calm down. You were married by an Arnold Schwarzenegger impersonator in Vegas," Jude says.

"Eff you. It was romantic as hell," Blair says.

"Oh yeah. Especially the part where he said, 'I'll be back,' when he forgot to bring his speech and had to go to the back to get it."

"I happen to love *The Terminator*! I'll have you know that part was the highlight of the wedding for me."

"You say the sweetest things." Nora lifts her eyes from the plates she's putting on the table.

I sigh again. This is going to be a long evening.

THE WEDDING and relationship jokes peter out after another hour or so, because even the best comedians run out of steam at one point. After a brief interrogation about our time in Maine that I leave entirely on Quinn's shoulders, the conversation veers to other topics, and I slowly relax and try to enjoy the rest of the evening.

I get thirty minutes of reprieve before the shit really hits the fan. Again.

It begins with my phone ringing in the hallway.

Family dinner is a no-phone zone, so I get the obligatory stink eye from Blair.

"I forgot to turn it off," I say. "Sorry."

I start to get up, but that only earns me another glare from Blair. "Don't even think about it."

I sit back down and lift my hands up. "I was only going to turn it off."

The phone stops.

"Problem solved," Blair says.

The phone goes off again.

I raise my brows at Blair. She rolls her eyes. "Just go already."

In the time it takes me to go to the hallway, the phone has stopped and started ringing once more. I go to turn it off, but the name on the screen stops me.

I stare at the word *Mom* while I debate what to do. Pick it up or emigrate to Australia? One of those options is more appealing than the other.

It's been a while since I've heard from either of my parents, but seeing that August is fast approaching, I imagine I'll be hearing more from them.

The ringing stops, but I'm under no illusion this is the end of it.

And I can't be here once I finally pick up the phone.

I silence it for now, stuff it in the back pocket of my jeans, and saunter back into the living room doorway.

"Hey, so, I'm gonna take off," I say.

Blair narrows her eyes at me. "Why?"

"I've got plans for dessert." I put as much innuendo in my tone as humanly possible and waggle my brows for good measure.

"You're not gonna blow us off because somebody hit you up on Grindr," Blair says.

I give a careless shrug. "What can I say, babe? The heart wants what the heart wants."

"Seriously?" Blair asks.

"We're almost done here anyway." I'm a shitty friend. No room for argument here. But when it comes down to being a shitty person or being honest, I choose the former.

Blair opens her mouth to argue, but my fucking phone starts vibrating. She takes a deep breath.

I pull the phone out and make myself glance at the screen again.

Mom.

I stuff the phone back into my pocket.

"See you, guys," I say and make my escape before anybody can start to argue.

Once outside, I pull in a slow, measured breath and dig out my phone.

My hands start to shake almost immediately.

Nausea rolls in my stomach.

You don't have to do this, Steph. You don't have to call them back.

I close my eyes. Bite the inside of my cheek.

Just leave it be. Go back upstairs.

It's impossible to unlock the phone when your fingers shake this badly.

I'm dead, Steph!

I curse and dig my fingernails into the soft part of my palm for a moment.

Take a few deep breaths.

And dial the number.

STEPH

HOTSPOT IS a strange mix of a bar and a pub, switching between the two based on whether Marlon, the owner, is in the mood to cook or not. The place isn't pretty, but it has its own charm and a steady set of regulars.

Like with many things in life, I ended up working here by accident. There was a Help Wanted sign on the window. It was haphazardly slapped there, half hidden behind an old open mic night poster like the person who put up the sign didn't care if it was even visible. I was on my way to another job interview, but there was something about the slapdash sign I liked, so I stepped in on a whim. Ten minutes later, I had a job. Just like that. Just because Marlon, who looked like an aging gang member but was actually a teddy bear, said he had a good feeling about me. His gut was lying, but I was in need of a job, so I didn't bother to inform him about that.

Most days I like my job just fine. It pays well enough for a bar, people are nice, and the tips are decent, so most days, I can't complain about anything.

Most days.

Today is not one of most days.

Because sometime around eleven thirty, an hour before closing, Quinn walks in.

Quinn, who I haven't seen since I took off from Blair and Nora's place a week ago.

Quinn, who's called me several times since then, and whose calls I've blatantly ignored.

Quinn, who takes the bar in with his usual sort of impassive, mildly unimpressed look on his face, which I can't even interpret as unimpressed anymore because now I know things about him I so wish I didn't.

Quinn, who's accompanied by yet another one of those despicably good-looking, suit-wearing men he seems to be partial to. Although, this one's not in a suit but jeans and a leather jacket, so I suppose this is Quinn spicing things up a bit? The dude's blond, though, so no change there. And really, disgustingly handsome—as usual.

It's not particularly busy today, so the moment Quinn glances toward the bar from his latest fuck buddy, our eyes meet across the floor.

And in a moment of pure idiocy, I duck down behind the bar.

Mona, the second bartender, sends me a funny look. "What are you doing?"

"I believe he's hiding from me," Quinn's voice answers somewhere above me.

I close my eyes for a moment before I look up and straight at Quinn.

"Am not," I say, and seeing that I'm currently crouching on the floor, I opt to elaborate on that lie. "I dropped something." I pick up the first thing I can find on the floor. "There it is," I say and lift up a beer cap. "What a relief." I inspect the cap and wipe over it with my hand like I'm polishing the family jewels.

"I bet that has great sentimental value," Quinn says dryly.

I stand up and adopt the most dignified expression that's ever graced a person's face. "This is a family heirloom. My great-great-grandfather brought it over from..." I completely blank out on all countries. After an embarrassing thirty seconds, I go with, "Scotland. During the gold rush."

Quinn squints. "Is that a beer cap?"

"Like you said. Sentimental value," I say and stuff the cap into the pocket of my jeans. Based on how things are going for me right now, I fully expect to somehow cut myself on the dick with it later. "What are you doing here?"

"This is a bar," he says.

"Well, yeah, but you've never been here."

"I didn't know that was a requirement. Do you have a sign-up sheet I should fill in?"

"Funny," I say. "Just..." I shake my head. This conversation, like every other conversation I've had with Quinn, probably won't end with me looking brilliant, so it's better to nip this thing in the bud. "What can I get you?"

Quinn glances behind himself to where his... friend has settled in a booth.

"Two beers," he says. "Whatever you have on tap."

I prepare his order in record time and slide it over the bar.

"Have a good evening," I say.

He stays put. "I'm sure I will."

The images of Quinn fucking that blond Adonis he came in with flash through my head like the most unwelcome movie premiere ever.

"Is your phone broken?" he asks.

I cross my arms over my chest and meet his gaze head on. "Nope."

"So you're just ignoring my calls," he says.

"Aww." I press my palm to my chest. "How sweet of you to notice."

"Any particular reason as to why?" he asks.

Fear. Debilitating, paralyzing fear because I don't understand you, and you look at me like I'm a puzzle that needs to be solved.

I put my palms on the bar and lean forward, lowering my voice. "Look, I did my part already. I came to Maine. I played your boyfriend. We're done."

He sends me another thoughtful look.

"No, I don't think we are, Stephen."

He takes the beers and goes back to his date.

And I don't understand anything anymore.

STEPH

I GET a few days of reprieve after that encounter, until one morning when I'm doing my usual circle around the neighborhood. It's barely six thirty in the morning, and my brain is extra loud today, because I'm on mile five already, and it just refuses to shut up.

I only give up running when my phone rings. I stop and pull it out from the armband.

"Yeah?" I say.

"Oh good," Blair says. "You're up."

I lean forward to get my breathing back under control.

"Early bird and all that jazz," I say.

"Ugh. Runners. Are you busy?"

"Not really," I say. This promises a distraction, so whatever she has to say, I'm game.

"I need a favor," Blair says.

"Sure. Lay it on me."

"Quinn forgot his phone at our place last night, and he needs it, but Nora's on her way to the airport and Hazel's running a fever, so could you just stop by, grab the phone, and drop it off at the pool for him?"

Shit, shit, shit, and a fuck for good measure.

"Steph?" Blair prompts.

"Yeah," I say belatedly. "No problem at all. I'll drop by your place in"—I check the time—"thirty minutes?"

Seeing Quinn is the absolute last thing I want to do, but considering how many times Blair has gotten me out of a bind, I owe her so many favors I'll need a few lifetimes to repay them all.

"Thanks. You're a lifesaver. I gotta run. Hazel's crying."

She drops the call, and I'm left staring at my phone with a sour face.

I run back home, take a lightning-fast shower, and am out the door again in less than ten minutes. Better to get this over with. I take the subway to Blair's place and then get back to Brooklyn and search out the address Blair scribbled on a piece of paper for me.

"The pool" is on the ground floor of a small office building. I don't know what I was expecting from a place where Quinn works. Something super modern and sleek where the rich and successful go to show off their skills in the water and pose by the poolside? I know he teaches swimming, but not much else, because if there's one topic I've always avoided, it's Quinn. Instead of sleek and sterile, though, this place is full of color. Drawings of sea animals, fish, plants, and coral decorate the walls that have been painted to look like the ocean. Large windows make everything seem light and bright.

I'm still busy taking everything in when a woman walks into the room, dressed in shorts and a tank top. She stops and sends me a confused look and a polite smile. "Hello. I'm sorry, but we're not open yet."

"Hi. I'm not here to... do anything," I say. "I'm looking for Quinn? Henris," I add in case they have more than one Quinn here. "I have his phone."

Her smile turns warmer. "And you are?" she asks.

"Steph. Stephen," I correct myself because Quinn doesn't call me Steph for some reason. "Stephen Hartley? But you don't have to let him know or anything. I'm sure he's busy. I can just leave the phone with you, and you can give it to him."

"He has time right now. He's outside. Go down the hallway and first door to the right. It's impossible to miss."

My shoulders slump.

"Thanks." I'm sure my smile looks pained and my "thanks" sounds insincere, but it can't be helped at this point.

So I trudge down the hallway and when I spot a glass door on my right, I go through it, and then I'm outside, as promised. I end up in a fenced courtyard type of thing where there's an outdoor pool.

And in that pool, there's Quinn, doing laps.

I develop a pretty unfortunate dry mouth syndrome while I stand still like a statue and watch him cut through water like he's a freaking dolphin. I used to think of water as my element, but I don't think I've ever looked like I belong quite like Quinn does.

I walk closer, hypnotized by the fluent way he moves, and stop at the edge of the pool. He turns around at the other end and swims back toward me, slower this time, almost lazily. I don't think he's noticed me yet. I could still drop the phone somewhere and sneak away.

But it's already too late.

He comes out of the pool like he's filming a scene for a movie, complete with water cascading down his body and him dragging his hand through his hair to get the wet strands out of his face.

This much muscle flexing cannot be healthy. Not for him. Definitely not for me. It's giving me ideas. Unwelcome, dumb ideas.

The only sign that he's surprised to find me standing by the pool is the slightly raised eyebrow.

"Stephen," he says. He looks me up and down, slowly and thoroughly, and I've never been more *aware* of a look.

What. The fuck. Is happening?

"Blair sent me over with your phone." I hold it out for him, but instead of taking it, he goes and picks up the towel and starts to dry himself.

"Thank you," he says. "I hope it wasn't too much trouble."

"I was out anyway," I say.

"Morning run?" he asks, and by now my throat is so dry from watching him rub the towel all over his chest I can only nod.

"You should invite me along one of these days," he says. "Turns out I quite enjoy running with you."

I snort out a laugh. "Sure you do. I'm slow, and I wish for death the whole time, so I'm real good company."

"I had fun."

"Just as I always suspected. When they handed out common sense, you were in the pool and missed out."

He smiles, all enigmatic and amused at my expense, and drapes the towel over his shoulders.

"You skipped dinner on Friday," he says.

I look away and try my best not to start fidgeting under the close scrutiny. "I'm taking a few extra shifts at work."

He nods slowly. "And here I was starting to think you were trying to avoid me."

I snort. "Wow. To think you managed to fit an ego of that size in the pool with you. Now there's an achievement."

His lips twitch, and he shakes his head. "There are days when I think I actually might have an ego if I didn't have you in my life constantly taking me down a peg."

"I live to serve."

I hold out his phone to him, and he takes it off my hand, fingertips grazing my palm, awareness racing up and down my skin from where he touched me.

"Well," I say. "Nice catching—"

"I stalked you online the other day," he says, so very casually while all my muscles lock in place and the temperature seems to drop from blazing hot to freezing cold.

"Why?" I ask carefully, trying my fucking best to fake nonchalance.

"Curiosity," he says with a shrug.

What did you find?

Not much, I presume. I've been careful enough, so my digital footprint should be pathetically uninformative. At least the digital version of *this* version of Steph should be. I don't think he did a deep dive into my past. Fuck me, I should've never told him I was from the Outer Banks. It's those breadcrumbs that ruin everything.

"Oh good," I say. "Next thing I know you're collecting my hair from the shower drain to make a sweater."

"For you or for myself?"

"A matching set."

"As sweet as it sounds, I don't think we're quite there yet," he says.

"Well I, for one, am heartbroken."

He's looking at me again. That intense, penetrative gaze that promises to slowly chip away at the protective layers until he gets to the heart of the matter. Until the mystery is solved.

"You know, you've met my family, but you've never told me anything about yours."

I feel slightly nauseated by now.

"You never asked," I say.

"Okay," he counters. "Tell me, then."

"I have a mother and a father."

"Groundbreaking revelations," he drawls.

I eye his bare chest and the indecently clingy swimming shorts.

"Shouldn't you put some clothes on? You don't want to catch a cold."

"I'm good. What do your parents do?" he asks.

I take a deep, slow breath. It's fine.

"My mother's an anesthesiologist, and my father is a software developer."

He just keeps looking at me. "Are you close?"

Nope. Not going there even if you paid me.

"Look, as lovely as this is, some of us have places to be and people to see. I can't just sit by the pool the whole day and work on my tan."

That all-knowing look of his really just invites shutting down with violence... Or kissing. I could violently kiss his face off.

And I'm not going there either.

"Later then," he says.

"Sure. Later." Right now, I'd promise pretty much anything that'd get me away from Quinn and his scrutiny.

I take off with a hasty, "Bye." When I peek over my shoulder at the door, he's still looking after me.

STEPH

MONA and I are on shift together again, along with Jack, Marlon's son. He helps out on the weekends because he's a grad student who needs extra cash, and nobody around here says no to an extra pair of hands. It's Saturday, so the bar is busy. Mona's always down for showing off her bottle throwing skills, so a lot of people have crowded around the bar to enjoy the show.

Mona laughs loudly as Jack tries to copy her and flip the bottle. He hasn't broken any yet, but he's come close a few times.

"Hopeless," she calls out with a laugh while she watches Jack's fumbling.

"I can do it. It's physics," he insists.

I smile to myself while I hand out drinks.

"Did I tell you all I had a date the other day?" Jack calls out conversationally to nobody in particular. His stories of failed dates are sort of legendary around here by now.

"We went to her grandfather's birthday party, and she tried to give me a handjob under the table."

I raise my brows at him. "In front of her grandfather?"

"Oh, no. Not just her grandfather. Her whole family. I tell you, nothing sounds as loud as a zipper being pulled down in the middle of your date's mother telling you about her vacation in Hawaii. She got mad at me and kicked me out when I said I wasn't in the mood. The date, not her mother."

"Poor baby," Mona says and pats him on his cheek when she passes him.

He shrugs. "It wasn't too bad. Her mom gave me a slice of cake to go just as I was waiting for my Uber. All in all, I've had worse evenings."

He looks around with a boyish smile on his face. People in hearing range laugh.

"Maybe I should switch teams," Jack muses and hands a margarita over the counter. "Steph? Thoughts? How's your side of the aisle looking?" he shouts from down the bar from me.

"Not too shabby," I call back.

"Will you show me the ropes?"

"Sure. Come here, and I'll give you a handjob under the bar."

I grin as people snicker around me. I hand a beer to the man in front of me and take the money he slides toward me.

"I'll have one of those handjobs, too, if you're offering," he says with a wink.

"I'll think about it."

The guy suddenly pitches forward and stumbles into the counter with a loud, "Oof," spilling beer all over the place.

"My bad, man. I didn't see you there," Quinn tells the guy, pats him on the shoulder and elbows him out of the way. His words are sort of nice, but the sneer he delivers them with is definitely not.

My heart gives an uncomfortable jolt in my chest and picks up speed at the sight of him. He looks... good. Too good. His dark hair is meticulously styled, and he's wearing a tux. A tux! I don't even like guys in suits, but I can't deny that Quinn wears the hell out of his.

I'm still a bit preoccupied with the suit, so it takes me a moment to notice the man at Quinn's side. The same blond dude he brought with him the last time. He's in a tux, too, so... Awesome. They match. How sweet.

The rush of blood in my ears and the tightness in my chest is idiotic and unwelcome. Another date, it seems. Good for them.

I clear my throat and force a smile on my face.

"You again. You must really like this place. What can I get you?"

Quinn's date leans his elbow on the bar and sends me a wide grin.

"What do you recommend?"

"Depends on what you're in the mood for."

He glances toward Quinn. "Shots?" he says with a smirk. "What are we thinking? A blowjob? A screaming orgasm?"

Quinn sends him a dirty look before he glances toward me. "Can I get a gin and tonic, please?"

"And a whiskey sour," Quinn's date says before he reaches his hand toward me. "Sutton Holland," he says.

I take his hand and shake it dubiously. "Steph," I say.

"A pleasure," he says.

I can feel Quinn's eyes on me the whole time I prepare their drinks. It's a relief when I can slide the glasses over the counter and move on to the next customer.

For the next hour, I can't stop myself from taking covert glances toward the table where Quinn's sitting. I say covert, but it's not that necessary to *be* covert seeing that he's occupied with his date. They're sitting close to each other, heads together, talking about something intently.

When the door opens and more people pour in, I'm grateful

because my chances of spying on Quinn go down the busier we get.

I finish with a customer just as Sutton reaches the bar. He grins at me and leans forward, raising his voice so I'll hear him over the noise.

"Can I have another round?"

"Sure thing," I say.

Even by Quinn's usual standards, Sutton is extremely handsome. Blond hair, cheekbones for days, large blue eyes fringed with thick, dark lashes. And the good looks come with a side of class and elegance that screams of wealth and money. It's in the way he holds himself. In the easy confidence and the polished edge that accompanies his tone.

I try not to think about the way he leaned into Quinn earlier, blond hair mixing with black. Two impossibly good-looking people.

Maybe this one will stick? Maybe, in a few months' time, Sutton will be the one who sits at Quinn's parents' dinner table? And they'll look back at that week I spent there and laugh. *Remember when you were dating that guy? Steph something. What a disaster he was.*

The tightness in my chest gets worse.

"So you're Stephen," Sutton says while I'm mixing the drinks.

I lift my gaze from the glass I'm holding.

"Steph," I say, because only Quinn has ever really called me Stephen. And I'm an idiot.

"Quinn talks about you quite a lot," Sutton says.

I put the glass down and look at him.

"Does he?" I say tonelessly. Fuck's sake, I'm really not in the mood for a jealous boyfriend act. The last thing I want to do is waste time debunking somebody's misplaced fears about my existence.

"It's like I practically know you already." He takes a sip of his drink.

I quirk my brow at him. "Can I get you anything else?"

"Your number," he says.

I stand very still as I stare at him. "Aren't you here on a date?"

He shakes his head. "With Quinn? He's business. You and I, though? We could be pleasure."

"Yeah... Somewhere down the line, somebody obviously told you that was a good line. They were lying."

His grin only widens. "I'm starting to see why Quinn's so obsessed with you."

I roll my eyes. "Quinn's not obsessed with me. Mostly he's annoyed with me, pissed at me, in dislike with me, or some combination of the three."

He just laughs. "Obliviousness is such a delight. It's so fun to watch."

He leans forward over the counter and grabs a pen by the register. Next thing I know, his fingers wrap around my wrist, and he pulls it toward him. The tip of the pen is against the inside of my arm, digits appearing on my skin, one after the other. He makes a real show of writing those numbers down, too. It takes forever before he pulls away and drops the pen on the bar.

I stare at my wrist. "I'm not going to use the number. You know that, right?"

"I imagine you won't. That wasn't the point, anyway."

"What was the point then?"

"I'm bored, and I like setting fires," he says.

And then he's gone.

My eyes involuntarily move to Quinn. If looks could kill, this would be a massacre.

I look away.

When did my life become so messy?

Eventually, I brave another look in Quinn's direction, but he's no longer there. The table has been occupied by new people. As much as I reprimand myself, my eyes still search for him for the rest of my shift. Pointlessly. He's gone.

I'm not disappointed.

It's a good thing he left.

Makes things easier.

It's already past one a.m. when the last of the patrons pack it in and leave. It's another hour before we've cleaned the place and set everything back in order.

Jack and Mona take an Uber, but I wave away their offer to share. Fresh air will do me some good. Plus, I've always liked the city at night. It's only a twenty-minute walk to my place anyway.

It's a good plan.

But when I step outside, I find Quinn leaning against the wall.

I stop.

He sends me a calculating look, his features set in stone.

"I thought you left," I say.

"I did." He straightens himself. "And then I came back."

He's still in his formal wear. He's lost the tux, but the dress pants remain, and he's rolled up the sleeves of his crisp white dress shirt, exposing his strong forearms.

"Why?" I ask.

He stalks toward me. There's intense, and then there's Quinn. Tension and ferocity swirl in his gaze, and I'm not sure if I want to fight back or capitulate.

His hand goes to the back of my head. Fingers grip my hair. The air is thick with terrible decisions.

"You drive me fucking insane," he says in a low, fierce voice.

"You're annoying and aggravating and impossible, and it's like you've made it your mission in life to get under my skin."

My breath gets stuck in my lungs, and for the first time in my life, it happens in a good way.

I force myself to swallow through the thickness in my throat. "That's a lot of words to say I get your dick hard."

The laugh that spills from his lips is decidedly unhappy. "I wish it was just my dick. You make everything hard."

When you light a match, you get to decide. Are you going to blow the flame out? Or are you going to add fuel to the fire?

I meet his gaze head on. "Then do something about it."

I don't even have time to quirk a challenging brow. My back hits the door with a loud thud when he collides with me.

My brain goes sluggish trying to process the feel of Quinn's lips on mine, the crisp dress shirt beneath my palms as my hands find purchase at his waist, the sting at the back of my scalp where his fingers are still wrapped in my hair.

Somewhere in the back of my mind is a film reel of magazine cutouts and teenage crushes and exchanged insults and two people sitting in an old oak tree, and I'm not quite sure how it all translates into *this*. How all of it results in Quinn's lips on mine, somehow angry and gentle both at once.

In my head, I'm trying to catalog this moment. Make it make sense.

He kisses me like he was made to do it.

That's all I have.

Because Quinn's tongue slides over my lower lip, and then my tongue brushes his, and common sense loses the battle.

It's like nothing I've ever felt before. And the breathless feeling remains. It should be terrifying, but it's just... not. Instead, it's safe again. Instead, I feel real. In this moment, my life isn't a play, and I'm not an actor. I'm cells and blood vessels and bones and skin and a wild heartbeat of a person, more alive than I've been in a decade.

His mouth leaves mine as suddenly as it found it.

Quinn takes an unsteady step backward, hands leaving my body, and I only stay upright because there's an old, grimy bar door behind me.

His eyes are huge and bottomless in the low light of the street.

My chest rises and falls rapidly.

"Oh," I breathe out, and the sound encompasses *everything*.

This is what it can feel like.

And you never knew.

"My car's parked on the next street," Quinn says. "I'll take you home."

His voice is hoarse.

I did that.

His meaning is crystal clear, and I have no arguments. Bad idea or not, I'm absolutely going to let him take me home and do whatever the hell he wants with me. Consequences are tomorrow's problem.

He turns around but stands still until I'm next to him, and only then do we start walking. Neither of us says anything.

It takes us only a couple of minutes, and then I'm sitting in the passenger seat of Quinn's car, and he's navigating through the late night streets.

In another few minutes, he finds a parking spot almost directly across the street from my front door.

The click of the seat belt releasing is as loud as a cannon shot. Quinn's hands grip the steering wheel so tightly his knuckles turn white, and then he's on me again.

His lips devour me. Own me. Claim me.

It feels just as safe as I was afraid it would. But even being scared is safe with him.

"Ask me inside," he says against my lips. "I have a lot of dishonorable intentions."

I only manage a nod.

STEPH

MY BEDROOM DOOR is dark blue, feels cool to the touch, and is nice and solid. I know because I'm currently pushed against it with Quinn mauling me. His tongue is so deep in my mouth he could probably check my tonsils, and my cock is so hard it's pulsing in my jeans like it's trying to hammer its way out of my pants.

We left a trail of debris in our wake when we stumbled into the apartment. Keys clattered to the floor. A wallet here. A phone there. A jacket thrown over the armrest of the couch. A T-shirt on the floor. Things thumped and fell and rattled as he alternately dragged and pushed me through the apartment, bodies smashing into walls, mouths exchanging wild kisses. We're an earthquake of need.

"Nice place," he says.

I snort out a laugh, my chest vibrating against his. "An interior design fan?"

"Not even a little bit." He goes in for the next kiss. He flicks the button of my jeans open and drags the zipper down. His hands sink into my pants, squeezing my ass cheeks.

"Going commando," he says. "I should've figured."

His finger strokes through my crack, and my spine tingles.

"Tell me more about those dishonorable intentions of yours."

He hums, lips against my throat. "I want to bend you over and fuck you. But if that doesn't appeal, I can be the one who bends over for you. I'm good either way."

I don't even have to think about it too much. Or really at all.

"Sounds good."

The words are out. I'll analyze the request later. Or not. Because Quinn's smile is downright feral now. His kiss is feral, too. All teeth, tongue, and bruised lips. I can't believe I ever thought he was robotic.

"Me inside you?" he asks, and all I can do is nod.

Yes. Do it. Get in me. Get in me and fuck me into the mattress. Turn my brain off. Take the lead. Take me somewhere where I don't have to think anymore.

He hums and pulls my T-shirt over my head. Takes a step back. Tilts his head to the side. And just looks.

He reaches out his hand, fingertips sliding over my abs.

"You're beautiful," he says, and lifts his gaze to me.

Why does that one simple sentence make me feel so vulnerable?

"Tested?" I ask to get rid of that awful feeling.

"Religiously," he says.

"Good."

He gets right to business after that.

Like marking a route on a map, he kisses his way down my body until he's on his knees in front of me. His fingers hook into the waistband of my jeans and pull them down, so my cock springs free.

He sends me another one of those addictive grins of his before he unceremoniously takes the head of my cock between his lips and sucks. I draw in a harsh breath and exhale with something that sounds suspiciously like a whimper. You'd think nobody's ever sucked me off before. And maybe they haven't. At least not like this. At least not while I'm in this strange headspace that makes everything feel not quite real.

Quinn's tongue digs into the slit, and my head thumps against the door loudly. He opens his mouth wider and takes me in farther. Strong fingers wrap around the base and squeeze. Talented tongue laves and licks.

"Motherfucker," I breathe out. Look down. Quinn's head bobs up and down, his eyes on me, a cocky glint in his eyes.

Sex is most often transactional in nature. I'll suck you because I know then you'll suck me. I'll make you feel good because then, in exchange, you'll make me feel good.

It doesn't feel like that right now.

Not with how Quinn goes down on me. With a single-minded, raw delight, like my cock in his mouth is the grand prize.

His tongue runs up the underside of my dick, pausing just beneath the head and pressing down on that spot that makes it feel like my head is going to explode. Not sure which one of the two. Maybe both.

My hands sink into his hair as he takes me deep into his throat and then slides his mouth up again. He keeps tonguing my slit, and it's steadily driving me insane.

I'm already breathing like I've just finished a marathon. Quinn licks his way up my body. His hands trap my face between them, and then he's kissing me again. Hard, bruising kisses, and I give as good as I get.

It's almost violent. This... thing between us.

And then it's not.

"Come on," he says and maneuvers me toward the bed. Turns me around.

Presses himself against my back. His clothes scrape against my skin. His lips latch onto the back of my neck.

"Lie down," he says. So I do. And then I wait while he undresses. Tosses condoms on the bed.

I'm not sure what I expect him to do, but him climbing on top of me isn't it. Him just casually settling in with his cock nestled between my ass cheeks isn't it. Him pressing his forehead against the back of my neck isn't it.

His hands are everywhere. Palms slide over my sides and my back and my ass. Calm and sure. It's starting to feel like I'm a skittish animal he's trying to calm down.

And it's working.

It's a very arresting thought once it reaches my sluggish brain.

I go completely still.

"Okay?" he asks, again with the spark of laughter in his tone.

I don't know how to answer that.

"Umm... what are you doing?" I ask.

"Enjoying the moment."

"Is that what you usually do with one-night stands?"

"You don't? You know that's the whole point, right? To enjoy yourself?"

I roll my eyes. "You know what I mean."

"I don't want quick and dirty with you, so I'm opting for slow and dirty."

A shiver runs through my whole body.

"Are you?" My voice sounds choked and needy, a combination I've never made before.

Instead of answering, he kisses my nape again.

This is vulnerability at its worst. I start to roll over. Quick and dirty. I'll choose quick and dirty.

He pins me in place.

"It's too…" I don't know how to finish that sentence without sounding like an idiot.

"You're overthinking this. Does it feel good?" he asks.

It takes a few measured inhales and exhales before I nod. Before I relax.

"Yes."

"Then enjoy yourself, for fuck's sake."

He slides slightly to the left, his thigh still holding me in place, and his hand starts moving. Up and down my back and sides and ass. Long, slow strokes of his palm that make me melt into the mattress.

I'm already a boneless mess when he replaces his palm with his lips. Kisses his way down. Kisses the backs of my thighs and bites the hollow at the back of my right knee. Then, a click of the cap and my ass is slippery with lube. He grinds down on me like we're teenagers dry humping, and I push myself to my elbows.

He kneels behind me. Pushes his thumb into me.

"Fucking hell, you're tight," he groans.

"Compliments will get you everywhere," I mutter into my arms.

His hand moves over the small of my back, the fingers of his other hand still lodged in my ass, stroking and scissoring and claiming. It's stupid to feel this way, but it's almost like he's marking his territory.

Quinn was here. And here. And here.

"You have a magnificent ass," he says. He casually curls his finger inside me. My eyes slam shut, and my forehead drops against my arm. Breaths leave my mouth in short bursts of air.

"You have no idea how badly I want inside you," he says.

I glance over my shoulder.

"Are you waiting for an official invitation?"

He laughs and spreads my ass cheeks. Both his index fingers

go inside me this time around. Spreading me wide open. He slides his cock up the crease of my ass until the tip rests against my hole. He presses his thumb against it and holds it there.

"Fuck me," he sighs, voice a bit more strained now.

"That's my line."

He laughs again.

"I will when you relax," he says.

"Your fingers are in my ass," I point out.

It's not so much about the fingers, though.

It's that it's Quinn.

Quinn's fingers.

Quinn above me.

Quinn on me.

Quinn in me.

"I've been told I have very relaxing fingers," he muses.

"You've been lied to."

He gives my prostate another stroke, and I groan. Sink farther into the mattress. A boneless mess of tension.

There's pressure. Constant and demanding. Skillfully applied. So damn patient.

Just shove it in, I want to snap. *Make it hurt, so I won't accidentally start to like it too much.*

His fingers spread me wider, and finally—fucking finally—the head of his cock breaches me.

"Look at this," he says, almost reverently. "I bet if I held still, you'd suck me inside you."

The sound that escapes my lips isn't quite human.

He inches forward, torturously slow, wickedly determined. I'd shove myself toward him, but he's holding me still with his hands and his hips and his weight on top of me.

I should hate this. The loss of control. Being at someone else's mercy. Not calling the shots.

Instead, I let it happen. I want it to happen.

Be inside me. Go as far as you can go. And then some more. Go so far you can say you've been where no man has been before. I dare you.

Quinn drapes himself over me. Rests himself on my back. Balls-deep inside me.

The empty spaces are quiet. There's no room for them in this bed. Not when Quinn's cock has set up camp so deep inside me I can feel him with my spine.

He lets out a shuddery breath and an unsteady laugh.

"Fuck me," he says. "Fuck me. Fuck me. Fuck me."

"Poetic," I gasp.

"It's a sonnet I'm writing about your fucking magnificent ass," he replies and nudges his hips so that he slides another impossible inch farther.

"Fuck, fuck, fuck," he chants.

He cants his hips experimentally. Pulls out a bit and jerks back inside.

Another chorus of fucks.

And he does fuck. It's not just words. He follows through.

His weight shifts and angles change. He alternates hard pumps with slow, languorous ones. I never know what the next move brings. It takes up all the space in my brain to guess what he'll do next.

His palm presses down between my shoulder blades, and he thrusts hard. I inch forward on the bed from the sheer force of it. Again and again until my head meets the headboard. I grab onto the black metal frame. Scramble on my knees. He's inside me again, but now his fingers wrap around my shaft while he slams into me. My back meets his chest. Movements turn uncoordinated and desperate.

His cock hits my prostate like he's some sharpshooting prodigy.

My weapon of choice is my dick, and my target is Steph's ass.

And he nails that target with unerring precision until my vision goes hazy and my ears fill with white noise. My stomach jolts and my toes curl. Pleasure races from the tips of my toes to the top of my head.

Quinn's sonnet for my ass—which, to be fair, was already mostly consisting of fucks—gets a ton of new lines of obscenities he hisses and moans into my ear before he collapses on top of me.

He covers me like a blanket, a heavy weight I'm in no hurry to remove.

He starts to laugh, his whole body shaking on top of me.

"Holy shit. This was one for the memory books."

I smile into my arms, a flood of happiness racing through my insides. "You have that?"

"I'm starting one in your honor. You'll be on page one, and it'll be a difficult act to follow," he mutters into my neck.

I hum. "Give me five minutes, and we'll see if we can get a few more pages filled in that book of yours tonight."

He chuckles, lips still against the nape of my neck.

"Consider it done."

STEPH

SLEEP REMAINS an elusive memory for the rest of the night. Sometime early in the morning, right before the sun comes up, I fall asleep with Quinn's weight still pressing me into the mattress.

A few hours later, I wake up to an empty bed.

My fingers slide over the cool sheet.

I'd think last night was an especially vivid dream, but my ass says otherwise.

Guess Quinn took off.

Good.

It's... good.

Absolutely great.

And whatever this weird feeling is inside, that's not disappointment. Even if I wanted anything to happen, it just can't. I'm a bit of a wrecking ball, and I have no intention of bringing anybody else down with me.

I sit up and clutch the back of my neck while I get my head back straight.

My eyes snap up as something clatters in the kitchen, and something simultaneously jolts in my stomach.

Don't be an idiot. It's just Jude.
I pull on a pair of shorts and head toward the kitchen.
It's not Jude.
It's Quinn.
Rummaging around in the cabinets like he lives here.

That jolt of *something* in my stomach travels up to my chest, where my heart picks up speed at the sight of him. Hair a mess. Bite marks on his neck and back. Boxer briefs riding low on his hips. Miles and miles of bare skin.

"My eyes are up here."

"Yes, but your ass is down here," I say before I look up.

He turns around. "There's no food here. No coffee either."

"I don't like coffee," I say. "And I don't know how to cook."

"I can teach you."

"People have tried before. I burn stuff."

"I'm a good teacher."

"Sure. Whatever. Why are you still here?"

He shrugs. "Didn't feel like going home yet."

"Yeah, okay, but as we've determined, there's no food or anything here, so unless you want to starve, you should probably head on out. It's Sunday. I bet you're one of those people who leave Sunday for chores, right? You should probably get on those."

"I have an assistant for chores," he says.

I stare at him. "You have an assistant?"

He shrugs again. "I'm a busy guy."

"Well then. All the more reason to head out."

He crosses his arms over his chest, ass leaning against the counter, an amused look on his face. "If I didn't know any better, I'd say you were trying to get rid of me."

"What gave me away?" I drag my fingers through my hair and huff out a breath. "We're done here. Why are we dragging this out?"

He laughs like I'm a cute little puppy performing tricks for his amusement.

And then he says something downright insane.

"Go on a date with me."

I stare at him while I try to figure out what he means when he says 'go on a date with me.'

I come up with a big, fat nothing.

His eyes sparkle, and he lifts his chin a bit as if he's preparing for a fight. Which he damn well should be.

"Why?" I ask. "We don't do that."

"We haven't done that," he corrects. "We *could*, though. There's not much stopping us. Unless you actually plan to take Sutton up on his offer."

He sends a glare at my forearm, where the digits are still visible on my skin.

"That's none of your business, is it?"

"Kind of is. You're not fucking doing that," he says.

I raise my brows at him. "Oh? Because you said so? Newsflash, I can do whatever and whoever I want. You don't have a say in it."

"I'm asking you out."

"Well... No. I'm saying no. Sorry."

He tilts his head to the side, mild curiosity on his face like we're debating something that doesn't really affect either of us personally. Something mundane and boring with no stakes in the game for either of us.

"Why not?"

All I can come up with is a spluttered, inelegant, "Because."

"That argument isn't really that convincing."

"It doesn't have to be convincing. We're not going out."

Still the same mild curiosity and infuriating calm, but with a dash of stubbornness now. "Why not?"

"I don't want to date! Jesus! Why would you?"

"Why would I what?"

"Why would you want to go on a date with me? It's a waste of our time. We're not arranging a relationship here. We wanted to fuck, so we fucked. You don't have to be a gentleman about it retroactively. I don't need dinner and flowers. In fact, I highly discourage you from wasting time with flowers and dinners. And we're done here anyway. This was a one-time thing."

The stubborn set of his jaw gets even more stubborn. "We'll see about that. I want a date."

"Oh, for fuck's sake!"

"I want to get to know you," he says.

This is hands down the unsexiest thing anybody has ever said to me.

"Why?" I ask. Confused. Bewildered. Flabbergasted. Baffled.

"Fuck if I know." He looks about as perplexed about it as I feel. "Believe me, I've repeatedly tried to talk myself out of it, but no dice."

I stare at the fridge and its shiny surface that reflects Quinn's back while I calm down a bit.

"We can barely tolerate each other. We don't need to spend extra time together to really make sure we both know it. Half the time we're in the same room, we get into a fight."

The only acknowledgment I get for my very valid point is a dismissive shrug. "We just argue from time to time."

"No, we fight."

"Argue," he says, infuriatingly calm while I get more and more pissed off.

"We're in a fight right now!"

"No. This is a constructive discussion about our next step."

"There is no *our* next step!"

He stalks toward me then, and I can't seem to make my feet move. His palm covers my cheek, unexpectedly gentle. My heart picks up speed, which is quite an achievement since it was already going haywire.

His lips come down on mine. And I don't stop him. Or pull away. Or do anything smart like that.

Instead, I open my mouth and let him kiss the fuck out of me.

My bare toes curl on the kitchen floor.

My stomach jolts like I've just jumped down from somewhere high.

Quinn pulls away all too soon, eyes searching my face.

"You want me," he says.

"So?" I glare at him. "You want me too."

"I do," he simply says.

"Okay, fine. I'll make you a deal. This technically still counts as the same night of our one-night stand, since you didn't leave. So let's get back to bed and fuck once more. For old time's sake."

"Tempting," he says. "But no. Not until you go on a date with me."

"Well, I won't."

He shrugs. "Then I won't sleep with you again."

I let out a growl of frustration and aim a disgusted look his way.

"Unbelievably, you got even more annoying," I say. "Quite an achievement. I'm gonna take a shower. Show yourself out."

I'm already halfway down the hallway when he says my name. I turn around and find him standing in the doorway. Brow quirked. A deceptively casual stance.

"Running," he says.

I immediately bristle. "Oh no, buddy. You're not going to pin this on me. I'm not running away. Just because we have differ—"

He lets out a loud, frustrated sigh that cuts me off.

"*We,*" he says pointedly, "will go running together. Like we did in Maine. We will spend some time together. It's called a compromise. I understand it's a new concept for you but try and keep an open mind."

"No," I say, and shake my head for good measure.

"See, the way it works is you meet me in the middle," he says.

"That does not sound like something I would ever do."

He breathes out slowly and does that thing where he counts to ten to get rid of the I'm-going-to-strangle-you urge.

"Rock, paper, scissors," he says. "I win, we go running. You win, I leave. We both have a fifty-fifty chance of getting what we want."

I stare at him for a moment, but it doesn't seem like he's planning to leave, and if this is the idiotic way of getting him out of here?

I sigh. "Fine."

He counts us down.

Paper versus scissors.

I'm the idiot who chose paper.

He sends me a smug look.

"Pleasure doing business with you," he says.

"Go suck an egg."

His grin widens. "Play your cards right, and I'll suck something else."

To my credit, I manage to wait until he goes to get dressed before I slump against the wall in an undignified puddle of lust.

QUINN

STEPHEN PICKS the Shore Parkway trail, so that's where we meet up later that same day.

He's changed gears again.

I expected he'd be crabby.

He's not.

Instead, he strolls toward me, not a care in the world, eating a chocolate croissant.

I watch him approach me. Messy hair. Shorts. A T-shirt with a large arrow in front that points downward and declares, "My eyes are down here."

Wanting him makes so very little sense.

And still, I do.

Being fascinated by him is dangerous.

And still, I can't stop.

It's not only that I want him. I also want to know him. I want to decipher him. Unlock him. Have him open up to me and see what's hidden underneath the jokes and calculated laughter.

"The crappy sneakers were bad enough," I say. "Don't even

try and tell me you're planning to run in those." I nod toward his flip flops.

He raises his brows. "Wait. You actually wanted to run? I figured it was just a euphemism."

"A euphemism for what?"

"Ideally sex, but in reality, probably an interrogation. It's hot as balls. Who in their right mind would exercise right now? And I only run early in the morning," he says with a shrug and fishes another pastry out before he hands the bag to me.

"Did you plan to feed the whole neighborhood?" I ask when I peer into the bag and see the sheer amount of treats inside.

"Those are for me. Sugar makes me mellow. It's why I'm nice enough to share with you right now."

I fish out a chocolate chip cookie, and we start walking. The early evening air is muggy, the heat of the day radiating from the concrete in waves. All around us, people are hanging out, enjoying the end of another hot summer day. There's sluggishness in the air. Oppressive heat tends to do that to people.

"If you hate running so much, why do you do it?" I ask.

"It's better than standing still," he replies, like that cryptic answer makes any sense at all.

"Meaning?"

He rolls his eyes. "Exactly what I said."

There is no highway to Stephen's mind. Only an endless maze of narrow roads where every once in a while you'll arrive at a cliff's edge.

"Tell me something real," I say once I've finished the cookie.

He's silent for a long time as we walk. I'm half expecting another movie summary, but he surprises me when he eventually speaks.

"I used to be in a band. Back when I was in high school."

I wait for a moment to see if this ends up being another

movie reference. He doesn't say anything else, so I suppose this is real.

"Of course you were. Based on my stalking, you did *everything* when you were in high school. I only swam. Way to make everybody else look like slackers."

"Aww. Is the itty-bitty sixteen-time Olympic winner feeling a bit self-conscious?" he asks. "Do you want reassurances? There, there. You're a good swimmer." He pauses for a second. "Not as good as Michael Phelps, but..."

He sends me a shit-eating grin, and I push his shoulder. He laughs out loud, dives into his bag of sweets again, and pulls out a cookie.

I shake my head when he extends the bag toward me, too busy with the realization that just hit.

"You know how many medals I've won," I say. "Huh."

He narrows his eyes at me. "Huh?" he says. "What does 'huh' mean?"

"Just... interesting. Seems like somebody's been keeping tabs on me."

He rolls his eyes. "Don't flatter yourself. You were a *Jeopardy* question once when I was at home with stomach flu. It's why my brain mainly associates you with nausea now."

"Once again you pick the weirdest thing to lie about," I say.

"I resent that. It's God's honest truth."

"Next thing you'll tell me you're honest to a fault."

"I really am."

"Uh-huh." I pull him to a stop and press my thumb against his left eyebrow. "How'd you get the scar?" I ask.

Stephen tucks into another cookie and chews slowly, eyes staying on me the whole time like he's daring me to call him out again.

"I was training at the Navy Fighter Weapons School," he

says. "Really elite stuff. Can't tell you more, though, since you're a civilian."

"Was your call sign Maverick, by chance?" I ask.

He widens his eyes. "How did you know?" He lifts his arm and speaks into his smartwatch. "We've been compromised. Eliminate the target. I repeat. Eliminate the target."

He turns and walks away from me, and I trail after him.

I'm like an archaeologist on a dig. I've got all these pieces I'm unearthing one after the other, but I have no idea how they fit together.

And I'm too curious for my own good to stop.

STEPH

DOING the wrong thing is a choice. It doesn't just happen. You don't accidentally stumble into bad decisions. You choose.

And when Quinn looks me straight in the eye and asks, "My place or yours?"

I choose.

"Yours."

QUINN UNLOCKS the door and pushes it open, and I walk past him.

I turn around once I'm inside and meet his gaze.

"Just to be clear, this is just sex," I say.

It's stupid and unsettling and enticing.

Quinn pushes himself off the door he's been leaning against and stalks toward me.

"You want something to drink?" he asks and heads to the kitchen.

"Did you hear me?" I ask his retreating back. "It's just sex."

"Yeah, I heard you," he throws over his shoulder. He goes and opens the fridge and peers inside. "Water?" he asks. "Beer?"

"I'm good."

He shrugs and pulls out a bottle, opens it, and takes a drink. He leans against the counter, one leg crossed over the other.

I give up the fight and go stand next to him. I take the beer out of his hand and drink. For a while, we just stand there, both leaning against the counter, sharing a drink in silence. And he doesn't protest or tell me about the imminent threat of mono or bacterial meningitis or something. Then again, I've had his tongue in my mouth, so I guess it's a moot point now.

Quinn keeps sending me looks from the corner of his eye, a small smile on his face.

"What?" I eventually ask.

He just shakes his head, still with that same smile on his face. "You keep looking around with a strange expression on your face, and I can't quite figure out what you're thinking."

"Mainly that you're a terrible host. What, no offer to give me a tour?"

"You've been here before," he points out.

"Blackout drunk and then impossibly hungover. The brain didn't retain much information. Imagine that."

"Do you want a tour?" he asks.

"I thought you'd never ask."

He drains his beer and puts the bottle on the counter.

"Any particular rooms you're interested in seeing?"

"The kitchen?" I say.

"We're in it."

"The living room."

He turns toward me, arms on either side of me, palms on the counter, trapping me in place, chest against mine, lips only inches away from my lips.

"It's behind you," he says. "Want me to show you my bedroom?"

"Can't imagine there's anything interesting there, so I'm good." My voice has gone all low and husky, the closer his mouth comes to mine.

"I'll be there," he says.

"Still not seeing the appeal of climbing all those stairs," I reply.

He takes a step back.

Grabs the hem of his shirt.

Pulls it over his head.

"How about now?" he asks. "Do you see the appeal now?"

It's actually quite impressive I manage to speak at all with all these abs right in front of me.

"You have to put more on the table if you're trying to get me interested," I say. "I don't usually sleep with the same person twice."

"Because?" he asks.

"I get bored easily."

The sexy half-grin I get in response nearly brings me to my knees.

"I don't think you have to worry about that too much."

"Somebody's confident," I say.

In response, he drops his running shorts.

"Feeling bored yet?" he practically purrs.

I swallow hard and force my gaze up from his cock that's straining against the fabric of his boxer briefs.

"Nothing I haven't seen before." I smile back at him sweetly. "You think I can't find someone else to give me what you're offering?"

"I'm sure you can. You won't, though."

"Or so you think," I say.

"Steph, you can't keep your eyes away from my dick. You're not going anywhere."

This whole situation is throwing me way off course. I can't really even understand what made me take him up on his offer again and meet up with him in the first place when I'd been crystal clear with myself that I wouldn't.

He drops the boxer briefs.

His cock springs free.

I've never once been shy or reserved or unsure about sex, so I'm not sure why my cheeks feel burning hot while I watch him. Why my breathing picks up. Why my heart won't stop hammering.

Sex has never been anything special for me. It's a nice distraction. Nothing else.

I'd spent the whole day trying to talk myself out of seeing Quinn again. In the end, my dick won the battle and common sense gave up the fight.

Because it's just sex. Nothing. Special. He wants me. I want him. What's the harm? The novelty will wear off after a few encounters, and we'll go back to ignoring each other or snapping at each other.

It doesn't have to mean anything.

It *can't* mean anything.

Not with who Quinn is.

Not with how high profile his family is.

Not with who I am.

An undetonated landmine. Hidden. Inconspicuous. But take one wrong step, and I will fuck up your whole life.

Quinn reaches over and touches my thigh. His palm runs over my skin, fingers sliding underneath my shorts. My heart goes haywire inside my chest.

His hand pushes higher and higher, fingers grazing my balls, gaze holding me hostage. The kitchen is deathly silent save for the rustle of fabric and my harsh breathing.

He steps closer. Lowers his head. Licks over the side of my neck.

My eyes slam shut as if it somehow helps combat the rush of lust that fills the space between us rapidly like somebody's set off a bomb.

"I'm gonna blow you now," he says, voice a rough whisper in my ear. "And then I'm going to give you that tour of my bedroom. How does that sound?"

I let out a shuddering breath, nowhere near coherent enough to say anything anymore, so I just nod.

He's on his knees in front of me. His fingers move to my waistband, and he drags my shorts lower, just past my balls. I can't quite believe it, so I lift my hand and slide my fingers through his hair. Too gently. He sends me a quizzical look.

I close my eyes.

He pinches my thigh, and my eyes fly open.

"This time," he says, sounding almost conversational. So fucking cool. "This time, I want to taste."

"Fuck," I say, and my head falls back.

He pinches my thigh again, and I yelp before I glare at him.

"Eyes on me," he says. "You're blushing. It turns my dick hard."

"I don't blush."

"You do with me."

"I don—"

He swallows me down.

My hips jerk forward.

"Holy fuck!" The words burst out, propelled by pure desperation.

Yes. Please. More of that. All of that.

Quinn's lips slide all the way to the tip. He sends me a quick, cocky grin, and goes down on me again.

My fingers grip Quinn's hair, way past gentle now.

It's sloppy and messy. My shorts are still around my thighs, the elastic of the waistband rubbing against the back of my balls. My shirt is still on, and I'm holding it up in a death grip, so it won't block my view.

Quinn sucks me, cheeks hollowed, tongue sliding up and down and digging into the dip underneath the head.

He cups my balls and rolls them between his fingers. My vision goes hazy, but I keep my eyes on him, nevertheless. The head of my cock pumps against the back of his throat, and he gags, and it's fucking hot. Anticipation tightens my muscles, and my hips move faster.

"Quinn," I rasp.

He sucks harder.

My hips punch forward, forcing my cock deeper into his mouth.

His hand wraps around the root of my dick, moving up and down in short, fast movements. He sucks the tip so hard it's just on the good side of painful.

I grab onto the counter with one hand, the edge of it digging into my palm. Quinn's palm cups my ass and pushes my hips forward.

With a harsh shout, I come. Spurt after spurt flood his mouth, and he swallows it all down.

He keeps sucking me until I go soft against his tongue, and my thigh muscles quiver with the effort of holding myself up.

"Fucking fuck," I manage to say when he pulls off, and the cool air hits my wet cock.

"Thank you," he says smugly and gets up. "I'm guessing this was five stars?"

"Out of ten? I'm feeling generous, so sure," I say, even though my voice is unconvincingly shaky.

He just grins and kisses me, my taste on his tongue, his still-hard dick poking my lower belly.

He pulls away, takes my hand, and tugs until I follow him after shucking my shorts.

Up the stairs.

To his massive bed.

Where he pushes me down, and I bounce on the soft mattress and laugh, and he smiles at whatever it is he sees on my face.

He crawls on top of me, naked and hard, and I wriggle and fight with my shirt until he helps me pull it off. His thighs are on either side of mine, straddling me.

I'm expecting hard and fast. Dick in my ass. Him taking what he's earned with that blowjob, but he just lowers his head and kisses me. Slow and gentle at first, more demanding after a while.

We're making out, I think, and almost want to laugh because it's so innocent and somehow soft and calm, and I've never had that. At least not when it comes to sex.

We grind against each other. My dick grows hard again, but I'm not in a hurry to do anything about it. I'm just content kissing him. And touching him. And having him touch me.

I should be more concerned about this. I should be concerned that I'm not concerned. But I don't have the energy right now.

So I just keep kissing him.

Kissing him until we're both breathless and needy and desperate.

Kissing him until he pulls away and looks down at me, eyes burning with desire. He puts his fingertips against my lips and quirks his brow. I open obediently and suck two fingers in my mouth.

"Make them wet," he whispers into my ear before he rolls off me and lies next to me on his side.

He nudges me with his toe. "Spread," he demands in that bossy voice of his that I hate in real life, but apparently love when I'm in his bed.

He lowers his head and licks over my right nipple, tongue teasing me while he works his fingers into my ass.

I spread my legs wider. Make myself comfortable.

He easily finds my prostate and strokes over it. The bolt of pleasure is so sudden and intense it's bordering on uncomfortable, but when he does it the second time, I relax back and just enjoy the feel of him above me, next to me, inside me.

His fingers tease and spread until my hips arch off the bed, my cock bobbing against my abdomen every time I move, painfully hard, but weirdly boneless at the same damn time.

Quinn's fingers inside me keep me hovering on the edge of the promise of something good. He keeps me just where he wants me, the coil of pleasure tightening inside me, ready to unfurl whenever he gives the go ahead.

It's almost never like this. I almost never let myself be in this position. Just taking. Just enjoying.

It's easier to be the one who gives. Because I can decide just how much of myself I will give in return.

Quinn takes. And decides how much he takes, and I find that I don't have it in me to argue. I give what he wants to take. It should be more terrifying than it feels right now.

His fingers move over my prostate again, and my eyes slam shut.

"Fuck! Stop," I gasp. "I'm gonna come."

Quinn doesn't say anything. Just squeezes the base of my

dick until I get myself back under control. I don't even have the energy to glare at him.

I try to roll onto my stomach when he leans over me to grab a condom, but he pushes me back down on my back.

"No. Just like this," he says.

I close my eyes.

"I can't," I grit through my teeth.

"Yes, you can," he simply says.

And then I find myself looking up at him, fingers gripping his hips as he pushes inside me, slowly and surely.

And it doesn't matter anymore that it's too much and too intimate and that I've never done it like this before. Nothing much matters with his thick cock inside me, forcing me to surrender to the bliss of it.

He sinks inside me, and fuck this. He can do anything he wants with me, and I'll take it. I'll even take the rush of unwelcome emotions that push past everything else.

Quinn lowers his head and captures my mouth with his. We exchange slow, open-mouthed kisses as he fucks me with slow, deep thrusts.

There's nothing frantic about this. Nothing accidental. When I look back tomorrow, there's no way I can write this off as getting caught in the moment. It's determination and purposefulness.

And when he reaches between our bodies and takes my dick in his hand, it's also done with quiet purposefulness. He strokes me.

Once. Twice.

A moan of pleasure escapes.

"I want to hear you come," Quinn says, voice wrecked and strained from holding back, but gaze steady and even.

He pushes himself up on his knees and holds my hips,

pulling me forward. I grab my cock and jerk myself off while he fucks into me.

Quinn's thumbs brush my stomach. I dig my heels into his ass cheeks for purchase. Slow and determined turns into wild and hard. Mindless. His thrusts fast and hard. Almost violent. Welcome.

The rising pleasure wipes away everything else in its path. When it crashes over me, it steals my breath and my thoughts.

My hips punch up and my whole body locks, back arching, dick pulsing, ass clenching around Quinn. He lets out a guttural moan and collapses on top of me, limbs tangled with mine, crushing me into the mattress. His heart beats wildly against my own.

I slide a shaky palm up his back and clutch his shoulder while I come down from the high of the orgasm.

He turns his head.

Wraps himself around me.

Kisses the side of my neck.

I'm not panicking.

Not really.

Couldn't even if I wanted to.

But I sure as hell know this is not good.

STEPH

IT'S scary how effortlessly Quinn inserts himself into my life. Where before he was happy staying on the outskirts, he's now bulldozing his way in, and I don't know what to do about it. What to do with him.

I start off determined to stay away from him, but I fail simply because after a little while, I'm not really trying that hard.

It's because the sex is excellent.

That's my official stance.

Every day, I wake up, determined to put an end to it.

But then somehow, somewhere along the way, I always seem to find myself either on my back, on my stomach, against a wall, or plastered against any other flat surface, with Quinn pushing inside me.

He's still annoying as hell.

We still get in a fight every other day.

But there's this thing. Something that helps make him much more tolerable than he usually is. Turns out we have something else in common besides liking nature documentaries. A thing we both really want—to fuck each other as often as possible.

It's all very straightforward.

Or it would be if there was less talking involved. Because we do that too. Hence the annoyance and fights.

But there are also those other times when we don't get into an argument.

Those times really are the worst.

I FROWN AT MY PHONE, my thumb moving over the screen as I scroll through my messages.

Nothing.

I mean, there are a ton of messages, but none of them from—

The phone is suddenly gone.

"Hey!" I snap.

Blair raises her brows at me.

"Oh, I'm sorry. Is this lunch date with your best friends in the whole world keeping you from something more important?" she asks sweetly.

I purse my lips and look away.

"No?"

"Good boy," she says and slides the phone over to Jude, who drops it into his backpack.

"I need that," I protest.

"You'll get it back after we eat," she says.

"But—" I start to protest.

"After," Blair repeats sternly.

Jude tilts his head to the side.

"What's in the phone?" he asks.

I clamp my mouth shut. "Nothing."

They exchange glances, complete with raised brows and suspicious expressions before they both turn back toward me, perfectly synchronized in their movements.

"You've been awfully difficult to track down lately," Blair says, almost conversationally. "Feels like I haven't seen you forever."

"Well, don't feel bad. You have a baby, and a wife," I say. "You're bound to be busy."

"I invited you to that concert two weeks ago," she says.

"I had a thing," I reply.

Quinn.

"And you skipped another family dinner," she continues.

"Work," I say quickly.

Quinn

It's technically not a lie. I *was* putting in a lot of work to get Quinn off before we had to leave for dinner, but then things got a bit out of hand, and before we knew it, it was already way too late to show up. So we ordered a pizza.

"It's weird," she says and looks at Jude. "Right?"

"Sure," Jude says. "Weird." He says it lightly, but his eyes stay on me for an uncomfortably long time. Like he knows something.

"Well? What gives?" Blair asks, turning her attention back to me.

"I'm sorry I have a life," I say testily.

"You've always had a life. You've kept an insane schedule for as long as I've known you," Blair adds. "No, no. This is something else. It's almost as if…" Her voice dies down, and she purses her lips.

"Almost as if nothing," I say. "I've just been busy with work and stuff."

"Jude totally did a disappearing act when he first started seeing Blake," Blair says.

I do the stupidest thing possible and look away from her in the clearest admission of guilt there could be.

"Oh my God!" Blair squeaks way too loudly. "You're seeing somebody?"

"No," I say at once, which is technically the truth. Hooking up with Quinn is *not* seeing him. I mean, I see him while I'm with him, but I'm not *seeing* him.

Blair leans forward. "Who? When? Where? How long?"

"I..." I blink and try to think of a lie. Any lie. It shouldn't be this difficult. I lie all the time!

"Is it serious? When do we get to meet them? How did you two meet?" Blair fires on like a machine gun.

"Uh..."

"You've never dated anybody. This means it's absolutely serious. Dude! I'm so excited for—"

"It's Quinn," I blurt out just to get her to shut up because my head is spinning, and I don't make good decisions.

"Quinn?" Blair says and frowns before her eyes widen. "Wait. Our Quinn?"

"It's not—"

"Jesus Christ," Blair says and starts to massage her temples, plummeting down from her happy high of a second ago. She lifts her head for a moment and looks at me before she goes back to digging her fingertips into the sides of her head. "Please tell me this is a joke."

"We're not seeing each other," I say. "We're just sort of... hooking up."

She lets out a short, mocking snort of laughter. "Oh, good news! You're *just* hooking up! Because obviously that always ends up well. How wonderful for us all."

"Can you calm down?" I ask. "Quinn and I both know what we're doing and what this is."

"Dear God, Steph," she says. "Steph, Steph, Steph! Sweetie. Honey. I say this with all the love in the world, but you never have any idea what you're doing. Ever."

I lick over my dry lips. She's wrong. But she's also not wrong.

"It's not real," I say. "Or serious."

"You just keep making it worse," Blair wails. I've never seen her like this, and she's been there for all of my greatest hits.

She turns toward Jude and waves her hand in my direction. "Please, talk some sense into him!"

Jude looks uncomfortable as hell as he scratches the back of his neck and avoids looking at Blair.

She narrows her eyes. "Wait a second. Why aren't you more surprised by this?"

Jude looks toward the ceiling studiously. "I kind of knew already? I... might've, sort of walked in on them a few days ago?"

"What?" I ask the same time as Blair snaps, "You what?"

Jude glances at me and raises both his hands. "Not like I did it on purpose. But I also haven't seen you in a while, so I stopped by Tuesday evening."

"No, you didn't," I say.

He scratches the right side of his nose. "You were both asleep on the couch."

I rub the bridge of my nose while I try to figure out how to fix this.

Nothing comes to mind.

When I look up, I find Blair eyeing me more seriously than she ever has before.

"When you say it's nothing serious," she says. "What does it mean, exactly?"

I look down. Then force myself to meet her gaze.

"It means it's not serious," I say. "He's hot. We fuck. That's it."

"You're not just saying it?" she asks. "You're not hiding some long-buried crush? You're not just saying it because the two of you need to figure things out before you break the news?"

"Come on," I say and force myself to grin. "It's Quinn. No, we're not serious."

I don't know why those words don't come out entirely naturally.

It's the truth.

"Then stop it," Blair says. "If it's just fucking around, find somebody else. He's Nora's best friend. This has messy written all over it in capital letters. Don't make her choose sides."

"I'm not—" I start to say.

"This is what it'll inevitably come down to," she says. "He's Nora's *best* friend. If it's not serious then you have to stop this."

I look down at my fingers. They feel weirdly numb.

She's right.

Of course, she's right.

Finally a voice of reason.

She's absolutely right.

So, so right.

I nod.

"Okay."

BLAIR TAKES a cab to her photo studio and leaves me and Jude standing in front of the restaurant.

I have this weird, not-quite-real feeling inside me. Some sort of hollowness. Like I've lost something.

It's stupid.

I haven't.

Jude doesn't look like he's preparing to take off yet, though. Doesn't even look like he's considering going anywhere. Instead, he just looks at me for so long I'm starting to feel extremely uncomfortable.

Eventually, when he still hasn't said anything, I roll my eyes. "What? Come on. Out with it."

"I'm not going to lecture you," he says.

"Really? How come? I was so looking forward to a good lecture," I say, voice thick with sarcasm.

Instead of calling me out on my shit, he steps toward me and pulls me into a tight hug. I stay stiff as a plank for a moment, but he keeps holding me until I relax and wrap my arms around him too.

"I just want you to be happy," he says, low voice in my ear. "That's all. I know what Blair says. I know the whole thing's a bit tricky, but if Quinn makes you—"

I pull away so abruptly Jude sways a bit.

"Don't," I say.

I should've known he wouldn't let up. Stubbornness is a part of Jude's factory settings.

"You deserve to be happy."

"Oh my God! Just, please, stop this fucking happiness bullshit!" The words burst out before I can stop myself. "Fucking no. Not everybody deserves to be happy. Some of us deserve to just get by, and that's the best we can hope for, so stop trying to fix me!"

He sends me a level look.

"It wasn't your fault. You didn't kill him."

Like a child, I slam my palms over my ears, so I won't have to hear him.

"Fuck off. Fuck off. Fuck all the way off!" I snap before I turn on my heel and walk away from him.

"Steph," he calls after me.

I don't turn around.

STEPH

SINCE I'M ALREADY on a roll, I march my ass straight to Quinn's place. This shit has been going on for far too long. Good sex or not, Blair's right. This has to stop, and it's going to stop now.

I reach the front door of his building just as Quinn's neighbor walks out.

"Hello there," he says with a friendly smile.

"Hi, Mr. Kaiserman," I say. He holds the door open for me, and I go inside. It's only when I'm climbing the first set of stairs that it registers. I know Quinn's neighbor's name. Because I ran into him one morning when I was sneaking out from Quinn's place. And one other time when I helped him carry an armchair up to his apartment.

Fuck's sake! The hell am I doing? I don't do this. I don't create meaningful relationships with people. Because I break things. People. I'm a fucking landmine. And sure, Quinn and I aren't anything serious or important, and we just have a lot of sex, but it's still too much.

I'm full of determination once I stand in front of Quinn's

door. Fuck it, I would've sent him a text and ended this, but Jude still has my phone, so I guess I'll do it in person, then.

I pound on the door with way more strength than strictly necessary.

And wait.

And wait.

Knock again.

And wait some more.

Finally, after I've almost given up, the door is pulled open.

"The fuck is the matter with you?" Quinn says with an abundance of very un-Quinn-like vitriol in his tone.

I frown at the sight of him.

"What's the matter with *you*?" I counter.

He looks rough, and that's me being nice. His eyes are red. He's leaning on the door like his life depends on it. His immaculate hair is a mess, and his golden complexion is way paler than people should usually look.

I'm still frowning when I put the back of my hand against his forehead. It doesn't seem like he's running a fever. Instead, he feels cold and clammy.

"You don't look too hot. Why aren't you in bed?"

"Oh, I don't know," he says and closes his eyes for a moment like speaking hurts. "Might be because somebody was trying to break down my door a moment ago."

"Well, it's a good thing you came downstairs, then. You're obviously ready to ride into battle."

He winces and starts rubbing his temples.

"I'm just feeling a bit off. It'll sort itself out in a second. I'd appreciate it if that second was quiet."

I hover in the doorway for a moment, but I can't exactly have my important conversation right now when he looks like death. Instead, I step inside and close the door. Quinn sways in his spot for a second before he gives up and slumps against the door.

"Come on, then. Let's get you to bed."

"I'm not going to bed," he grumbles. "I've got stuff to do. I have an afternoon class in an hour."

I nod. "That's a great idea. I bet not a lot of people have seen a dead body in the water, so it'll be a real teaching moment. And it'll be memorable. Real life examples tend to be."

The scowl deepens. "My lessons *are* memorable. Even without corpses."

"That's one way to advertise yourself." I nudge him toward the stairs. "You need to rest. I don't want to come and identify the body if you drop dead and nobody notices until the neighbors start to complain about the smell."

"Don't be so fucking dramatic."

"I have no experience with migraines, but I assume they suck, so I won't take the attitude personally."

"My God! Has your voice always been this loud?" he mumbles.

"Get in the bed, or I'll perform some heavy metal screams for you and show you loud."

He squeezes his eyes shut again before he opens them and sends me a dirty look, like it's my fault he's feeling terrible.

"I can handle myself."

"You're hurting," I say.

"No. It's a small headache. I can handle myself."

"You're lucky you look so pathetic. Otherwise I'd whistle."

Even the thought of that makes him wince. I sigh and go and wrap my arm around his waist. "It's not a weakness to rely on somebody else once in a while. You don't always have to be in control."

"Yes, I do."

"Well, tough luck. Because for the time being, I'm in charge."

I start steering him toward the stairs and then up them. Once we're in his bedroom, I lean my shoulder against the wall and watch him gingerly sit on the bed and then sink down on his back agonizingly slowly, legs still dangling over the edge. I feel a strange urge to tuck him in. To try and make him more comfortable, somehow.

It's not weird. It makes sense. The quicker I nurse him back to health, the quicker we can put this... thing we're doing to rest.

I go to the bed and poke his shoulder. He opens one eye and looks at me blearily.

"Can you get up for a second?" I ask. "And take off your jeans. Why are you even wearing jeans when you have a migraine?"

"I'm just resting my eyes. I'm going out in a second," he mumbles.

"Sure you are, buddy." I reach out my hands and start to unbutton his jeans.

He slowly pushes himself up on his elbows and frowns. "You want to have sex? Fine, but we have to be quick."

I quirk my brow at him and pull the zipper down. "Oh yeah. You know, the moment I saw you swaying by the door and wincing at the sound of my voice, I was all, 'I need to get me some of that.'"

"I'm fine!" he says. "I'll prove it to you. Let's have sex right now."

"Absolutely. You just lie back down and let me do all the work." I pull his jeans off and then grab his hand and pull him up enough to remove his T-shirt. He starts to shiver the moment I'm done. I tug the comforter out from underneath him, push him onto his back, and tuck him in.

"That's a weird foreplay," he mutters and burrows deeper under the comforter.

"You don't like it?" I ask.

"It lacks mouth on my dick."

I gasp dramatically and press my palm to my chest. "Well, excuse me for trying to bring some excitement into our lives and spice things up a bit by trying something new."

"You don't need to spice anything up. You're already dangerously good in the sex department."

I ignore the way my insides go all hot at his words.

"Aww. I'm the best you've ever had, huh?" I ask.

"I didn't say that."

"You kinda did," I say.

He pulls the edge of the comforter over his head. "Well, even if I did—which I didn't—but if I did, it doesn't count. Because my head hurts like a bitch."

"Is that how it works?" I ask with a laugh.

"It's in the rulebook," he mutters.

"Well, if that's the case, is there anything else you want to tell me while your words don't count? I promise I won't be offended."

He's silent for so long I figure he's fallen asleep. I'm turning around to go downstairs when he says, "Stay? I know we don't do that, but stay. I like you here."

My heart jolts in my chest. I try to ignore it. It's impossible.

Instead, I go back and carefully sit on the bed, making sure I don't jostle him while I do. I tug the comforter lower and slowly slide my thumbs over his eyebrows to his temples.

"That's good," he mutters.

He doesn't say anything else, and neither do I, and eventually his breathing evens out, and he's asleep.

"I wasn't going to go anywhere," I say softly.

There. Not a lie. Spoken to somebody who's basically unconscious. I'm a fucking hero.

I trek downstairs and grab Quinn's phone. I find the contact information from his website, and call in to his work and let them know he's not coming in.

Then I hesitate for a moment.

Fuck it. He has a migraine. Whatever insanity I'm engaging in right now doesn't count. We established that.

I find *Mom* in his contact list.

I dial the number.

QUINN

I WAKE up without feeling like my head is about to explode and without nausea. Instead, I'm burrowed nose-deep in a mountain of blankets, somebody's legs are tangled with mine, and I'm finally warm instead of that sweating-from-pain-and-then-freezing-my-ass-off feeling I had going on earlier.

I blink blearily. It's dark outside, but the lamp on the nightstand is on, bathing the room in soft golden light.

"How are you feeling?"

I look up and find Stephen's eyes on me. There's concern in his gaze. Something that I've never seen there before.

"Like shit, but a little less so than in the morning." I don't dare move because there's still a dull ache in my temples, and I don't want to risk making it worse. I don't get headaches like these often, but every once in a while they hit, and it's always terrible.

"You think you could sit up for a bit? I have soup for you."

"Soup?"

"Give me a few." He gets out of the bed. I shouldn't feel his absence. But I do.

True to his word, Stephen is back shortly with a steaming bowl.

I slowly push myself to a sitting position. The dull throbbing remains, but doesn't escalate.

I take the bowl.

My eyes fly to Stephen. "Is that—"

"Some weird vegetable soup you supposedly like, yes," he says. "Your mom said you'll be hungry once the worst of the pain starts to go away."

"When did you talk to my mom?"

He's starting to look so uncomfortable now that I catch on, even though my brain isn't exactly firing on all cylinders.

"I called her," he says, and starts fixing the comforter unnecessarily. "I figured she'd know what to do to make you feel better, and since we're not technically broken up yet, I thought it was okay."

"I'm not complaining," I say slowly.

"Well... good," he says.

I look down at the bowl. Then at Stephen again.

"Wait, did you make this?"

"It's edible," he says defensively. "I tasted it. And your mom was keeping an eye on me every step of the way. She said it looks good."

"Mom was here?"

"Video call," he says.

I have no idea what to say to that. How to feel about that.

Or, more specifically, how to feel about the fact that I like that he's taking care of me.

"Eat your soup," he says, and points toward the bowl with a scowl. He starts to turn around, but I grab his wrist and stop him. He looks down at where my hand is. Then at me.

"Thank you," I say.

He's back to feeling uncomfortable. And he's standing by the side of the bed like a guard, watching me eat.

"Just come back to bed," I say. "What were you doing anyway? Just watching me sleep? 'Cause I have to say, you don't seem like the type."

He hesitates for a moment before he rolls his eyes.

"I was correcting your math," he says, leans over me and picks something up from the bed. He waves some papers in front of me and points to a row of numbers. "You made a mistake here, so then this here is wrong, and then the rest of the page too, because of that."

I don't have it in me to deal with numbers right now. Paperwork is already the bane of my existence, so being sick only deepens my aversion to it.

"You fixed it?" I ask.

"Well I couldn't exactly leave it like that. It'd come back to haunt me later," he says. "I used a pencil. You can erase everything if it's not correct."

Defensive again, but at the same time resigned. I've never really noticed how often he does that—prepares himself for failure.

Huh. I wonder why that is? I mean, you can't possibly be the culprit here in making him feel that way, can you, Quinn?

In my head, Stephen and I are standing on the shore in Maine.

"I know you, Stephen. It's a when, not an if."

"You never deal with the fallout yourself. Why should this time be any different?"

He's still hovering by the bed, frowning at the bowl of soup I'm holding.

"It's perfectly safe to eat," he says tonelessly and reaches his hand toward the bowl. "I was supervised every step of the way, I promise. But if you don't want it, just give the bowl back, and I'll get you something else."

I clutch the bowl tighter. "No, I want it."

He sends me another cautious look, like he doesn't quite believe me and suspects I'll hide the soup underneath my bed when he isn't looking.

So I take a spoonful. I've heard stories of Stephen's kitchen mishaps over the years, but this is pretty good.

After the first taste, my stomach catches on to the fact that I haven't actually eaten anything since last night, and I'm starving.

"It's good," I say. "Really good."

"Well... good," Stephen says. He's still throwing glances at me as he goes to the other side of the bed and climbs back in.

"You know," I say between mouthfuls. "If you get bored and want to check over the rest of the papers, I wouldn't exactly fight you."

"Figures you'd bring me here and make me work," he says, but then he takes the papers, and I swear he looks pleased.

For a while, the room is silent, save for the clank of the spoon against the bowl and papers rustling.

"What's with all the bids?" he asks after a little while. "I mean, why do you have them?"

"Need to renovate the pool," I say. "I've been putting it off for a while because it's a real hassle dealing with the contractors and the paperwork that comes with it. And I have to close the place for at least a month, probably closer to two, which will be a headache."

When I look up, I find him frowning at me. "You said you teach swimming. That's a weird amount of responsibility for that."

"I do teach swimming," I say. "I just happen to also own the place."

"Of course you do."

He shakes his head. And smiles. And I smile back. And it's nice. More than nice.

"You teach kids?" he asks.

"Yes." I put the empty bowl away and yawn. "Kids with autism."

He tilts his head to the side. "Why autism?"

"Reid," I say. "He's autistic. He was one of those kids who loved water, and he kept wandering off. Really freaked us all out over and over again. There was an incident when he was six. We couldn't find him for hours, and then eventually somebody saw him climbing on a seawall. So my parents tried to enroll him in lessons, but nobody was offering them to autistic kids. And, well, my parents have the money, so they found somebody eventually. There are so many families who can't afford it because having an autistic kid is already expensive and anything extra is simply out of reach. So we offer them classes for free."

He looks at me for the longest time with the most curious expression. Almost as if he's seeing me for the first time in his life. As if I'm a stranger.

"That's really nice," he finally says softly.

"You look surprised," I say.

He's frowning again. "Guess I've just never really thought about... you. In that capacity," he quickly adds. "In the what-you-do-for-a-living capacity," he finishes.

My lips twitch. "Well... now you know."

"Now I know," he agrees. His gaze is still locked with mine. Green eyes that hold so many unspoken words and secrets.

How did you ever think he was shallow?

"Do you need anything else?" he asks, all business all of a sudden. "I can go to the pharmacy and buy you something if you tell me what you need. Or do you have, like, a prescription? You should probably sleep some more, too."

"I've slept the whole day. I don't think I physically can anymore."

"How about a movie?" he asks.

I shake my head and wince at the stab of pain. "I can't do screens today."

He nods and looks around the room, lips pursed. "Want to read something?"

"Can't really read right now either."

"Well I can. Read, that is," he says hesitantly. "For you." He huffs out a laugh and rolls his eyes. "I mean, I can read to you."

That is the last thing I thought he'd offer, so for a moment, I just stare at him.

He lets out a self-conscious laugh and scratches the back of his head. "Yeah, no. Dumb idea. I can just—"

"I'd like that," I say.

His eyes snap to mine.

"Okay," he says. "Yeah. Okay. Uh... What are you in the mood for?"

"You choose."

He looks at me for a little while longer before he points his thumb toward the stairs. "I'll just go find something, then."

He's back in a few minutes and lifts up *The Hobbit* with raised brows. Still with a moment of that hesitancy here, too.

"Perfect," I say.

He smiles and crawls back under the covers.

Opens the book.

And starts to read.

STEPH

WITH EVERY EVENT IN LIFE, there's a turning point.

That moment when gears shift and course changes.

That moment you later look back on and think, *Ah. This is where I should have gotten off the ride.*

But you didn't

And now you're screwed.

THE BOX IS SHOVED into my hands the moment I open the door. I look at it and then at Quinn.

"What's this?"

"Oh," he says and frowns. "My bad. I didn't know I had to tell you how boxes work. See, the trick is to lift the lid."

"Have I ever told you you're so funny?" I ask.

"No."

"Well, don't hold your breath," I say sweetly.

He grins back as he stalks toward me. Stops. Grabs the back of my head. Presses a kiss on my lips. Moves past me.

That whole ending-things-with-Quinn plan is obviously going really well.

In the kitchen, he pours himself a glass of water and leans his ass against the counter, making himself at home. I put the box on the table and eye it suspiciously.

He lets out a loud sigh. "Dear God, Stephen, what the hell do you think's in there?" he asks after a few moments of observing me silently and with growing impatience.

"A tarantula," I say, eyes still on the box.

"Must be a sneaky one to get in there without me looking."

"Anthrax."

"Where would I get anthrax?"

Instead of answering, I flick the lid open. And frown.

"What are those?" I ask.

Quinn pushes himself off the counter and comes and stands next to me. "Were you one of those smart kids that thrived in school but is helpless in real life settings? Those are running shoes."

"For me?" I ask, frown deepening.

"No. No, I bought those for me and just wanted to brag." He rolls his eyes. "Yes, for you."

"Why?"

"Because if you keep running in your crappy sneakers, you will ruin your knees by the time you're thirty. And I happen to like you on your knees."

My gaze flies to his. The air in the apartment feels a thousand degrees hotter in a snap. I should get an award for ignoring the boner his words create.

"My sneakers are fine," I grumble.

"A fine addition to the trash can?"

"Still not funny. You do try, though, so credit where credit is due," I say.

He shakes his head, and the smile is replaced by a serious

expression. "You need proper running shoes with how much you run. These are it. Use them."

I have no idea how to feel about this. I don't want to like the gesture. But it also feels good. To have somebody care about something like this.

"Fine," I say. "I'll wear your stupid shoes."

He raises his brows.

"What?" I ask.

"I fully expected I'd have to steal all your shitty sneakers and destroy them to get you to wear those." He nods toward the box.

"I'm not that unreasonable."

"You absolutely are. Unreasonable." He turns himself toward me and slides his arms around my waist. "Unreadable." He lowers his lips toward mine. "Unexpected," he murmurs just before he kisses me.

My heart jumps into my throat. Beats there in an erratic rhythm. And then slowly settles down.

Safe.

"How much do I owe you?" I ask, lips still against his.

He pulls away and sends me a sour look. "And you've ruined it." He makes a whole show out of looking at his watch. "And it took you a hundred and seventy-eight whole seconds. This is a personal best."

"Me? What did I do?"

"It's a gift," he says pointedly. "I don't want you to pay me back."

I take a step back and cross my arms over my chest. "We don't do that."

"You say that a whole lot. You should really consider adding some different tunes to the setlist."

I glare at him. "You can't just buy me shoes. Expensive shoes at that."

"Yes, I can. I just did."

"Well, then I don't want them."

Another deep sigh escapes his mouth. He looks toward the ceiling. "Why do I do this to myself?" He aims his gaze back at me. "You do know I've got a shit-ton of money, right? This is nothing."

"Bragging about your wealth. Classy," I say, and yelp as he pinches my ass. "Wait. Does that mean you're my sugar daddy?"

"Would that make you stop complaining about the shoes?"

"Huh," I say slowly. "Well, this puts things in a whole different light. My God! I've been selling myself really cheap, haven't I?"

"This took a turn," Quinn says dryly.

"We should really talk about my benefits," I say, and send him a thoughtful look.

"As in?"

I wave my hand in the air. "You know, regular things. A brand-new car, shopping sprees on Fifth Avenue, trips to St. Barts."

"And now it's escalated."

"It's a small price to pay for all the forbidden things I let you do to me."

"Just say thank you," he says. "It's not that difficult."

I mean... I guess?

I lean forward and press a brief kiss on his lips.

"Thank you," I say.

He nods.

I nod.

"Just to clarify, that's a no on the car?" I ask.

He laughs, wraps his fingers around the back of my neck, and pulls my mouth against his.

I press myself against him and nip the side of his neck with my teeth. "Want me to make my case and give you a preview of those dirty, forbidden things?"

I don't wait for his answer. I grab his hips and turn us around, so his ass is against the counter once again.

Then I drop to my knees in front of him and pull his pants down.

It's a good sight. All of Quinn is. Not that it's a surprise, exactly. I know his body intimately by now. The way there are two perfectly symmetrical dips right above his hip bones. Exactly how soft the hairs that make up his happy trail are. There's a faint appendectomy scar on the right side of his abdomen, and he gets ticklish when I dip my tongue into his navel.

I kiss his hip bone, and his cock jerks. My tongue drags a diagonal line downward until I lick over the spot where his thigh meets his groin.

His fingers clutch the edge of the counter, eyes locked on me, taking in every move I make, every swipe of my tongue with the kind of intent attention nobody's ever paid to me.

His thick cock slides over my cheek, and he hisses out a breath. I ignore it. Bury my nose in his pubic hair. Inhale.

His hips snap forward, and the tip of his cock slides from my cheek to my ear, leaving a wet trail of precum behind.

"Fuck," he says. "Just do it, or…"

The words are commanding, but the hand he slides into my hair is gentle.

I glance up and blink at him innocently. "What's the matter? A bit quick on the trigger?"

He closes his eyes, and a pained laugh escapes.

"It hurts," he says. "You should blow me and make it better."

I wrap my fingers around his base and squeeze. Hard. Hard enough that it makes him yelp.

"I hate you," he says.

"You really don't." I open my mouth and suck the swollen tip in. His skin is smooth and salty against my tongue. I suck him farther into my mouth. As far as I can take him. The fingers in my hair tighten. I look up, my mouth full of cock, straight into Quinn's eyes.

His head is bowed, fingers still in my hair. Hooded blue eyes and flushed cheeks. Parted lips and harsh exhales.

The blowjob is fast and sloppy. The more enthusiastically I go at him, the better sounds he makes. Low moans interspersed with curses that sound like praise.

My own cock is throbbing in my pants, but it's easy to ignore right now.

I cup Quinn's bare ass. Run my fingers up the crack. Push my forefinger against his hole.

He shudders, and his fingertips dig into my skull, forcing me to take him in as far as he wants to go.

He sucks in a breath and pushes his ass back against my fingers. His fingers tighten in my hair.

"Steph." His voice is a harsh rasp. He loses the e and n, as if he can't possibly manage more letters than strictly necessary. "I'm gonna—"

His entire body stiffens for a moment and then jerks forward, pushing deeper into my mouth.

I swallow.

And suck.

Until his body goes lax.

I press a last sticky kiss somewhere on his hip and fall back on my heels, my breathing mirroring the harshness of the breaths that come out of Quinn's mouth.

Our eyes stay fixed on each other.

He's never looked better.

I want to be the only one who gets to see him like this.

It's perilous ground. Wishing.

But there's bliss on his features and hazy happiness in his eyes, and I can't stop myself from wanting.

Wanting... more. More of him. More of this. More of us.

Cracks are forming in the armor I've built over the last ten years.

And I let them be.

He lowers himself to his knees in front of me and cups my chin in his hand. Kisses me. My fingers go to the back of his neck. Dig into his skin. Hold him in place.

Maybe we could just stay like this forever. In the here. In the now. Without the outside world. I don't think I would mind.

He leans his forehead against mine and looks me so deep in the eye I think he might see my soul.

Every dark corner.

Every ragged edge.

"What if we would be good?" he says in a low voice.

"What if we would be horrible?" I counter, searching his eyes. For what? I don't know.

I find only certainty.

He smiles. Open and brilliant and hopeful. "Go on a date with me."

Do the right thing.

Say no.

End this.

"Okay," I say.

STEPH

HE PICKS me up the next afternoon. There's been just enough time between me saying okay to him and him knocking on my door that I've been able to freak out. But I also haven't completely lost my shit and pulled a runner.

He's dressed in a pair of shorts and a T-shirt, a gray backpack thrown over his shoulder.

His eyes wander up and down me, and he smiles.

"You look hot."

"Don't I always?" I say with a casualness I don't really feel.

"There is a pattern there," he agrees.

I step forward, slide my arm around him, and squeeze his ass. "How about this. We stay in. And take advantage of my hotness."

He lowers his head and nips at my bottom lip, and I'm almost convinced things will go my way.

Sex is easy.

Quinn is complicated.

He grins at me, presses one last quick kiss on my lips, and says, "No."

My shoulders slump, but I grab my keys and lock the door behind me.

"I think you looked about as excited about spending time with me when we first went to Maine," Quinn muses as we trudge down the stairs. "I'm trying not to take it personally."

"I've never been on a date," I mutter once we're out on the street.

"So you're just generally opposed to new experiences? Is that it?"

"Pretty much. So what are we doing?" I ask. "Something first date-ish? Are you going to take me to a fancy restaurant, and then we'll awkwardly stare at each other across the table and try and fill the silence with small talk?"

"Aren't you supposed to be the optimist out of the two of us?"

"Not about this," I say grimly.

"You're going to enjoy yourself," he says, confident as ever. "Because when I set my mind to something, I win. And my mind is set on having a good time."

So I clamp my mouth shut and let him drag me to the subway.

In about twenty minutes, we get off the train and head back outside, where we cross the street and...

I stop.

"We're going to a park?" I ask.

"It felt more like you than dinner in a stuffy restaurant," he says.

I can't seem to speak for a moment. My mouth opens and closes. And opens and closes.

He's not supposed to *know* me.

But he does.

I'm not supposed to like it.

But I do.

We find a spot on the grass, and he lays down a dark blue picnic blanket and pulls a frisbee out of his backpack.

"Loser buys dinner?" he says with a grin.

I laugh and nod.

"Bring it," I say.

He goes over the rules, firing the few there are out in rapid succession. A step back for each successful catch. Missed catches are points for the other player.

He hands me the frisbee and jogs away from me.

"Good luck," he calls with a smirk.

I never knew he was such a dirty player. He sends the frisbee flying to my left and to my right. High above my head or aimed toward my calves. Soon enough, I'm returning the favor.

There's running. Taunts. Laughter. Diving toward the aquamarine disk. The front of my shirt is green from throwing myself on the grass over and over again. My knees and the heels of my palms are covered in streaks of dirt.

Quinn's laughter rings out all around me until my chest is vibrating with his joy.

Rules go out the window.

Instead of catching, we're now trying to steal the frisbee from each other. The picnic blanket becomes a makeshift end zone where we both try to aim our throws, arguing about points and whooping and hollering when we score.

I fling the frisbee into the air, and it soars past Quinn's head.

We take off at the same time, chasing after the frisbee. I dive for it, but Quinn's arms wrap around my waist and pull me to a stop. My back slams against his chest. He loses his balance, and we topple to the ground.

Quinn twists his body so that he cushions my fall, and we end up hitting the ground, me on top of him, legs tangled, chests rising and falling in rapid pants.

I can see the frisbee above Quinn's head, just out of reach.

My eyes meet his for a moment before I scramble forward to get my hands on it. We abandoned keeping score a long time ago, but somehow we both know with unmatched certainty that this point matters.

His fingers wrap around my wrist just as I reach for the frisbee, his arm goes around my hips. He licks over my collarbone, and I lose my concentration. He makes a dive for it.

We struggle and wrestle and laugh.

There's so much laughter.

Eventually, I drop on my back on the grass, frisbee abandoned, still smiling. Quinn leans over me.

His palm cups my chin. Thumb moves over my cheek.

His mouth comes down on mine.

He smells like grass and dirt and sweat and summer, and I inhale until I can't anymore.

Until my lungs start to burn.

LATER, we buy dinner from a nearby deli. Wraps so big we need both hands to hold them. Bags of chips and bottles of freshly squeezed orange juice.

I lie on my back, my head in Quinn's lap. His head is propped on his backpack, the bill of an old New York Yankees baseball cap pulled low over his eyes to shield them from the sun.

His fingers play in my hair absently. We share a bag of chocolate chip cookies. He takes a bite and holds it out for me, until I take a bite of my own. Cookie after cookie, until the bag is empty save for a few chocolate chips in the bottom. He angles the opening of the bag against my mouth and tries to pour the stray chips in. Most of them end up somewhere between my collar and my skin.

He laughs.

I lick over one chip I fish out of my shirt and press it against his cheek.

He tries to wipe it away with his tongue.

His laugh is loud and brilliant and free.

And we talk.

About pointless things that become important when the person you're talking to is important.

Quinn's first concert was Metallica.

The best place he's ever visited is Melbourne.

He doesn't like watermelon.

His biggest pet peeve is people who chew with their mouths open.

His eyes crinkle in the corners when he laughs.

The tips of his ears turn pink in the light of the setting sun.

The hairs on his thigh are soft to the touch.

There's a birthmark underneath his left earlobe.

His kisses taste like chocolate.

And I'm in so much trouble.

STEPH

I LOOK around the crowded bar until I see a glimpse of a very familiar back. I tug at the hem of my shirt self-consciously. It's another first for me. Caring about whether or not I'll leave a good impression.

I haven't in forever. I know I usually do fine, but I don't give a shit if I don't. Even with Quinn's parents, it didn't exactly matter in a real, honest way. It would've made for an awkward week if they had hated me, sure, but I wasn't necessarily worried about it. I was never going to see them again. Who cares?

I do now. Doesn't even matter that it's Rubi and Sutton, and that I've met them before. Doesn't matter that Rubi already knows me as Quinn's boyfriend and seems to like me just fine. This is my first official outing as Quinn's... date, and it matters so much that even the hypothetical prospect of failure makes me queasy.

"Get over yourself," I mutter underneath my breath.

A palm slaps on my back, and I jump and snap my head up.

Sutton grins at me. "We're over there," he says, and nods toward a booth in the back.

He throws his arm over my shoulder and steers me toward their table.

Quinn lifts his head, and his smile widens as he watches me approach, his eyes moving between me and Rubi, who's telling him something that makes her gesture wildly with her hands.

I slide into the booth next to him. Quinn smiles at me, and nods at something that Rubi said before he presses a kiss on my lips, and then smoothly continues his conversation with Rubi.

It's the casualness. It turns the air hot and makes my heat thunder in elated beats. The way he does all this so naturally. Like I belong. Like I'm a part of his life. Like I fit in so goddamn easily.

I haven't belonged in ten years.

It's terrifying.

And safe.

Quinn throws his arm over my shoulder, still laughing at whatever Rubi is saying. Easily. Casually.

Like I belong.

I sidle closer. Slowly. Hesitantly. Then with more determination.

Like I belong.

"No, no, no," Rubi says with a loud laugh. "Oh my God. No. Listen to this, Steph," she says and jumps into a story. Including me.

Easily.

Casually.

Like.

I.

Belong.

Quinn slides his glass toward me, and I take a drink. His arm brushes against mine whenever either of us takes the glass, and we listen to Rubi and Sutton bicker and argue.

"How do you three know each other?" I ask when there's a lull in the conversation after a while.

"Rubi here was stalking me," Sutton says.

She gives him the finger. "I was not."

"She used to watch me sleep. Caught her in the act and everything," Sutton says.

"It was once, and I didn't watch you sleep. I was trying to put your hand in warm water to get you to wet the bed."

"A disturbing behavior for a twenty-nine-year-old woman, but I guess we all have our kinks," Sutton says.

"I was thirteen," Rubi says with a sigh. "I'm still not convinced you didn't pee your pants with the way you screamed when you opened your eyes and saw me there."

"You try and stay cool when somebody stands above you in a white nightgown and smirks like she's come to collect your soul."

"Mom was so pissed," Rubi says, and laughs at the memory.

"You've all been friends for a long time," I say.

"Most days it feels like too long." Rubi smirks and squints at Sutton.

He just waggles his brows at her before he meets my gaze over the table. "I was Lukas's stepbrother once upon a time. But don't hold it against me. I never liked the little shit."

There's that name again.

I glance toward Quinn. His expression is completely unreadable.

"I absolutely do hold it against you," Rubi says. "How very dare your father shack up with the woman who birthed the spawn of the antichrist?"

"Antichrist?" Quinn says dryly. "A bit overly dramatic, don't you think, Rubs?"

She shrugs, not even the least bit apologetic, clearly deciding to stand by her words.

"It's actually very much in character for dear old Dad," Sutton says thoughtfully. "Like attracts like."

"Clearly. Is Lukas in town? We should go egg his front door," Rubi says.

"It's been years," Quinn says. "Let it go."

"I'm more of a revenge person," Rubi muses. "And I never got to have it."

"Seeing that you weren't the one dating him, there's really no reason for you to start harassing him now," Quinn says.

Rubi shakes her head. "You're too levelheaded for your own good. It's really annoying."

"I like it," I say. No one is probably more surprised than me at those words, but… it's true. I do like that he's levelheaded. It makes me feel like he can handle anything. Maybe even me.

Hope is a dangerous thing.

"Oh, no, no, no," Rubi says. "Nick just left for Seattle for two weeks this afternoon, so no couple-y shit in front of me, or I will become all mopey."

"Right. Very sorry, Rubs," Quinn says. "We'll try and be less happy."

"Please do," she says.

Quinn glances at me from the corner of his eye, lips turning up in the corners with a subtle smile that feels like a secret only the two of us share.

Am I happy?

I've never asked myself this question. It used to be that I didn't have to. I just was. And for the last decade I simply haven't bothered to contemplate happiness. I just wasn't.

But lately…

Days hold possibilities.

The what ifs are quiet.

I wouldn't trade this moment.

This moment is good.

Rubi launches into a story about her job as a political research analyst.

And in the middle of her story, I move my hand so the back of it brushes against Quinn's hand.

I'm enough of a coward that I don't really dare to look at him. If I do that, I'll probably chicken out. So instead, I forge ahead. I very slowly slide my palm over the back of his hand and then my fingers between his. It feels like each inch takes forever because all the while I feel stupid and not really sure if I should even be doing it. My face heats. My heart is going a mile a minute.

I should absolutely add to the already somewhat unstable impression Quinn probably has about me and throw in another panic attack because I've never held a guy's hand before, and somehow that simple gesture feels *big* and *important* and *meaningful*.

I'm almost prepared to pull my hand away when Quinn curls his fingers and traps my hand in place.

My heartbeat is still too loud and wild and uncontrolled, but with each passing second it starts to settle.

His hand in mine still feels *big* and *important* and *meaningful*, but now it's also *good* and *right* and *safe*.

It stays there for the rest of the evening. Through drink orders and stories and laughter—his fingers stay linked with mine.

His hand is in mine when we pay the bill.

His hand is in mine when we walk outside.

His hand is in mine when we say bye to Sutton.

His hand is in mine when we wait with Rubi for her cab.

His hand is in mine when we start to walk home.

And it's *big* and *important* and *meaningful* and *good* and *right* and *safe*.

His hand is in mine when I say, "Tell me something real."

Fingers squeeze mine.

He's silent for a little while.

But then he starts to speak.

"I met Lukas when I was in high school," he says. My eyes snap up and stay on the side of his face. "Sutton introduced us when their parents got married. He was a swimmer too. We became friends quickly. Then more. He was... We just fit. Sort of perfectly. Friends first. We started dating the summer after we finished high school, and somehow it was even better." He drags his hand through his hair and shakes his head. "We were together for so many years. And I thought... I thought he was my safe space.

"I've spent so much of my life being careful. Constantly aware of myself. Never say the wrong thing. Never step out of line. Never show your true feelings to anybody. There's always somebody watching you. It's exhausting.

"And with Lukas... He made me feel like it was okay to be real. To do everything. Make mistakes and try things I'd never done before and say how I really feel, and it'd be okay because it was between us. Because he was going to keep my secrets."

I've never hated a person I've never met more than I hate Lukas right at this moment.

"But he didn't?" I say. Pointlessly. I don't think there would be a story here if he had.

"No," Quinn says. "He sold me out. Quite spectacularly, too. There was this series of articles about 'the real Quinn Henris.' Years of building a life together only to have it reduced to detailed descriptions of our sex life. And he didn't even stop there. He was part of the family, so he'd been privy to a lot of private information, and that kept trickling out over the following months."

"I'm sorry," I say softly. Uselessly.

I try to ignore the hollow crater that starts to open up inside me as his words settle. Its edges crumbling in, expanding and widening as what happened to him fully registers.

"Dad was planning to run for president," he says. "But then he didn't. He's writing his books and giving an occasional guest lecture, and Mom is doing her thing as a Goodwill Ambassador. They both stepped out of the limelight. Because of me. I've never liked being in the public eye, but this was a whole other level of awful. And I couldn't handle it. There were a lot of PR people involved right after. A lot of plans about how to spin this, so it wouldn't hurt any of our careers. The phrase 'damage control' was used *a lot*. They planned a press conference where I was supposed to give a speech, and I couldn't do it. I stood there, in front of fifty reporters, and then I just walked out."

He stops speaking for a moment, a distant look in his eyes, before he continues, "My parents never had the same hang-ups about privacy I did, and I didn't ask them to step away from the public eye, but they still did."

"And you retired," I say.

"It sounds stupid. It's a few articles, years ago. I should be over it."

I try to ignore the queasy fear that takes up residence in the bottom of my chest. The resignation that comes with the knowledge that this thing between us really, truly will never work out.

Because it's Quinn. Fiercely private Quinn Henris. Even when he was at the height of his career, he rarely gave interviews, and when he did, his personal life was always strictly off limits.

"Things from a long time ago can still hurt," I say, echoing what I told him in Maine. "And I don't think it's the articles. It's the betrayal that's painful."

"You're doing a terrible job at being shallow with all that insightfulness," he says softly.

I force a smile onto my face. "As long as you don't tell anybody. I've got a reputation to maintain."

We walk in silence for a little while.

"Why'd he do it?" I ask.

Quinn shrugs. "The thing with swimming is only very few people make actual money."

"He wasn't good enough?" I guess.

Quinn shakes his head, and then he snorts. "Exactly how messed up is it that after everything, I still feel guilty admitting it? No. He wasn't. He was good. But not good enough."

"So... you got better, and he got bitter?"

He nods. "In hindsight, things were tense between us. At the end. I just figured... Relationships have ups and downs. I thought we'd work through it, and it'd be okay again."

"That's not on you, though. You get that, right? He's the asshole."

He sends me an amused look. "I know," he says before his voice turns serious again. "By now when I think about him... I don't miss him. I don't hate him. I don't really think about him that much at all. But I feel guilty. Bitter pills are easier to swallow when *you're* the only one who has to swallow them. If you make everybody else swallow one too, it gets much more complicated."

"Yeah," I say. "Your family doesn't seem like they're exactly bitter about anything."

He stares straight ahead into the distance for a little while. "They say they're not."

"You don't believe them?"

"I think they're happy. But... I think they would've been happy in that other life too. I would've preferred if they'd gotten to choose which of those two lives they lived."

I stop and pull him to a stop too.

"They did get a choice," I say. "They chose you."

He looks at me for so long I'm starting to think I overstepped, but then he hauls me against himself and kisses me, arms wrapped so tightly around me I can't breathe, but it's okay. It's always okay when I'm with him.

He runs his tongue over mine and presses his body more firmly against mine. I grip the back of his shirt, tugging him even closer.

His chest vibrates with laughter, and he slows the kiss down. Leans his forehead against mine.

I don't know how much courage it takes to trust somebody else after something like this. Mountains of courage, probably.

I wouldn't know.

Can't really even imagine that much strength.

I've always been a coward.

"You're very wise," he says.

"I know," I reply. "I'm unbelievably smart."

Let's add another lie to the tally, why don't we?

He chuckles, takes my hand, and we start to walk again.

And he doesn't know.

Doesn't know that I'm a landmine.

That he's trudging so close.

That he's about to step on me.

That if my parents find out about him... I'll give him an act two of everything he hates so much.

And then he'll hate me, too.

QUINN

STEPHEN IS ODDLY quiet the whole way to my apartment. It's almost as if he's moving on autopilot. I suppose it makes sense. I did unload a whole lot of crap on him earlier.

I'm not sure what to make of his mood right now, though. He almost looks scared. Of what, though, I have no clue.

I unlock the door and hold it open for him. He stuffs his hands into his pockets and walks inside. The look he sends me is pensive. I don't know what to make of it. I've never seen that expression on Stephen's face.

"You okay?" I ask.

He opens his mouth.

Closes it.

And simply nods.

"Are you sure?" I ask.

He nods again before he finds his voice.

"Yeah," he says.

He empties his pockets on the side table. Phone. Keys. Wallet. On autopilot again. Before he blinks and starts putting them back in his pockets.

"What are you doing?" I ask.

He looks up, hand hovering in the air, midway to the table.

"I'm not really sure," he says. The laugh that follows is strange too. Not his real laugh. Not the pretend one either. It's as if he's really laughing, but he doesn't find the joke that funny.

He leaves the phone and the keys be and goes to the window. He turns around in a slow circle, eyes moving over my home like he's never been here before he turns to look out the window.

"You know, I never would've pictured you'd be living in a place like this," he says, sounding marginally more like himself again.

"What did you expect?" I ask.

"A sleek, modern bachelor pad," he says.

I go to him and wrap my arms around him from behind. "Is that the impression I give off?"

He tilts his head to the side, and I press my lips against his neck.

"Not really," he says. "I just don't like sleek, modern bachelor pads, and since I really wanted to think that you're an asshole, then in my head you lived in one of those." He waves his hand around. "This feels very much like you, though."

I lean my chin on his shoulder, and his head falls against mine.

I splay my fingers wide on his chest. His heart beats against my palm. "Can I ask you something?"

He hesitates for a second before he says, "Shoot."

There's something grim in that word, too. Like he's preparing for an actual bullet.

"When we first met... why didn't you like me?"

He turns his head to the side and glances toward me, lips twitching.

"Don't say it," I warn with a laugh.

"What?" he asks and widens his eyes innocently. "You

asked me a question, but now you don't want to hear the answer?"

"You weren't going to answer me. You were going to have a go at my ego."

"I don't even have to actually make the joke for you to get it. This saves a lot of time."

"Just answer the question," I say and nuzzle into his neck.

"It's not really important anymore," he says.

"It is to me."

"It really isn't. Trust me."

"Please?" I say.

He looks out the window for a little bit.

"The first time we met wasn't really the first time we met," he says.

I frown. "What do you mean?"

"I ran into you in Central Park a few years before Nora introduced us. I..." He looks down and chuckles. "I was... I used to swim too, and I watched your competitions a lot when I was younger," he rushes out.

I did not see that one coming at all.

"Okay?" I say slowly.

"I approached you. I guess I just wanted to tell you... I don't even know what I was planning to say. Something about admiring you, I guess." He falls silent again.

"But?" I prompt.

"I didn't get that far. You told me to fuck off."

I blink slowly.

I try to remember.

I can't imagine *not* remembering him. I've never met a more memorable person than Steph. How can I not remember him?

"I don't remember," I finally say, and frown. "How can I not remember you?"

"It doesn't really matter," he says. "It's not like I've been going out of my way to be nice to you over the years."

"I've always kind of liked it," I admit.

"You liked that I was a dick to you?"

"Yes," I say, and laugh. "People don't do that with me. Some are genuinely nice. Some are dicks behind my back, but nice to my face. But there's always this veneer of politeness to it. You don't give a shit about being polite to me. You're sarcastic and snarky and downright fucking annoying some days. But you're real. You make me real too."

He closes his eyes and lets out a choked laugh, but he doesn't say anything.

"When was that?" I ask after a bit. "When I told you to fuck off."

His hand goes to my arm, fingers clutching it like he's holding on to me. "Almost exactly five years ago."

"Two thousand and eighteen," I say slowly. "Oh."

"Yeah," he says. I can feel his heart pick up speed, and he swallows hard. "I was... It was... Uh..." He stumbles over his words, fingers digging deeper into my arm. "I was having a... It was August, so I was..."

"Right around the time of the thing with Lukas," I say since he doesn't seem to be able to get the words out for some reason.

He clutches my arm even tighter before he relaxes his fingers quickly. Let's out a deep breath. His eyes stay on the floor for a moment, but then he looks up and nods.

"Right around that time," he says, and his shoulders slump a bit.

"Ancient history," I say.

He's clutching my arm again.

"Yeah," he whispers. "Ancient history."

I've talked and thought about Lukas more than I have in the

last year tonight. It's high time to push him back where he belongs—out of my head.

"Bed?" I say.

He nods.

I unwrap myself from around him and take his hand. Now that I know how it feels in mine, I find it hard to let it go even for a second.

We go upstairs.

In the bathroom, we stand side by side and brush our teeth, he sends me a toothpaste-y grin in the mirror, and I snort, which only spurs him on until we're both making faces at each other.

He rinses his toothbrush and peels his clothes off. Meets my eyes in the mirror and winks before he saunters into the shower. I drop my own clothes and follow him. Under the warm water, I take the soap and wash him, and he returns the favor.

His fingers massage my scalp as he rubs shampoo into my hair. His eyes stay locked on mine, water cascading down his body.

This moment is beautifully simple.

Once we're clean, he steps out of the shower. Hands me a towel and grabs one for himself. I watch him dry himself. My cock's been half hard ever since he pulled off his shirt, but now it goes full mast.

He sends me a slow, sly look, eyes moving up and down me before they settle on my dick. He looks up and slowly licks over his lips before he drops his towel, turns around, and walks out the door.

"Brat," I call after him with a laugh before I drop my own towel next to his and follow him.

When I enter the bedroom, he's lying on the bed, back propped against the headboard, lazily stroking himself.

I don't stop to admire the view. Instead, I climb on the bed and straddle him. So quickly he doesn't have time to pull his arm out from underneath me, so the back of his wrist remains somewhere between us, smothered between my balls and his crotch.

He snorts out a laugh, and I grin at him. He's still holding his cock, so he taps it against my ass, the tip of it moving over my lower back.

It's easy. And fun. Because that's what Steph does. He makes things fun.

He rolls his eyes and pulls his arm free. Grabs my face and pulls me forward until he's kissing me again.

"Quinn," he says, that rasp in his voice that makes me so fucking glad I have a bed where he can lie and say my name just like this.

I gently bite his lower lip, and he lets out a shuddering breath that goes straight to my balls.

My thumbs press into his hip bones and slide up and down his skin. My own cock is resting against Stephen's abdomen, and every slide of our bodies makes me feel a little bit like I'm about to lift off this bed in a moment, gravity forgotten.

I pull my mouth away from Steph and look at him below me. Eyes foggy with slow-building pleasure and kisses. Cheeks flushed. Lips red and swollen.

"Do you ever top?" I ask.

A flame of heat makes his forest green eyes burn.

He nods.

"Good," I whisper before I lower my head and kiss him again.

My mouth stays fused to his as he reaches out to get the lube and condoms.

It stays on his as he fumbles to open the cap.

My lips are on him while he squirts a whole glob of cool liquid on my back and laughs as I jerk in surprise.

"Oops," he gasps, fingers trailing through the mess and

down the crack of my ass, spreading it around and inside. I slide my thumbs over his cheeks and laugh into his mouth.

"Christ, that's good," I mumble when his fingers go deeper, and Steph looks like he's going to start laughing again from sheer happiness.

He's a little clumsy and a little unsure as he fumbles with the condom.

"Shit," he says, and laughs again.

It's as if he can't quite believe I'd ask him to do this, and he's not quite sure how to feel about this, but at the same time, he won't argue or second guess because he wants it too.

And when he slides inside me, he bites his lip and closes his eyes and throws his head back on a long, rough exhale.

I slot our mouths together again. Swallow down his moan when I start to move my hips. Ride him until his breaths turn to gasps and his fingertips tattoo themselves on my hips.

Chests rise and fall rapidly. Skin slaps against skin.

I find his hands. Link our fingers. Lift his hands above his head. Slam myself down on him.

He groans, and his head slams against the headboard, but he doesn't even react.

His eyes screw shut.

"Fuck! I can't—" he says.

His body tightens, muscles lock.

He lets out a shuddering breath and goes slack underneath me.

I wrap my hand around my cock and give it a rough tug and come all over his chest before I collapse on him.

We'll be glued together come morning.

Good.

THE BED IS empty when I wake up. No note. No message on my phone.

I was hoping we'd wake up together, but it's Steph, and he's sort of predictable in his unpredictability.

He probably went for his run like he always does when he can't sleep. I'm not sure how it's possible to not fall into a coma after last night, but, well, Steph. Unpredictable.

The shirt he was wearing last night is still in the bathroom.

My favorite hoodie is missing.

I chuckle and go downstairs to start my day.

STEPH

I GO to Quinn's place after he's done with work, but he's not there, and he doesn't pick up the phone when I call him, so I drag my ass back home.

I miss him.

And I'm relieved.

One more day of mercy where I can pretend things will be okay in the end.

One more day when I don't have to tell him just how much of a fuckup I really am.

My phone rings later that evening, and I dive for it so fast I knock it off the table before I can pick it up.

"*Hey,*" he says, distracted, tired, but there's also that warmth in his tone he seems to reserve just for me. "*I have a broken pool pump, so I'm trying to figure out if we can fix it, and it's taking fucking forever!*"

Somebody yells something in the distance, and Quinn laughs, his voice muffled for a moment. "*Yeah, fuck you too.*" He comes back online. "*It's been a shit day. And I miss you.*"

My insides go all warm.

"Come here when you're done?" I say.

"I'll be late."

"Who cares?"

He laughs.

"Not me."

TURNS out the pump is fucked, so after a day of sitting on the phone and yelling at people, Quinn throws in the towel and goes ahead with the renovation.

"It's warm outside for at least another few weeks, so we can use the outside pool for most of the classes. Just have to reschedule and negotiate a bit," he says. "It'll be a bit of a nightmare because you can't count on the weather to hold, but I guess one crisis at a time."

When he's not at work, he's on the phone trying to coordinate and mediate and work out solutions.

I bring him lunch every day, and we eat it outside on a bench, and he vents about contractors and tiles and lessons and kisses me between bites of sandwiches and pizza and tacos.

He also texts me.

A lot.

Turns out he's exceptionally talented at being dirty in writing.

And he's very prolific, even if he's busy.

A week later, Mona sprains her ankle, so I take on extra shifts at the bar to cover for her, which means I'm working every night and Quinn's and my schedules go even more out of sync, and I only see him when I crawl into bed late at night when we both have just enough energy for a quick fuck before we fall asleep, him wrapped around me or vice versa.

And all the while, my parents keep calling me.

Because 'we have to have a plan' and 'this is our chance to get people interested again. Our one shot, Steph.'

It's the same thing every year.

Has been the same for a decade.

Ever since August 10th, 2013.

I'm exhausted.

I'm living on borrowed time.

I know I am.

But I just want to keep Quinn. For as long as I'm allowed.

I know I don't deserve it.

I don't deserve happiness and good things, and I'm a fuckup.

But I just really want to keep him, and please, please, *please* can I just have him, and I will never ever ask for anything else ever again?

JULY ROLLS INTO AUGUST.

The countdown timer resets in my head like it does every year.

Tick-tock-tick-tock.

Nine days to go.

What if you could make a deal with the devil, Steph?

Eight days to go.

What if you could get the other half of you back?

Seven days.

What if you could trade?

Six days.

All the people you now have in your life.

Five.

All the people you now love.

Four.

Jude. Blair. Nora. Hazel.

Three.
Quinn.
Two.
What if they disappeared out of your life for good? But you get Sky back. Would you make the trade?
One.
For the first time, the answer changes.
No.

QUINN

I CHECK MY PHONE AGAIN, but there's still no reply from Stephen. I throw the phone on the couch, rub my palms over my face and sigh.

He's been AWOL the whole day. No calls. No texts. No spontaneous lunch visits.

I'm not worried.

But I'm not *not* worried either.

Mostly, I feel useless.

For the last week and a half or so, he's been distant.

When I talk to him, I have to say his name two, three times before he snaps back into the present.

He's restless.

He runs like a maniac. Early in the morning. Late at night. And even so, he tosses and turns those few hours he actually manages to stay in bed.

He crawls into my bed late at night, drops a condom on my chest and tells me to "make it hurt."

We get into a fight.

He storms out.

He comes back a few hours later.

Apologizes.

He gets even quieter.

At night, he wraps himself around me so tightly it's as if he's afraid I'll disappear unless he holds on to me.

I can see he's not okay.

But he refuses to talk to me.

He's not sleeping.

When his phone rings, he looks at it as if it's a ticking time bomb that'll detonate when he picks it up.

Every time I get a look at the display, it says either *Mom* or *Dad*. He never picks it up when I'm near him. Instead, he goes out, doors slamming, tension clouding everything around him for the rest of the day.

"Tell me something real," I tell him one day.

He looks at me, silence stretching out between us.

He swallows hard.

Looks away.

"It was a few years ago," he says. The pretend lightness makes his voice hollow. "After an unexpected storm, I got stuck on Mars."

"Fuck's sake, Stephen!" I snap.

He squeezes his eyes shut and clenches his teeth.

"I'm sorry," he whispers. "I'm sorry."

I go to him. Throw my leg over his. Straddle him.

"Tell me something real," I repeat.

He meets my gaze. Holds it.

"I love—"

I slam my palm over his mouth.

"Don't. Not like this."

"I'm sorry," he says again.

I take a deep breath. Press my thumb on his left eyebrow. On the scar there.

"How did you get this?"

He looks me straight in the eye.

"I don't know."

I sigh and start to get up, but he grabs my wrist.

"I don't know. I don't remember," he says, words rushing out. "I was on a boat. Below deck. Something hit me. Or I fell against something. I don't know. I blacked out, and I never... I don't know what it was. I... Blood started dripping into my eye. That's when I noticed. But I don't know how I got it."

He looks like he's about to throw up once he's done talking.

I lean my forehead against his and close my eyes.

"I don't know what to do with you," I admit.

"Jump ship," he suggests tonelessly.

I snap my eyes open.

"No! Fuck. No. Unless..." There seems to be less oxygen in the room suddenly. It's all sucked into the black hole that's opened up inside my chest at his words. "Is that what you want?"

"No," he whispers. He drops his head back so my forehead is now against his lips. "I'm sorry," he says, lifting his hand and rubbing it over his eyes. "My head's a mess right now."

"But why?" I can hear the desperation in my voice. *Just tell me what's wrong. I'll fix it for you.*

"I mean, take your pick. I'm generally a mess, if you haven't noticed yet."

We're back to lying, it seems.

"Maybe... Just hold me for a little bit?" he finally says, voice timid like he's afraid I'm going to say no.

I lie down on the couch and pull him down with me. Wrap him in a hug and hold him. He falls asleep soon after and while I listen to him breathe, I drift off too.

When I wake up, he's gone.

I sigh and pick up my phone again.

Still nothing.

I can't seem to sit still, so in the end, I pocket my phone and head outside. I go to Steph's place and pound on the door long enough to wake the dead, but there's no answer.

"Fuck," I mutter before I head back outside. It's as if my feet have a mind of their own, because next thing I know, I find myself in front of Jude and Blake's building.

I press my thumb on the buzzer.

Jude is already standing in the doorway when I make it upstairs.

"Hey," he says, more than a little bit of surprise ringing through, which is understandable, I suppose. Jude and I are mostly friends because of our friends. Not to say I don't like him or anything like that. We're just not close. We're not the call-me-anytime-anywhere type of friends.

He opens the door wider and motions for me to come inside.

"What brings you by?" he asks.

I don't take off my shoes. Just stand there, hand in my pocket still clutching the phone.

"Do you know where Stephen is?" I ask, point-blank. I'm not really in the mood for small talk. "I can't get a hold of him."

There's a beat of silence, followed by a heavy, resigned sigh, the weight of which settles heavily on my shoulders.

"He said he was spending the day with you," Jude says.

I shake my head. "I haven't seen him at all today."

There's another lengthy silence, and then...

"Fuck!" Jude clutches the back of his neck, and his head drops back. "Fuck, fuck, fuck!"

"Uh... What's going on?" I ask.

He lets out a deep breath and shakes his head. "Fucking fuck," he mutters.

His fingers roll into a fist, and he taps it against his forehead, muttering more curses.

"Are you planning to explain?" I ask, impatience ringing

through loud and clear, and it seems to snap Jude out of his cursing streak.

A mirthless laugh escapes his mouth. "It's August tenth."

"And a Thursday," I say. "Thank you for clarifying. So what?"

Jude just keeps shaking his head. "Figures he's still not talking about this. Fucking Morgan and Shae have screwed him up so badly by now he's just..." He lets out a frustrated growl before he says, "August tenth is the anniversary of Steph's brother's death."

I blink and stare at him until Jude waves his palm in front of my face.

"You still with me?"

I clear my throat and try to process what I've just learned.

"Yeah. Yeah, I'm still here."

"I'm guessing he hasn't told you about Skyler," he says.

"First time I'm hearing that name," I say dully.

Why is this the first time I'm hearing that name?

"Yeah, don't try and find any sense or logic there," Jude says. "I've known Steph since high school. He was there when I fucking found out my parents had fucking kidnapped me. You know how I found out about Sky?"

I shake my head.

"Steph's grandmother," he says, and now he's marching back and forth in the narrow hallway. "She was using a photo of Steph and Skyler as a bookmark, and it fell out when I was leafing through the book. I thought it was photoshopped at first, but nope. Twin brother. An eerily similar twin brother. Like... to the point it was impossible to tell them apart." He scrubs his palm over the top of his head. "Evelyn told me and Blair everything. The one time I tried to talk about it with Steph he moved to fucking Seattle for a year. Fucking Seattle. Like, he was here one day, then it's August tenth, his parents arrive in town, guns blazing. He gets totally wasted and is arrested. Drunk and disorderly. I try and talk to him. He fucking takes off!"

I drag my hands through my hair and pull at it.

"You think this is what he's doing?" I ask.

He stops pacing and turns to look at me. His shoulders slump.

"I don't know," he says. "I don't think so? But then it's Steph. And it's August. And Steph and August is a terrible combination. Ah fuck!" This outburst is followed by a glum look. "I guess we'll just... I guess we'll just have to wait and find out."

I straighten myself.

Fuck that.

"No," I say. "I'm not giving up without a fucking fight, and if he thinks he can move across the country and get rid of me, he has another think coming."

Jude cocks his head to the side and studies me. "Okay. How do we find him, then?"

"You're living with a hacker," I say. "Is he home?"

Jude's lips pull into a grin, and he nods.

"Yeah, he's home."

STEPH

"SORRY! So sorry. Oops! Sorry. My bad." The girl pushes her backpack into the luggage compartment and drops into the seat next to mine with a huge sigh of relief. She sits still for a moment before she turns her head toward me, a friendly smile overtaking her whole face.

"Almost didn't think I was going to make it," she says. "But then they pushed the flight back, and I'm like, 'Summer, this is your lucky day.' You know what I mean?"

"Sure," I say. My voice is hoarse from disuse because I've barely said a word to anybody since I left Quinn's place last night.

She thrusts her hand toward me. "I'm Summer, by the way. If that wasn't clear yet from me talking to myself."

I stare at her fingers for a moment before I take her hand and give it a quick shake. "Steph."

"I'm flying home for my sister's birthday. Taking a long weekend. How about you?"

How about me?

"Going home?" Summer continues. Clearly, she's decided

to have a conversation with me, even though I don't think I've demonstrated any enthusiasm for the prospect.

And now my hands are shaking again.

What are you doing, Steph?

When did North Carolina stop being home? I can't pinpoint the exact moment. I just know that when I think of home, the only thing that comes to mind is Quinn.

I shake my head. "No. Not home."

"Just visiting?"

"Yup," I say.

My short answers do not deter her in the least.

"Well, you're going to love it there. We have the nicest people you've ever met, I swear. The food is great. I'll give you the address of my favorite place for shrimp and grits. It's going to change your life. And oh my God, don't even get me started on the—"

"I'm actually really tired," I say, cutting her off.

"Oh." She visibly deflates. I'd feel bad, but I'm already maxed out, so possibly hurting Summer's feelings doesn't even make it onto the list of the top fifty things I regret.

I turn my head away and stare out the window for a little while.

"I wonder what's taking so long," Summer mutters.

I squeeze my eyes shut in case she gets any ideas to draw me back into the conversation.

And then I just keep them shut because it feels good. Like hiding. Like when little kids haven't mastered object permanence yet. Hide something under a blanket, and it's gone for good. So I'm hiding myself behind my eyelids. I'm not really here. I'm fine. I haven't been actively fucking up my life for the last decade.

You kind of are screwed up, aren't you Steph?

Well, I wouldn't fucking be if you hadn't fucking died on me, would I?

It's been ten years, dude. Maybe it's time to stop holding a grudge about that?

I take a deep breath.

I'm hiding.

You can't see me.

I can't hear you.

There's some commotion somewhere in the front.

I ignore it.

I do my best, at least.

But when a very familiar voice says, "Hi there," my eyes fly open.

Quinn leans his elbow on the back of the seat in front of Summer and sends her the kind of wide, charming smile I've never once seen on his face. He's more of a glowering type in my experience. Or maybe it's just with me.

Summer's eyes widen.

"Oh my God. You're—"

"Quinn Henris," he says and reaches out his hand. Since when do we volunteer that information with such gusto? Summer has a dazed expression on her face as she shakes Quinn's hand.

"Summer," she says. "Levy. Summer Levy. Oh my God! I've seen you on TV! This is so cool." She starts patting her hair and then her T-shirt. "Can we... I mean, can *I* take a photo? With you. Not of you. But us together. In a photo?"

"I would absolutely love that," Quinn says. "Sounds like a great plan."

I stare at him.

What?

Summer finds her phone and hands it to me. "Would you, please?"

Quinn lowers his face until it's right next to Summer's, and they both smile.

So I take a photo of them. I'm not sure how I manage, exactly, because my fingers are completely numb, but somehow I do.

I hand the phone back, and Summer flips through the shots I've taken. "My brother is going to die on the spot if he sees these," she says. "He's a swimmer too. In University of Florida."

"Go Gators," Quinn says. "Hey, Summer? I was wondering if you could maybe do me a favor?"

"Sure," she says. "Anything."

Quinn's still looking at her with that wide smile he's been aiming her way the whole time.

"I have two first class tickets," he says. "And I was wondering if you'd maybe want to switch seats."

Summer blinks at him. "What?"

"Two seats," Quinn repeats. "First class. You'll get both for yourself. There'll be lots of leg room. I think they're offering champagne there, too."

"And... you're just... You just want to give those tickets to me?" Summer asks.

"In exchange for this seat, yes," Quinn says.

"Uh... Why would you do that?" Summer asks.

Quinn lifts his eyes then, and looks at me. I guess he used up all his smiles on Summer, and all he has left for me is burning anger.

"See that guy sitting next to you?" he asks.

Summer sends a quick look my way. "Yes?"

"That's my boyfriend."

"Oh!" Summer says. "Oh my God! Really?"

"Yup." Quinn nods. "The apple of my eye. The light of my life."

Those words just don't have the same ring to them when they're uttered in a complete monotone.

"And you wanted to surprise him. Aww!" Summer says. "God, I'm so single. No, of course. This is so sweet. Of course you want to sit next to him." Her smile gets even wider. "You don't have to give me your tickets. I mean, I'm sure you two would like to sit in first class together, instead."

"No," Quinn says, eyes still locked on me, blazing wildfire still in his gaze. "No, no. Stephen here doesn't really deserve first class seats. At all. If it was up to me, he'd be running after the plane to... wherever the fuck it is we're going."

"Raleigh," Summer inserts helpfully.

Quinn just keeps scowling at me now.

"So..." Summer says, finally cluing in to the fact that this isn't a happy reunion. "I'm just gonna go, then."

"Enjoy the seats," Quinn says.

It takes her a minute to gather her things, but then she's done and gone, and I'm left with an extremely pissed off seatmate, who crosses his arms over his chest and stares right in front of himself, huffs every once in a while, and mutters under his breath.

"Well," I say eventually when the plane is somewhere above Maryland, and Quinn is still giving me the silent treatment with the added bonus of angry muttering. "This is fun."

He's still scowling at the back of the seat in front of him.

In total silence.

WE GET off the plane in total silence.

We walk through the airport in total silence.

We go and rent a car in total silence.

It's like sitting on top of an active volcano.

I throw my bag in the trunk and slam it shut.

I go to the driver's side door.

Quinn's glaring at me over the roof of the car.

I sigh.

"Look, can you just—"

"You're a fucking asshole," he says in a low voice.

"Okay, well, that's—"

"I don't think I've ever been this angry in my life."

"I can see that, yes, but..."

He drops his head back and scowls at the deep blue sky above us before he shakes his head and lets out a short, bitter laugh before he starts to pace.

And the volcano explodes.

"You know, this is just fucking fantastic," he says. "You act like a fucking basket case for weeks. You won't talk to me. Then you ignore all my calls and texts, and then you take off to fucking. North. Carolina. And do you tell anybody where you're going? Of course fucking not. Oh no. That would be way too normal and sane, right? So I have to hire a fucking hacker to track you down!"

"I hear they're not cheap, so I guess I'm flattered?" I mutter, which earns me another murderous look.

"And then I have to do a mad dash through the whole fucking city to get to the airport on time. I have no fucking clue where I left my keys, and I forgot my phone somewhere. Might be at Jude's place. Might be in the fucking Lyft. I have no. Fucking. Clue. And you know, if you're going to fucking dump somebody, at least have the decency to do it in person. What kind of absolute fucking dick just runs off without saying a word? I really didn't think you were that much of a fucking coward. And now I'm in North fucking Carolina. So yeah, I'm having an absolute fucking blast."

His voice has gotten progressively louder. So clearly the

hour and a half of silence on the plane didn't do anything to improve his mood.

I take a deep, *deep* breath.

"Okay. Maybe we should just—"

"I don't know why I'm surprised," he barrels on. "Somehow I had this naive idea that if you find the right person, it'll be easy. But my fucking God, not a single thing about you is easy. And not because it can't be. No, no. It's because you fucking make everything so goddamn difficult for no goddamn reason at all! Half the time it feels like I want to tear my own hair out when it comes to you!"

"Then why the fuck are you here?" I ask.

He whirls toward me sharply, eyes narrowing. "Oh! My bad I can't just turn my feelings off and go on my merry way as easily as you do."

The keys dig into my palm as I hold them in a death grip.

"That's not what's happening here," I say, hurt and annoyance and exhaustion turning into a painful lump in my throat.

He takes a pointed look around the parking lot. "Could've fooled me!"

"Stop being a sarcastic jackass!" I snap.

"Stop being a fucking stubborn idiot!"

"It's so nice you're here," I say. "I do really enjoy when somebody pushes their company on me just to yell at me. It's really an underrated quality in a road trip buddy."

"Yeah, well, running away without saying a word is an underrated quality in a boyfriend, so I guess we're even, huh?"

"I'm not running away!"

I'm actually surprised there's no steam coming out of his ears.

He laughs out loud.

Cold.

Downright icy.

And then a fucking inferno of anger.

"Oh, that is rich. We're in North. Fucking. Carolina!" he roars.

"If you hate North fucking Carolina so much then why the fuck are you here?" I shout back as the little patience I have left snaps.

"Why am I here?" he asks, voice dangerously calm for a moment. "Because I fucking love you!" he thunders in the next breath.

We stare at each other, chests falling and rising rapidly.

I should be happy, right?

That's what people should feel when somebody you love tells you they love you too.

Instead, it's a moment of pure panic.

My ears ring and my heart is trying to beat itself out of my chest and it's not warm and lovely and overwhelmingly wonderful but scary and terrifying and awful.

"Well... maybe you shouldn't," I choke out. Whatever smidgen of courage I had in me flees.

Quinn stares at me in disbelief. "What?"

"Maybe... maybe you shouldn't. Maybe you're right, and maybe you should find somebody who's... better and less fucked up and easier to deal with."

He rounds on me, and he's seriously starting to look like he's contemplating tackling me.

"What?" he snaps once again.

"Maybe that's what you should want," I say.

He drags both his hands through his hair and stares at me. There's a muscle in his jaw that keeps twitching, his whole body vibrating with tension.

"What the fuck, Stephen?" he demands. "I don't want you to tell me what I should want. I already *know* what I want. I don't need you to throw out idiotic guesses."

"Well, what do you want, then?" I choke out.

He's in front of me once again, so close I can feel the warmth of his skin.

"I want you to fucking fight for me," he says. "I want you to fight for *us*. I want you to tell me you love me and that you want me and have me and keep me and be with me. Forever. But most of all, I want you to be happy. I want you to stop all the lying and hiding and just be fucking happy. With or without me."

I close my eyes.

I want him. I want all of him so much that my fingertips itch with the need to reach out and grab everything he's offering.

"It's not that simple," I whisper.

He's standing so still it looks like he's even stopped breathing.

"You're going to hate me," I say.

He stares at me. "I just told you I love you."

I swallow hard.

"Can I show you something?" I ask.

STEPH

IT'S GETTING dark by the time I park the car. There used to be a row of lights on each side of the driveway, but those are long gone now. The flowerbeds have been replaced with grass, and the blinds are always drawn.

Everything is very still and quiet.

This place has got the feel of a cemetery, which I suppose it is. A mausoleum to a life that doesn't exist anymore.

I get out of the car, and Quinn follows me silently.

We walk past the house.

"There was a rope swing there." I point to a maple tree. "I fell off when I was nine and broke my arm. So... I had to have a cast on my arm, and Sky threw the mother of all tantrums in the ER because he wanted them to put a cast on his arm too. Because... otherwise people could tell us apart."

Quinn draws in a sharp breath.

I don't stop. Just keep walking. Through the backyard. Jiggle the handle of the rusty gate until it opens. Past the trees. Down to the beach. To the dock.

I sit down, and Quinn settles in next to me.

I dig out my phone and scroll through my photos.

I hand the phone to Quinn.

He takes it.

Looks.

And keeps looking.

"Which one is you?" he asks after a long moment of studying the screen.

Two boys on a boat. Arms thrown over each other's shoulders. Wide smiles. Tanned faces. A bucket of water at their feet. Sponges and brushes littering the deck.

I shrug, eyes on the horizon. "No idea. Mom used to label the family photos in the albums when we were younger, but she gave up at one point, so nobody really knows anymore. Not that anybody ever looks at those albums now. There's a bunch in the house, but nobody goes inside anymore either."

Quinn is quiet for a little while, eyes still on the photo. Every now and then he taps his thumb on the display to keep it active.

"I'd like to see them," he says. "Are there a lot?"

"Mom and Dad loved taking photos. There are albums and numerous boxes in the attic with photos that didn't make it into the albums."

"Then maybe you'll show them to me one day," he says.

"Yeah," I say and look down at my hands. Roll them into fists and then stretch out my fingers. "I'm gonna tell you things. And then... I mean, you might not want me to. After. You might... You might not want *me*."

He puts the phone down.

I lie down on my back.

He lies down on his back.

Ocean under and universe above us.

He doesn't say anything. Just waits.

"I was fifteen," I finally say. "We were supposed to move. To Washington, D.C. Dad got a job there. A really good job. And it's not that Mom wanted to move, but we were a team. All four of us. And Dad wanted the job, so she was all in. They broke the news, and Sky and I ran away from home."

Quinn snorts next to my ear, his chest vibrating with quiet laughter, and unbelievably, I start to laugh too.

"I was dramatic back then," I mumble.

I can feel his eyes on the side of my face.

"Obviously you grew out of that."

"I did," I say indignantly. "I'm chill."

"So chill," he says, and snorts again. "You don't dramatically run away anymore at all."

I half-heartedly smack at his chest, and he catches my hand and holds it still, his heart beating steadily against the back of my hand.

"I wasn't running away from you. I came here to say goodbye," I say softly.

Quinn squeezes my hand more tightly. A reassuring presence. Port in a storm. Calm and safe.

Big and *important* and *meaningful* and *good*.

"We took our boat," I say. "And just stayed out there for the whole day. Because they were going to sell everything. And we didn't want to move anywhere. It was the kind of lame protest you stage even if you know it's not going to change anything. And when it started to get dark, we went back.

"It was getting cold. Sky was at the wheel, and he told me to put on warmer clothes. And I went below deck. I couldn't find his jacket. I searched for so long and... Maybe I would've been up there with him. But I wasn't. He called my name, and I... I just thought he was bitching at me for being too slow." I swallow hard. "Next thing I knew, I was flying through the air. I hit my head against something, and I blacked out. I don't know for how long." The words are coming more quickly now. As if my mouth is trying to get them out as fast as possible to get it over with.

"And when I came back to and got up on the deck again... Sky... He was gone."

The world gets blurry, and I squeeze my eyes shut. No matter how much I swallow, the lump in my throat stays put.

"They think it was a rogue wave," I finally say.

"What's that?" Quinn asks.

"This... unusually large and powerful wave that suddenly appears. Seemingly out of nowhere. There doesn't have to be a storm or anything. It just suddenly happens. The official version is that it swept him overboard."

He's squeezing my hand so tightly now it's starting to hurt, but I'm grateful. It makes speaking easier.

"Lost at sea," I say. "Presumed dead."

"Steph," he whispers.

But I can't stop now. I have to get it all out.

"My parents think he's still alive," I say.

Quinn's hand goes slack around my hand, his eyes still locked on the side of my face like they have been ever since I started speaking. I turn my head to look at him.

"And now comes the part where you'll hate me."

QUINN

"WHAT—" I start to say, but he snaps his eyes toward the sky again and speaks over me.

"There was a search and rescue mission, but they never found him. And my parents think there's still hope. That somewhere out there, he's still alive."

"Do you?" I ask carefully.

"Do I think he's still alive?" he asks.

I nod.

He's silent for a long time. "I drowned with him. So no, I don't think he's still out there stranded on some deserted island off the coast of North fucking Carolina."

He takes a deep breath and pushes it out through his teeth.

"They were going to call off the search," he says. "And... the story was mentioned in the papers in passing when it happened. Missing teen. Boat accident. That kind of stuff. My mom... she said we need to get more attention on Sky's case. Raise public awareness. Keep the investigation open. Keep the search going."

He licks over his lips and keeps going, even though his voice keeps cracking and stalling every few sentences, but he barrels on.

"They sat me down. Her and Dad. And they said... that it's possible there were other boats nearby. That this wasn't... That this might've been kidnapping. Because if he was dead, we would have a body. So he's not dead. He's either stranded somewhere. Or somebody took him. And the most important thing is to keep the search going. We'll find him if we're given a chance to find him."

He sounds almost feverish now, staring determinedly at the sky, silent tears rolling down his temples, into his hair.

"And they kept asking me if there were other boats nearby, and there had been. Of course there had been. Glimpses of sails in the distance and occasionally the sound of an engine and... And I was passed out below deck, so if somebody stopped next to our boat, I would've never known. So all I had to do was tell the police there had been other vessels. It wouldn't even be a lie. And if you love your brother, you'll do anything to find him." His next words come out in a whisper so soft I can barely hear it. "So I did."

"Steph," I say again and try to take his hand, but he pulls it away sharply.

"No, no. Wait. It gets better," he says, still with the same fiery, hectic tone. "I lied to the police, and we got all those stories in the newspapers. I mean, the press really picked it up after I pointed fingers and said there were other boats nearby. Because now it was intriguing. There was the possibility of a crime. They ran all these stories about what a tragic family we are. About how close Sky and I had been. It felt like everybody in town got to give an interview. Our photos were everywhere. Like, missing posters? We... my parents and I, were giving interviews to news stations and making appearances on talk shows. I barely remember any of it. Just... I was doing all of it, but I wasn't really there. It was a media circus, and since there was so much public interest and pressure to solve this case, they kept searching. And..." He swallows hard. "They found this man, who... He'd been out with his boat at the same time. And... you're supposed to be innocent until proven guilty, but the word got out he was a... person of interest? Is that... is that what you call them?"

I nod, even though he's not even looking at me.

"He was a bit strange. Like... a loner, I guess? Living alone and not really communicating with neighbors or anything. So the police searched his place. And they found nothing. But then people started... They started sending him all these threats and harassing him. I mean, they vilified him with no evidence. There were protests to arrest him, and..." He swallows again and again. "People started digging into his past, and it turned out that guy... He used to be a teacher, and he'd been fired because he'd had a relationship with one of his students when she was a senior. And then things got really off the rails because the police kept saying there was no evidence, that he'd done nothing wrong, so a bunch of people... they took matters into their own hands. They marched into his place and tied him up and trashed his home and beat him up. Some hikers heard shouts and noise and called the police. And I don't know what would've happened if they hadn't." His voice lowers into a whisper. "He could've died because of me. I had to... I came clean. About how I lied. And... Well, let's just say nobody was happy with me after that."

He swallows hard.

"They stopped searching soon after that. Missing at sea. Presumed dead."

"Do you really think this will make me hate you?" I ask.

"It should. You keep telling me I lie. Well, I do. All the time," he says. "But if that's not enough for you, here's some more. My parents are still searching. They keep fundraising. And they're in the news whenever they have a chance. There's a newsletter. A website. They're all over social media. Every now and then when there's a slow news day, they're doing interviews on local news stations. They try to... raise awareness. That's what they call it. It's almost impossible to get people invested in the story of a missing person from ten years ago. But then you..." He finally turns his head and meets my gaze. "You'd be like a jackpot."

A soft breath escapes when it all sort of starts to make sense.

"The tragic surviving twin in a relationship with a famous swimmer. Your name would get all the attention necessary," he continues. "And if you have the attention, the money will follow. And if it hurts anybody along the way..." He shrugs one shoulder. "Means to an end. I'd be your Lukas two point oh. And that's why you'll hate me, and we should just... not do that."

It takes a bit of time to process everything he's just told me.

"It's not the same," I say.

He lets out a wet laugh and presses the heels of his palms against his eyes.

"Damn it!" he mutters before he says, "It is the same."

"Let me ask you this. Did you plan to screw me over?"

He licks over his lips and shakes his head.

"Well, then it's not the same."

He takes a deep breath and lowers his hands. The smile he sends me is pure sadness.

"The final destination is the same."

He starts to get up.

So I do the only thing I can think of and roll myself on top of him.

All breath whooshes out of him.

"What are you doing?" he asks.

Breathless. I like him breathless. With me, he's the good kind of breathless.

His eyes are the green of a bottomless sea in the dying light of the day.

"I love you," I say.

He studies me for a long time before he lifts his hands up in clear frustration.

"Did you hear anything I just said?"

"All of it."

"Well... then you're an idiot. I always suspected. It's nice to finally have the confirmation."

"You could say you love me back," I suggest.

"No."

"Another time, then," I say.

He shakes his head.

I lower my head and capture his mouth with mine. The headshaking lasts for another few seconds before he gives that up and kisses me back.

"You're an idiot," he says once our mouths part. "And you don't have any standards."

"You should be happy I don't have any. Otherwise I might find somebody who'd actually appreciate everything I have to offer."

He looks to the side and avoids my gaze. "Well then. You should definitely go find that person."

I hum thoughtfully. "You know, it might be nice to be with somebody nice."

"I imagine it would be," he says, still avoiding my gaze.

"I mean, life would definitely be easier."

He swallows hard.

"Tons," he says.

"But instead I got you."

His gaze snaps to mine. He licks over his lips. There's unmistakable hope in his eyes.

"Talk about drawing the short straw," he says hoarsely.

"I won't leave," I say. "I just think you should know that. I can do scandals and attention and whatever else if I get you in return."

Finally, he lets out a resigned sigh. "There's clearly no point in arguing with you right now, so we'll recuperate and revisit. And... don't be some noble gentleman about this. I hear what you're saying, but when you change your mind and come to your senses, you can leave. You should leave. I'll understand."

"You've said some dumb shit over the years," I say. "But this is probably the dumbest. The gold standard of dumb."

"It's not, and I mean it," he says.

"Yeah, yeah. Mean away."

There's a long pause.

Hesitation.

A battle being waged.

He licks over his lips.

Swallows.

Hard.

"I do too. You know that, right?"

"Do what?" I ask with a grin that makes him roll his eyes.

"Love you. I love you too," he says.

It doesn't feel easy. Nothing with Steph ever does. But it does feel light. And warm. Like sunrise inside my chest.

"We'll figure the rest out," I say.

LATER, much later, I stand in front of Stephen's childhood home.

My eyes stay on the boat dock where Steph's still sitting.

I don't know what exactly he's saying, and it's not my business anyway.

This is between Steph and Sky.

A goodbye.

An 'I'll see you again someday.'

It's so dark I can barely see him by the time Steph gets on his feet. He stands still for a long time.

I go to him then.

He looks up at the moon and then back at the water underneath our feet.

"You know what I feel like?" he asks, voice scratchy and uneven, but there's a new kind of calm in it. A steadiness that's always been missing.

"What?" I ask.

"A swim," he says.

I laugh and nod. "Okay."

He glances toward me. "Yeah?"

I grab the hem of his shirt, and he turns toward me and lifts his arms in the air. I drop the shirt on the dock.

"I don't know if you know this about me," I say while I pull my own shirt off, "but I really like swimming."

He dashes his arm across his eyes every now and then, but there's a small smile on his face. "Really? I would never have guessed. I thought you were an accountant."

He drops his pants, and I push mine down too.

"Sweetheart, accountants don't have bodies like mine," I say.

He laughs out loud then as he quirks his brow and takes my hand.

We run together to the edge of the dock and leap.

QUINN

"HEY, CAN I ASK YOU SOMETHING?"

Stephen lifts his head and stops shoveling pancakes into his mouth for a second. After barely eating anything and picking at his food for the past few weeks, he's now making up for lost time.

We're in a small diner. It's very, very early, and neither of us has slept at all, but I don't think either of us really feels how tired we are. Not just yet.

"Shoot," he says. Easily, this time. No metaphorical bullets anymore. No fear.

"I Googled you," I say. "And I got no decent results. Don't get me wrong, I'm very proud you're the two-time winner of a composting awareness week poster contest, but it's not really..." I'm not quite sure how to finish that sentence.

"Not the juicy stuff?" Stephen asks.

I shrug one shoulder in acknowledgment.

He stuffs another forkful of pancakes into his mouth and chews for a bit, eyes on me the whole time. I quirk my brow when he swallows and still doesn't answer.

"Might have something to do with the fact that you didn't search my real name," he finally says.

I lean back.

Somehow, after everything he's told me in the last twelve hours, this is the one thing that hits hardest.

"Are you serious?" I ask.

"I'd say so." He leans over and helps himself to my eggs and toast that now sit abandoned in light of this latest revelation.

"So you're telling me I'm in love with somebody whose name I don't know."

He stops, still bent over the table, knife and fork on my plate, and looks at me. "Huh. That certainly makes things a bit more interesting, doesn't it?"

"A bit more interesting," I repeat. "I'm sorry, are you saying this"—I motion between me and him—"is not interesting enough for you?"

"We have our moments," he says, and goes back to eating.

I watch him for a little bit before I gently kick his shin under the table.

He lifts his gaze.

"Are you going to tell me your name?"

He leans back and stuffs the last piece of toast in his mouth.

"Barry," he says. "Barry Burt Hartley. Super nice to meet you."

"Be serious. Your name isn't Barry."

"Yes, it is. Can't you just imagine calling it out in bed?" He throws his head back and closes his eyes. "Oh, Barry! Yes! That's the spot. Harder. Harder!"

"That was... weirdly arousing," I say. "I don't know how to feel about that."

"Barry doesn't sound so bad anymore, huh?" He grins. "Don't worry. We can keep that one for role playing."

"We'll table that for now. What's your real name?" I ask.
"Oh shit, it actually is Barry. No, it's not. Or is it?"

He laughs. "You can breathe easy. It's Stephen. I only changed my last name. Hartley is Evelyn's—my grandmother's—last name." His eyes move away from me and get stuck on the wall somewhere just above my shoulder. "Stephen Christopher Adler," he says.

"Is that a common name?"

"Not really, no," he says. "Makes it pretty easy for people to find you and send death threats and hate mail."

His tone is light, but the smile that goes with it is made up solely of jagged edges. Underneath the table, I move my foot so the side of it is pressed against his.

"I know I kind of deserved it after everything," he says. "But after a while it becomes a bit... disheartening. And then it's pretty difficult to not think people have a point when they say the wrong twin died."

I swear out loud.

"You didn't deserve any of it. You were fifteen," I say.

"There are plenty of fifteen-year-olds who won't lie and cause the witch hunt of an innocent man."

"Most fifteen-year-olds don't go through what you did, either," I say.

He shakes his head. "It doesn't make any of it right and doesn't make me less of a villain in this story."

"You're not a villain," I say.

"Depends on the perspective. I'm a villain for that guy. Martin Hoffman. I'm a villain for a lot of people who were trying to help while it was all going down. To an extent I'm a villain for my parents. I didn't exactly make things easy." He looks down.

I have a few choice words about Steph's parents, which won't help at all, so I keep my mouth shut about that.

"So," he says and grins. There's a veneer of hiding in that smile again, but I let him have this one. For now.

"Think we should go find somewhere to sleep for a few hours?" he asks.

I nod. "Sounds like a plan."

"And then I have one more thing to do before we can go," he says.

"Whatever you want."

THE TINKLE of a bell announces our arrival, and a rush of cold air hits me in the face as I follow Steph inside.

The cream walls are covered with framed drawings. There are two comfortable-looking armchairs in the corner, and a window seat with a narrow bookcase next to it.

"This looks more like a day spa than a tattoo parlor," I say as I look around.

Steph smiles. "You should tell that to Marley. She'll be happy to hear that."

As if summoned, the beaded curtains move, and a tall woman walks out. She's wearing shorts and a tank top, and her strawberry blonde hair is piled up in a messy bun. A brilliant smile takes over her face as her eyes land on Steph. She squeals and jumps into Steph's arms. And Steph laughs. There's no better sound in the world than Steph's laugh.

"Look what the cat dragged in," the woman says.

"Always good to see you, Marley."

"You too, Stephie," she says, palm on his cheek. "How've you been?"

"I have my moments. You?"

"Can't complain." She nods toward me. "Who's the dude?"

"Boyfriend," Stephen says. He does it so easily. Sunshine in my chest again.

"Hi, Steph's boyfriend," Marley says.

"Hi," I say without giving her my real name, because I like her calling me Steph's boyfriend instead. It's got a ring to it.

"We'd like to get matching tattoos," Steph says.

I blink.

"Cool." Marley goes to the counter and grabs a pad and a pencil. "Ideas about what you're getting?"

"Uh…" I say.

"Lightsabers but shaped like penises. Ours." Steph glances toward me. "Babe, drop your pants so Marley can get it just right."

"I'd rather skip that bit," I say.

"We'll do it by memory, then." Steph leans over the counter and tilts his head to the side as he studies Marley's drawing pad. "Whoa, you're being way too optimistic. Thinner. Definitely thinner. And shorter. By at least half."

"I take back the I love you," I say.

Marley laughs and leafs through her drawing pad before she slides it in front of Steph.

"This one?" she asks Steph when she's done snickering.

"Yeah," he says, and touches whatever Marley's showing him with the tips of his fingers for a moment.

"Let's do this, then."

Steph and I follow her to the back. Steph pulls his shirt off and hands it to me.

"Take a seat anywhere," Marley tells me while Steph sits down, his back to me.

It doesn't take her long to add another dragonfly to Steph's back.

Ten of them now flying over Stephen's shoulder blade.

"All done," she says after she puts a bandage on the finished dragonfly.

Stephen nods.

"Thanks," he says quietly.

"No problem, honey. See you next year?"

Steph hugs her goodbye, and then we get out of there.

We walk back to the rental car in silence. Once inside, Steph leans his head back and closes his eyes.

"My parents used to call us dragonflies." He doesn't need to explain further. I get it.

Ten dragonflies.

Ten years.

"It's funny," he continues. "When I was fifteen, I never wanted to leave this place. And now I can't wait to get out of here."

I take his hand and thread my fingers with his.

His gaze remains somewhere outside the window, a faraway look in his eyes.

"I feel guilty," he admits softly.

"For?"

He looks at me then. "When I'm with you, I feel good. You make me feel alive."

I caress my thumb over the back of his hand. "It's okay to feel that way. It's okay to be alive."

He looks down at where my thumb is moving over his skin. "It's like my brain knows it, but my heart isn't so sure. Whenever I start to feel even remotely okay, I do my best to fuck it up. Because it feels fair. Not being okay feels fair."

I choose my words carefully, navigating between past hurts, heartbreak, and harsh truths.

"Life isn't fair, Steph. You don't have to balance the imaginary scales by purposefully making yourself unhappy."

He looks at me for the longest time.

"You're very smart."

"That's definitely a step up from being an idiot."

"Well, even a broken clock..." he says. The smile is small. Tiny. A bit hesitant and a touch watery. But it's real.

I squeeze his fingers. "Have you ever considered talking to somebody about this?"

He shrugs, which isn't really an answer at all.

"I think you should."

"Can you..." His voice drops off for a moment, and he clears his throat. "I don't think it's fair to even ask you that, but—"

"Just ask," I interrupt him. "You can always ask."

He looks down to our linked fingers. "Please be patient with me," he says, so quietly I can barely hear him.

"I think that can be arranged," I say.

And he smiles.

His real smile.

STEPH

"MAYBE WE SHOULD JUST EASE them into it," I say, and kick a loose pebble with the toe of my sneaker.

"And by easing them into it, you mean..." Quinn raises his brows at me.

I stuff my hands deeper into the pockets of my jeans. "You know. Instead of outright telling them we're doing this love thing, let's pretend to fall in love over time. Make it less likely that Blair and Nora will dismember me for corrupting you."

Quinn's lips twitch. "Did you corrupt me? Is that the official stance?"

"I did. Scandalously. I'm just saying. Blair has warned me off you. Nora has warned me off you—"

"When was that?" Quinn interrupts.

"I told you about that lunch I had with Blair and Jude."

"No, the Nora warning."

"That was before we officially met. It went something like, 'I'm about to introduce you to somebody who's very important to me. Sleep with him and die.'"

"Okay, well, we're not just fucking around, though," he points out.

"Easy for you to say. You're not going to be the one they blame for this." I gesture between the two of us.

"Well, I obviously see your point." Quinn nods seriously. "What's the plan, exactly?"

"So glad you asked. I have a great one. We'll get them used to us. Let them witness the natural progression of our connection until they start pushing us together themselves because they don't even really understand why two people who suit together as well as we do aren't dating. We'll reprogram them. Psychological manipulation is a great tool, and we should use the hell out of it. Here's what I'm proposing. This week, for example, we won't fight. Next week, you laugh at my joke. One joke. We don't want to overdo it. The week after that, subtle eye contact across the table. The week after—"

"Exactly how many weeks does this plan take?" Quinn interrupts.

"Like…" I do a quick calculation in my head. "Thirty-seven? Give or take a few weeks."

"So they'll be fully on board with us sometime in the beginning of next summer?" he asks.

"Yeah. That sounds about right."

He nods. "Seems like a great plan. I'm totally game. So I laugh at one joke today?"

"No. Today we won't fight," I say with exasperation. "Try and keep up, will you?"

"My bad." He pulls open the front door of Nora and Blair's building and lets me in before him.

I stop once we reach their door and grab Quinn's arm just as he's about to knock.

"Wait. I don't think we should arrive together. It looks suspicious. I'll go hide around the corner for a second and then arrive a few minutes later."

"Great idea," he says and lifts both his thumbs.

I slink around the corner just as the door opens.

"Hey," Nora's voice says.

"Hi," Quinn replies. "I'm in love with Stephen. I figured you should know. He's hiding around the corner. What smells so good?"

My head falls back against the wall with a loud thump, and I sigh.

I try to will myself to disappear for a few seconds, but since that doesn't seem to work, I come out and walk to the door, where Nora greets me with raised brows. I think we've managed to shock her. I'm actually quite pleased with the achievement.

"Okay. So that wasn't a joke," she says slowly.

"When have you known Quinn to joke?"

"Point taken." She nods, still blinking at me like a baby owl.

I look down at my feet and then force myself to meet her eyes. "I can't promise I won't fuck it up or hurt him, but I promise I'll do my best not to," I say in a low voice. "So can we maybe skip the lecture and threats tonight? I know I'm not—"

Nora rolls her eyes. "Give me a break. I wasn't going to threaten you."

"You already *have* threatened me about Quinn," I point out.

"That was before." She eyes me thoughtfully. "He's been different lately. Lighter. Happy."

I have no idea what to say to that.

"Keep up the good work," she says, turns around, and goes inside the apartment.

DINNER IS MOSTLY dinner as usual.

Save for Quinn's thigh against mine when we sit.

His hand grazing mine every time he reaches for his wine.

Hot looks.

Soft smiles.

Warm feeling of belonging.

I didn't know I was missing it so badly.

He laughs at something Blake says and rests his arm on the back of my chair.

His thumb brushes over my back where the dragonflies are.

Casually.

Easily.

And this, too, is *big* and *important* and *meaningful,* but at the same time so very *simple* and *easy* and *perfect.*

After dinner is done, we put away the dishes, and when Hazel starts to get fussy, Blair picks her up.

"Steph, can you give me a hand?" she says.

Here we go. I knew it was coming. Nora didn't yell at me, but Blair will. I've been trying to prepare myself.

I'm not ready.

But I ignore the urge to run and go with her. She dresses Hazel in a pair of blue PJs and washes her tiny hands and face while she screams bloody murder.

"Can you get her bunny?" Blair asks and nods toward the light purple dresser in the corner of Hazel's room where the security blanket stuffy thing resides during the day.

Blair puts her palm on Hazel's back and sings her a song, and the crying peters out bit by bit until Hazel starts to snore softly.

We get out of her room. Blair closes the door behind her and leans against it. Muffled voices carry toward us from the kitchen.

She looks at me, all serious and grave, and doesn't really say anything.

I break first.

"I didn't mean for it—"

"I was a dick," Blair cuts me off. "A really selfish dick."

"It doesn't really matter," I say.

"It does! I should've been your friend. But I chose to be a dick. Who does that? 'Oh, don't be happy. It might not work out.' God!"

"Don't beat yourself up about it. It's not like I have a great track record."

"Oh my God! Just let me grovel," Blair snaps.

I raise my palms in the air, and she squares her shoulders.

"I'm sorry," she says.

I wait for a bit, and when she doesn't say anything, I quirk my brow. "That was it? Because it was kind of lame."

"Yeah, well. I'm usually right, so put it down to my lack of practice."

We both smile. Tentatively. Carefully.

"I don't like fighting with you," Blair says.

"We weren't fighting."

"We were in my head. You were really pissed with me, and I felt really bad."

"Did I give an epic speech and really let you have it?"

"The epic-est," she assures me.

"Good for me. I do like it if I don't have to put in any real effort," I say.

She slowly sits down on the floor, back sliding against the wall, and then she pats the floor next to her. I go and sit down.

She leans her head on my shoulder.

"I really am sorry," she says. "And I promise you, I'm a hundred percent in your corner. If somebody hurts you, I will mess their shit up. Even if it's Quinn."

I smile and press a kiss on the top of her head. "Thank you. You are officially accepted as my white knight."

"Do I get a pony?"

"Sure."

Her shoulders shake as she chuckles.

"Hey, do you know—" Jude walks into the hallway and tilts his head to the side. He looks at us for a moment before he comes and sits down on the other side of me.

"What are we doing?" he asks.

"We're having a moment," Blair says.

"Ah. Okay," he says, and leans over until the side of his head is against mine.

We sit like that in silence for a minute before Jude asks, "Have you heard from your parents?"

"I turned my phone off when I got on the plane. And I haven't turned it on since," I say.

"Good," Blair says.

I sigh and rub my fingers over my eyes. "I have to talk to them, don't I?" I ask. "Actually talk to them. Not just nod and go along with whatever they have planned, but put my foot down and tell them we can't keep doing this."

"I vote for yes," Blair says.

"Do you want us to go with you?" Jude asks.

I shake my head. "No. I think I have to do this on my own."

"If you change your mind, just say the word," Blair says.

I nod.

There are footsteps, and then...

"What do we have here?" Quinn leans his shoulder against the wall and looks at me, a soft smile on his face.

"We're having a moment," Jude informs him.

"Nora. Blake. We're having a moment," Quinn calls.

They all file into the hallway and sit down on the floor, side by side, heads against heads and shoulders against shoulders.

And then we just sit for a bit.

And the emptiness inside me fills up until I'm overflowing with love.

Because I have so much to live for.

And I think it's high time I finally do just that.

STEPH

THREE PEOPLE STARE at each other from three sides of the small table in the kitchen of my parents' condo in Wilmington. My childhood home has too many memories for them, so they moved here when I moved to Maine.

My mother is clutching the coffee cup so hard her fingertips are turning white around it.

"I don't understand what you're saying," she says. "Stop what we're doing? He's still out there, Stephen."

"He's not." I look down at my hands. Golden skin from all the hours in the sun this summer. The birthmark on the soft flesh between my thumb and index finger. The faint scar on the knuckles of my right hand.

I have never realized this acutely how much life there is in every single part of my body.

She laughs. A short burst of disbelief.

"I can't believe you're just giving up," she says.

"He's your brother," she says.

"You can't," she says.

I brace myself for the surge of guilt.

How can you just give up?

It's there, but it's not so overpowering I'll be buried under it.

The feathers of hope are still there.

Maybe I'm wrong. Maybe he's alive.

Maybe. Maybe. Maybe.

But I don't believe in that hope anymore.

It's a cold kind of hope that doesn't offer any comfort.

An uncomfortable hope.

Something I'd prefer wasn't there at all but will also likely never leave, because aren't we all wishing for a miracle?

"I want to live," I whisper.

"No one's stopping you," she says.

"Why are you doing this?" she says.

"I don't understand," she says.

"None of us live," I say, "because it's so much easier to just stay in this infinite state of pause, hoping life will be the same one day. It will never be the same again. He's gone."

"Stop saying that," she says.

"I don't want to hear this," she says.

"I can't be here when you're like this," she says.

"I still want you in my life," I say. "You're my family."

My father still hasn't said anything. My mother's face is an expressionless mask.

"Family doesn't behave like you do," she says.

"Family doesn't give up!" she says.

"He's somewhere out there. Waiting for us to find him," she says.

I close my eyes and hide my face in my hands.

"I felt him die," I say. "I stood on that deck, and I drowned with him. Please, just…"

I don't know what I'm asking. Believe me? Trust me? Be here for me?

Choose living.

Choose me.

Stop trying to catch a ghost.

"I need a moment," she says, and gets up. The chair clatters to the floor, and she leaves it there.

I stare at the table. The surface is swimming in front of my eyes.

My father stands up and pours himself a glass of water. He looks so old.

"There's going to be a documentary," he says. "About his disappearance. We've been trying to talk to you about this."

"Is there a point in asking you not to go through with this?"

"We have to see it through," he says.

"We have to try everything," he says.

"We have to exhaust all avenues," he says.

"Haven't you already run out of roads?" I ask tiredly.

"He's my son," he says.

"I will never run out of roads," he says.

I nod.

"I'm not going to be a part of this anymore," I say.

"Please don't ask me to," I say.

"Please don't use me," I say.

"I wouldn't," he says.

"You already have," I whisper.

I get up.

"I'm going back home. I have a flight to catch."

He looks startled for a moment.

In the doorway, I close my eyes.

Breathe.

Turn around.

"I'm your son, too," I say.

He stares at me for a long moment.

"You're my son, too," he says.

He frowns like something is dawning on him.

"You're my son, too," he repeats, softer and slower.

"I'm going home," I repeat.

Because I have a home to go back to.

He nods.

Follows me into the hallway.

"If I call you, will you pick up?" he asks as he watches me put on my shoes.

I nod. "Always."

"If we visit... Can we visit?" he asks.

I nod. "Always."

I find myself engulfed in a hug.

"I'm sorry," he whispers.

"I'm sorry too," I choke out.

ONCE OUTSIDE, I pull out my phone. I tap it against my palm for a second before I open my conversation with Quinn.

Steph: I miss you. I know what I said about how I need to do this alone, but I really wish you were here right now.

I slide the phone back into my pocket. I don't expect an answer. He's supposed to be at work right now.

My phone chimes.

Quinn: How did it go?

I sit down on the front steps of my parents' building.

Steph: It went.

Steph: I feel sort of empty. I don't know if it's normal.

Quinn: Baby, you've never been normal. Don't start now.

I laugh out loud, still grinning like an idiot when the phone chimes again.

Quinn: I love your smile.

Steph: Careful. Your sappy side is showing.

Quinn: Thanks for the warning. Better tuck that out of sight quickly.

Quinn: I'd really like to peel you out of those tight jeans. Better?

Steph: Marginally. Tell me more. In great detail if at all possible.

Quinn: The fact that you're wearing my T-shirt gets my dick hard.

Steph: Everything gets your—

I snap my head up and look around. My heart is trying to beat its way out of my chest. Pure fear. I don't know if I can take more disappointment today.

My eyes land on a pair of leather sandals. Travel up the sinfully defined calves to a simple pair of dark blue shorts. Up the wide chest hidden beneath a casual, printed shirt, to the easy smile that somehow chases all the sadness away.

Home.

I get up. Take a step. And another one. And then I'm running. Sprinting across the street, and I don't stop, just barrel into him. Jump. He catches me, and I wrap my legs around his waist.

He laughs out loud, and I kiss him.

"What are you doing here?" I ask once I manage to tear my mouth away.

His eyes shine in the sunlight, impossibly blue.

"I was hoping you'd change your mind about doing this alone." His expression goes serious. A fierceness that I feel in my bones replaces the smile. "Because you're not alone. You have me."

He sets me back on my feet, and I bury my face in his shoulder.

"Hey," he says softly. "You okay?"

I lift my head and send him a watery smile. "Yeah. I'm getting there. I'm just doing a shit job showing it."

He laughs.

"You're doing fine."

His mouth covers mine again. Warm lips. Strong fingers in my hair. Arms around my neck.

His kiss tastes like home.

"Want to go on a road trip?" he asks, lips moving against mine.

"Road trip?" I ask.

He pats his palm against the hood of the cherry red convertible behind him.

"Do you have any plans for the next few days? Because I thought we'd take this instead of the plane."

I let my eyes wander over the car before I grin at him. "Nice."

"You in?" he asks.

I nod. "With you? Yeah, I'm all the way in."

AUGUST 10TH, 2028

THE SUN IS a ball of fiery red, and the clouds around it a riot of oranges and purples as it sinks below the horizon. Slowly. Inch by inch.

It's warm. The new dock is lower, so when I sit on the edge, my feet are in the water.

The sea is calm.

Not a wave in sight tonight.

"Let's see. What else have you missed this past year?" I say, and tap my fingers against my cheek. "We bought a house. Yeah. I'm a suburbanite now. Well, not really. It's still in Brooklyn. You should've seen Quinn's face when I said I'd always felt like deep down inside I was a suburban kind of guy. It was exceptionally entertaining to watch him try and say Hoboken without gagging."

I laugh softly and shake my head.

"I finally went back to school. I know, I know. About time, right? Took me long enough. I just couldn't seem to figure out what I wanted, so I circled through every option and then finally landed on... Want to take a guess? No? Obviously I landed on marine biology in the end. If you were wondering if I'm still a bit of a mess, here's your answer. I was ranting about it to Quinn, but he said he'd start suspecting alien body snatchers if I suddenly emerged a normal, functioning adult."

My toes curl in the water.

"We're thirty," I say. "Can you believe it? Or, well, *I'm* thirty. I don't really know how things work on your side. Do you get older? Are you whatever age you want to be? If I eventually get there—in another sixty or so years—will you be fifteen, and I'll be a ninety-year-old fart? Doesn't really sound that good... So how about this, we agree that we'll both be thirty. Because thirty is kind of great, right? Grown up, but not too grown up."

I look down and swallow hard. "It's been a bit difficult this time around. It's been fifteen years. After tonight, I've officially lived without you longer than with you."

My voice breaks for a moment, but I lie down on my back to distract myself and keep going.

"David says it's okay. You remember I told you about David last time I was here? My therapist, in case you need a refresher. I have a standing date with him once a month. It's a pretty sweet deal. I get to talk about myself for an hour, and I've discovered I kind of like talking about myself because I'm such a fascinating person. Anyway, David seems to think I'm okay, and I'm paying him a lot of money to say that, so I choose to believe him.

"Speaking of therapy, Dad started going. It's only been a few months, but... They're still searching for you. Maybe they'll never stop. We had lunch with them a few months ago. It was... nice. Weird. But nice. We talked about you a lot. And our family. Not plans. But memories. Yeah. It was more nice than weird."

I stare at the sky and listen to the faint sound of footsteps approaching.

"Wedding plans are going okay," I say, louder this time. "It's going to be a small and intimate ceremony." I let out an exaggerated sigh. "Which is fine, I guess."

A pair of legs appear above my head.

"I mean, it's good enough for my first marriage, because this will be like a practice run anyway," I say. "The next one will be to an old, rich guy, who'll mysteriously die on our wedding night, but not before putting me into his will. I'll go all out with that wedding."

Quinn snorts and lies down next to me. He leans his head against mine. Just like he does every year. Somehow, he always knows when I need him. Every time. Year after year of coming here.

"Okay?" he asks.

I nod.

A gentle breeze moves over my skin and ruffles my hair.

"I've been thinking," I say.

"About?" Quinn prompts when I fail to elaborate.

"That thing you said."

His lips twitch.

"Care to narrow it down a bit? When? Where? About what?"

"Maine. Five years ago. About... wanting kids someday?"

He goes very still.

"What about it?" he asks carefully.

"Well, I've been thinking... I want them too. Someday."

He turns his head to the side and presses his lips against my temple.

"I think you'd be a great dad," he says. "And I really think it'd be a shame to deprive a kid of a dad like you."

I turn to my side and throw my arm over his chest.

"I have the potential. And with you there, we'll probably avoid screwing anybody up too much. Just, like, a regular amount?"

"Sounds like a plan," he says, and hugs me to his side.

And then we just lie there together.

It only takes one moment for a life to change.

One moment for a we to become an I.

But sometimes, through sheer dumb luck, or fate, or through hard work, or what have you, that I can also become something else.

Something *big* and *important* and *meaningful*.

And *good*.

Unexpectedly, wonderfully *good*.

"We've got this," I murmur into Quinn's chest. "You and me."

"You and me," he echoes.

The End

A NOTE FROM THE AUTHOR

Curious about how Jude and Blake found their happily ever after? Find out in Until You, the first book in the series.

The best way to find out about new releases by your favorite authors is to join their newsletter.

With that being said, here's a link to mine: briarprescott.com/contact

---

Reader reviews can make a huge difference, so if you love whatever you're reading, sing about it from the rooftops. Or leave a review on Amazon, GoodReads, BookBub, Instagram, TikTok, etc. Or tell a friend. The choices are endless, and you'll make an author very happy.

ALSO BY BRIAR PRESCOTT

Until series:
Until You

Standalones:
Project Hero
Rare
Inevitable

Better With You series:
The Happy List
The Dating Experiment
The Underdog
The Inconvenient Love

ACKNOWLEDGMENTS

A huge thank you to my alpha readers, Alexandra, Michelle, Kuba, and Kristy. You all have the patience of a saint because you've read all the different versions of this story, and none of you blocked me whenever my messages started with a "sooo, I rewrote the whole book…"

A thank you of the same size to Heather and Kate for the edits. Just out of curiosity, do you ever curse me out loud when yet another book comes and goes, and I still haven't learned the difference between further and farther? Or use the phrase "squint his eyes"? Or butcher every single preposition?

A third huge thank you to all the reviewers, ARC readers, and bookfluencers for everything you do. For all the beautiful edits. For your enthusiasm for books. For filling my TBR with awesome recommendations. For just generally being genuinely nice and wonderful people.

And last but not least, thank you to my family. As far as having to share a house with people goes, you four are not too bad.

ABOUT THE AUTHOR

Briar Prescott is a work in progress. She swears too much, doesn't eat enough leafy greens and binge watches too much television. It's okay, though. One of these days she'll get a hang of that adulting thing.
    Probably.
    Maybe.
    She hopes.

Printed in Great Britain
by Amazon